P9-CPX-468

Praise for the spectacular Playful Brides series by
VALERIE BOWMAN

NEVER TRUST A PIRATE

"Thrilling, delicious, and suspenseful." —*Kirkus Reviews*

"Another enthralling Bowman romance."
—*RT Book Reviews* (Top Pick!)

"An engaging literary treat for all romance readers."
—*Booklist*

"Bowman blends a lighthearted romp through Regency
London with a secret spy mission for a perfectly lovely
novel." —*USA Today* bestselling author Maya Rodale

"A delicious mix of intrigue and red-hot romance."
—*BookPage*

THE LEGENDARY LORD

"A sweet and fulfilling romance." —*Publishers Weekly*

"Graceful writing enlivened with plenty of dry wit, a
charming cast, and a breathtakingly sexy romance
make Bowman's latest addition to her Regency-set
Playful Brides series another winner." —*Booklist*

"The words funny, smart, sensual, and joyous come to
mind when readers pick up Bowman's romance."
—*RT Book Reviews*

THE UNTAMED EARL

"An enchanting romance." —*RT Book Reviews*

"*The Untamed Earl* is an engaging and romantic love story."

—*Fresh Fiction*

THE IRRESISTIBLE ROGUE

"Bowman's novel is the complete package, filled with fascinating characters, sparkling romance, and a touch of espionage." —*Publishers Weekly*

"With its lively plot, heated sexual tension, surprising twists, engaging characters, and laugh-out-loud humor, Bowman's latest is another winner."

—*RT Book Reviews* (Top Pick!)

"Exactly what romance readers want."
—Sarah MacLean, *The Washington Post*

THE UNLIKELY LADY

"An entertaining renewal of a classic plotline and well worth reading." —*Kirkus Reviews*

"Rich with fully developed characters and a plethora of witty banter." —*Publishers Weekly*

"A definite must-read!" —*San Francisco Book Review*

The Right
Kind of Rogue

VALERIE BOWMAN

St. Martin's Paperbacks

This is a work of fiction. All of the characters, organizations, and events portrayed in this novel are either products of the author's imagination or are used fictitiously.

THE RIGHT KIND OF ROGUE

Copyright © 2017 by June Third Enterprises, LLC.

All rights reserved.

For information address St. Martin's Press, 175 Fifth Avenue, New York, NY 10010.

ISBN: 978-1-250-12171-4

Our books may be purchased in bulk for promotional, educational, or business use. Please contact your local bookseller or the Macmillan Corporate and Premium Sales Department at 1-800-221-7945, ext. 5442, or by e-mail at MacmillanSpecialMarkets@macmillan.com.

Printed in the United States of America

St. Martin's Paperbacks edition / November 2017

St. Martin's Paperbacks are published by St. Martin's Press, 175 Fifth Avenue, New York, NY 10010.

10 9 8 7 6 5 4 3 2

For my stepfather, Stanley Rhodes,
who put up with my teenaged histrionics
and taught me how to drive a stick shift.
Mom was right, she picked a good one.
I love you.

CHAPTER ONE
London, May 1818

"I'm afraid I have some unhappy news for you, Meg."

Meg Timmons's head snapped up to face her friend Sarah, Lady Berkeley. "Unhappy? How unhappy?" Meg's hand stilled on the swath of embroidered yellow taffeta she'd been inspecting. They were strolling through a shop on Bond Street. Unlike Sarah, Meg couldn't afford any of the lovely trappings. Sarah's husband was a wealthy viscount. Meg's father was a destitute baron. The two ladies had come from vastly different monetary, if not social, situations, but they never allowed that to hinder their friendship. No. The only thing that served to make their friendship difficult to maintain was the fact that Sarah's father, the Earl of Highfield, and Meg's father, Baron Tifton, were sworn enemies. The two men had detested each other for years, which was why their daughters were forced to meet at shops and other public locales. Upon occasion, Meg was allowed to come to

Sarah's father's town house, but rarely and always with the censure of Sarah's highly disapproving parents.

Sarah winced and bit her lip, never a good sign.

"What?" Meg asked, her hand trembling against the fabric. "You're not permanently moving to Northumbria, are you?" Her closest friend, her *only* friend, had married last year. Viscount Berkeley's estate was far to the north. To date the couple had spent equal time in London and Northumbria, but Meg had worried all winter that Sarah wouldn't return to help her navigate the dreadfully dull waters of her *third* London Season. If Sarah left town, Meg would have no one.

Sarah left off examining some luxurious green silk. She turned to her friend, her face solemn. "It's Hart."

Meg's stomach dropped. Her fingers dug into the taffeta.

Sarah's older brother, Hart, the heir to the earldom, a viscount in his own right, was clever, handsome, witty, and extremely eligible. He was also entirely off limits to Meg but she had loved him for years.

Her heart in her throat, Meg scanned Sarah's face, her fingers digging deeper into the innocent taffeta. "What's the matter with Hart? He hasn't been injured in another racing accident, has he?"

Hart was always drinking and carousing and doing things like challenging his friends to races on the moors outside London. Last autumn, during a particularly dangerous chase when he was particularly foxed, he'd flipped his phaeton and broken his leg.

"No." Sarah shook her head. "It's worse than that. Much worse."

Meg's stomach dropped straight into her slippers. She forced herself to release her death grip on the taffeta.

She took a deep breath. "He's getting married, isn't he?" She swallowed hard and braced a gloved hand on the wall next to her.

Sarah leaned over and wrapped her arm around Meg's shoulders. "There, there, dear. We both knew this day would come. I'm sorry, Meggie."

Meg swallowed again. Her hand remained planted on the wall for support. The room spun around her, colors blurring. Nausea gripped her. It was true. She'd known this day would come. Hart obviously needed to take a wife and sire an heir to secure the earldom. Meg was penniless. Her father had gambled her dowry away. She owned two outdated ball gowns, one set of ever more shabby-looking slippers, a satin reticule that sported an unfortunate tea stain, and a pair of graying kid gloves that were near to disintegrating. She was only allowed in Society events due to her father's dulled title and her friendship with the popular Lady Sarah. Every year at *ton* events, Meg sat on the sidelines, a perpetual wallflower, withering by the moment. At nearly one and twenty, she was a veritable spinster. But that didn't matter. Even if she *weren't* a wallflower, even if she owned gorgeous gowns and possessed a hefty dowry, Hart's father and her own would never allow a match between them. And even if *that* weren't a problem, there was the tiniest issue that Hart had never once indicated in any way that he might be interested in her. In fact, if anything, aside from one notable exception, he'd steadfastly ignored her over the years.

Yes. Meg had always known the day would come when Hart would have to take a wife. She simply hadn't expected it to be so . . . soon.

"Who is she?" Meg closed her eyes to stiffen herself

against the pain that hearing the name of Hart's future countess would inevitably cause. She pulled her hand from the wall and pretended to calmly fold her gloved fingers together in front of her. "It's Imogen Hamilton, isn't it? No! It's Lady Mary Asterton." Both ladies were considered diamonds of the first water this Season.

"No." Sarah shook her head again, still squeezing Meg's shoulders. "It's no one . . . yet. He's merely declared his intent to *choose* a wife this Season."

Meg exhaled. She could breathe a bit easier. She and Sarah both knew this was still a large step for Hart. After what he'd been through with one Lady Annabelle Cardiff, Hart had been steadfastly against so much as considering a wife in the past, despite his father's constant nagging. This year, apparently, at the ripe old age of nine and twenty, Hart had changed his mind.

"He told Father he agrees. It's time," Sarah finished.

Meg nodded solemnly. "I see," she murmured.

"Oh, Meg, don't be sad," Sarah said. "Allow me to purchase some of this silk for you and have it made into a beautiful new ball gown." She pulled her arm away from Meg and held up a swath of the rich, soft material. "This green would be perfect with your golden hair. It will match your eyes. You'll look wonderful at the first ball of the Season. It's time you searched for a husband in earnest, too, you know."

Meg pressed a knuckle against the center of her forehead, where an awful headache was beginning to form. "No thank you, Sarah." Meg tucked a wayward curl beneath the brim of her bonnet. "We both know it'll take more than one beautiful ball gown for *me* to find a husband."

Sarah's eyes filled with tears, and she blinked solemnly at Meg. Indeed, they both knew all the reasons why Meg and Hart could not be together. It wasn't just because of their families and Meg's lack of a dowry. Sarah had told Meg often enough that Hart was not the sort for Meg. "He's a rogue, an unrepentant charmer," Sarah liked to say. "I've never known him to pay more than a passing interest in any woman. He'd break your heart for certain, Meggie, and I couldn't live with it if that happened. You're *such* a dear, so sweet and kind and unassuming. You'd give your last shilling and the gown off your back to someone in need. Hart is devil-may-care, only looking for a good time from moment to moment. He'd hurt you. I know it. I love you both dearly, of course, but my brother simply isn't the right man for you."

Meg reached out to pat her friend's hand where it still rested on the swath of emerald silk. "You're kind to worry about me, Sarah, and I quite agree, it's time I tried to find a husband of my own." She did her best to muster a smile.

Sarah's pretty face momentarily brightened. "Oh, Meg, I'm so happy to hear it." Sarah had been exhorting her for years to give up her hopeless infatuation with Hart and look for a man with less at stake, perhaps a wealthy mister with no interest in a dowry, someone who would love her and treat her like a princess. "What's made you change your mind?" Sarah continued.

Meg merely smiled a half smile. She wasn't about to tell Sarah. It would only worry her friend. But she hadn't changed her mind at all. In fact, in the few minutes they'd been speaking, Meg had firmly determined. Yes. It *was* time to try. Time to try to make Hart fall in love with her. She had a chance. A small one, to be certain, but a valid one all the same, for Meg knew something that Sarah did not. Meg knew what had happened between herself and Hart on the night before Sarah's wedding.

CHAPTER TWO

"How in Hades's name can you drink at this hour of the morning, Highgate?"

Hart tossed back his brandy, swallowed, and laughed at his brother-in-law's words. The two sat across from each other at Brooks's gentlemen's club. It was decidedly before noon. The only reason Hart was up at this hour was because he'd promised to meet Lord Christian Berkeley. His brother-in-law rarely asked for favors and Hart suspected this meeting was his sister Sarah's doing, but he would humor the viscount just the same.

"Berkeley, old chap, you don't know the half of it." Hart clapped the viscount on the back. "Helps with the devil of a head left over from last night, don't ya know?"

Berkeley lifted his teacup to his lips. "No. I don't. But I'll take your word for it."

That reply only made Hart laugh harder, which made his head hurt more. Hart liked his brother-in-law a great deal, but the man was decidedly humdrum when it came to amusements. Berkeley rarely drank, rarely smoked, and preferred to spend his time at his estate in the north of England or his hunting lodge in Scotland. Berkeley enjoyed quiet pursuits like reading or carving things out of wood much more than the amusements London had to offer. But Viscount Berkeley was a good man and one who clearly adored Hart's sister, and that was what mattered.

The viscount had gone so far as to dramatically interrupt Sarah's wedding to a pompous marquess and claim her for himself, thereby not only proving his commitment to Sarah but also saving Hart from having the self-involved Marquess of Branford as a brother-in-law. Overall it had been quite a fortunate turn of events for everyone. Everyone except Hart and Sarah's enraged, thwarted parents, that is.

Berkeley tugged at his cravat. "How are your—ahem—parents getting on?"

Hart cracked a smile. "Still angry, of course, even after all these months. You and Sarah made a good decision, staying up north for the winter. Gave Father and Mother time to calm down." His father's anger at having a scandal mar his family name and his daughter marry a mere viscount as opposed to a marquess who had the ear of the Prince Regent had barely abated over the winter, but no need to tell Berkeley as much.

Berkeley leaned back in his chair and crossed one silk-stockinged ankle over an immaculately creased knee, his hands lightly clutching the arms of his chair. He shook his head. "They're not calmed down, are they?"

"A bit." Hart stopped a footman and ordered another

brandy. "Don't worry. They'll be civil when they see you. For Sarah's sake."

"Well, that's something. Are you *seriously* ordering another drink?"

"Are you *seriously* surprised?" Hart scratched his rough cheek. He'd been running late and hadn't bothered to ask his usually drunken valet to shave him this morning. For Christ's sake, that man drank more than *he* did. Not exactly someone he wanted near his throat with a straight razor. "Besides I have quite a good reason to drink today."

"Really?" Berkeley tugged at his cuff. Ever since Sarah had taught him how to dress properly, the viscount was much more attentive to his clothing. He was downright dapper these days. "Why is that?"

"I'm getting married." Hart emitted a groan to accompany those incomprehensible words.

Berkeley's brows shot up. He set down his cup and placed a hand behind his ear. "Pardon? I must have heard you incorrectly. I thought you said *married.*"

The footman returned with the drink and Hart snatched it from the man's gloved hand and downed nearly half of it in a single gulp. "I did," he muttered through clenched teeth, wincing.

"*You?* Married?" Berkeley's brow remained steadfastly furrowed, and he blinked as if the word were foreign.

"*Me.* Married." Hart gave a firm nod before taking another fortifying gulp of brandy.

"Ahem, who is the, uh, fortunate lady?" Berkeley lifted his cup back to his lips and took a long gulp, as if needing the hot drink to banish his astonishment.

"I haven't the first idea." Hart shook his head. He was giving serious thought to the notion of ordering a third brandy. Would that be bad form? Probably.

"Now you're simply confusing me," Berkeley said with an unmistakable smile on his face. With his free hand, he pulled the morning's copy of the *Times* from the tabletop next to him and scanned the headlines.

Hart took another sip of brandy and savored it this time. "I haven't made any decisions as to the chit yet. I've merely announced to Father that this is the year I intend to find a bride. The idea of marriage has always made my stomach turn. After all, if my parents' imperfect union is anything by which to gauge the institution, it's a bloody nightmare."

"Why the change of heart?" Berkeley asked.

Hart scrubbed a hand through his hair. The truth was, he wasn't less sickened by the prospect of marriage these days, but he couldn't avoid the institution *forever*. At some point he'd have to put the parson's noose firmly around his own throat and pull. Wives were fickle, and marriages meant little other than the exchange of money and property. His own father had announced that fact on more than one occasion. His parents treated each other like unhappy strangers, and his father had made it clear that they were anything but in love. That, Hart supposed, was his fate. To live a life as his parents had in the pursuit of procreating and producing the next future Earl of Highfield. So be it, but was it any wonder he'd been putting it off?

"Seeing Sarah marry had more of an effect on me than I expected," Hart admitted, frowning at his not-quite-empty glass. "And if you ever tell anyone I said that, I'll call you out." He looked at Berkeley and grinned again.

"You have my word," Berkeley replied with a nod. "But may I ask *how* it affected you?"

Hart pushed himself back in the large leather chair and crossed his booted feet at the ankles. "I started thinking about it all, you know? Life, marriage, children, family. I expect you and Sarah will be having a child soon, and by God I'd like my children to grow up knowing their kin. My cousin Nicole was quite close to Sarah and me when we were children. Nicole's marriage isn't one to emulate, either. She hasn't even *seen* her husband in years. Last I heard, she's living somewhere in France, childless. By God, perhaps I *should* rethink this." Hart pulled at his cravat. The bloody thing was nearly choking him what with all of this talk of marriage.

Berkeley leaned back in his seat, mirroring Hart. "Perhaps you should focus on the positive aspects of marriage. I assure you, there are many."

"Believe me, I'm trying," Hart continued, reminding himself for the hundredth time of the reasons why he'd finally come to this decision. God knew it hadn't been an easy one. "Whether I like it or not, it's time for me to choose a bride. Sarah is my *younger* sister. While she wasn't married, it all seemed like fun and games, but now, well, seems everyone is tying the proverbial knot these days what with Owen Monroe and Rafe Cavendish marrying. Even Rafe's twin, Cade, has fallen to the parson's noose."

Just this morning when Hart had woken with a splitting head for the dozenth time in as many days, he'd thought yet again how he needed to stop being so reckless.

He wasn't able to bounce back from a night of debauchery nearly as quickly as he used to when he was at university. Seeing Sarah marry had made him consider his duties, his responsibilities, and his . . . age. For the love of God, he was nearly *thirty*. That thought alone was enough to make him want another brandy. It was his duty to sire the next Earl of Highfield, and duty meant something to him. What else mattered if he didn't respect his duty? Hadn't that been hammered into his head since birth by his father, along with all the dire warnings not to choose the wrong wife?

"It's true that several marriages have taken place lately in our set of friends," Berkeley replied, still leisurely perusing the paper while sipping tea. "But I thought *you* were immune to all of that, Highgate."

"I have been." Hart sighed again. "But I've finally decided it's time to get to it."

Berkeley raised his teacup in salute. "Here's to the future Lady Highfield. May she be healthy, beautiful, and wise."

"Thank you," Hart replied. He tugged at his python-like cravat again.

Berkeley regarded Hart down the length of his nose. "Any ladies catch your fancy?"

Hart shook his head. He braced an elbow on the table beside them and set his chin on his fist. "No. That's the problem. I'm uncertain where to begin."

Berkeley let the paper drop to his lap. "What sort of lady are you looking for?"

Hart considered the question for a moment. What sort of lady, indeed? "She'll need to be reasonable, well connected, clever, witty, a happy soul. Someone who is honest, and forthright, and who isn't marrying me *only* for my title. Someone who doesn't nag and has an indecently large dowry, of course. Father puts great stock in such things. Not to mention if I'm going to be legshackled, I might as well get a new set of horses out of the bargain. I'm thinking a set of matching grays and a new coach."

"Oh, that's not much of a list," Berkeley said with a snort.

"I don't expect the search to be a simple one, or a quick one." The truth was Hart had no earthly idea who he was looking for. He only knew who he wasn't looking for . . . someone like his mother. Or the treacherous Annabelle Cardiff. He wanted the exact opposite.

Berkeley tossed the paper back onto the tabletop. "Knowing your father's decided opinions on such matters, I'm surprised he hasn't provided you with a list of eligible females from which you may choose."

Hart rolled his eyes. "He has. He's named half a dozen ladies he would gladly accept."

Berkeley inclined his head to the side. "Why don't you choose one of them then?"

Hart gave his brother-in-law an are-you-quite-serious look, chin tucked down, head tilted to the side. "I'm bloody well not about to allow my *father* to choose a bride for me. Besides, after seeing you and Sarah, I hold out *some* hope of finding a lady with whom I'm actually compatible."

"Why, Highgate, do you mean . . . love?" Berkeley grinned and leaned forward in mock astonishment.

"Let's not go *that* far." Hart took another sip of his quickly dwindling brandy. That's precisely what confused him so much. He knew love matches existed. He'd witnessed one in his sister's marriage. On the other hand, her choice had so enraged his parents, they still hadn't forgiven her. Hart didn't intend to go about the business of finding a wife in quite so dramatic a fashion. Love matches attracted drama. However, his parents' unhappy union was nothing to aspire to, and he'd nearly made the mistake of marrying a woman who wanted nothing more than title and fortune before. It was a tricky business, the marriage mart, but he'd rather take advice from Sarah and Berkeley than his father. The proof of the pudding was in the eating, after all.

Berkeley laughed. "What if you fall madly in love and become a devoted husband? Jealous even. Now, *that* would be a sight."

"Jealous? *That's* not possible." Hart grinned back at Berkeley. "I've *never* been jealous. Don't have it in me. My friends at university used to tease me about it. No ties to any particular lady. No regrets." He settled back in his chair and straightened his cravat, which was tighter than ever.

"We'll see." Berkeley took another sip of tea. His eyes danced with amusement.

"I was hoping you and Sarah might help me this Season. Sarah knows most of the young ladies. She also knows me as well as anyone does. Not to mention, the two of you seem to have got the thing right."

Berkeley glanced up. "Why, Highgate, is that a compliment on our marriage?"

"Take it as you will." Hart waved a noncommittal hand in the air. He avoided meeting Berkeley's eyes.

Berkeley settled further into his chair. "I shall take it as a compliment, then. I have a feeling Sarah would like nothing more than to help you with such an endeavor. She fancies herself a matchmaker these days."

"Will you two be staying in London for the Season?"

"Yes. Sarah wants to stay and I, of course, will support her, at least as long as I can remain in the same town as your father without him calling me out." A smirk settled on Berkeley's face.

Hart eyed the remaining liquid in his glass. "I'll be happy to play the role of peacemaker to the best of my ability."

"I'm glad to hear that." Berkeley inclined his head toward his brother-in-law.

"Who else is Sarah matchmaking for?" Hart sloshed the brandy in the bottom of the glass.

"She's not merely matchmaking. No. To hear her tell it, she has an important mission this Season."

Hart set down the glass and pulled another section of the *Times* off the table and began scanning it. He'd talked enough about marriage for one day. Odious topic. "A mission? What mission?" he asked, merely to be polite.

"To find Meg Timmons a husband."

Hart startled in surprise, grasping the paper so tightly it tore in the middle. Tossing it aside, he reached for his glass and gulped the last of his brandy.

Meg Timmons. He knew Meg Timmons. She was Sarah's closest friend, the daughter of his father's mortal enemy, and a woman with whom Hart had experienced an incident last summer that he'd been seriously trying to forget.

CHAPTER THREE

Meg knew precisely whom she needed to enlist in support of her mission. The perfect person. The ultimate strategist. One Lucy Hunt. The young, dashing Duchess of Claringdon was a favorite of the *ton*. She was rich. She was beautiful. She was outspoken. And she was master of planning plots, the sort of plots that ended up matching couples together and ensuring weddings took place. The *exact* sort of plot that was in order if Meg was to have any chance at Hart. Meg had met Lucy through Viscount Berkeley, who was thick as thieves with the duchess and her set.

Yes. A visit to the duchess was necessary. Immediately. The Season was about to begin, and Hart might well find his bride at the first ball of the Season.

Meg dressed in her best day gown, did what she could to clean her old kid gloves for the hundredth time, and put on her paste jewelry. She called for the

well-traveled family coach and took her severely un-
derpaid maid—one of the few servants her parents kept
employed—with her to the duchess's town house during calling hours the next day.

The duchess greeted her warmly and welcomed her
into the stunning mansion. Lucy was dressed in a gorgeous emerald gown, her curly black hair piled high
atop her head, her unusually colored eyes—one was
blue, the other green—sparkling. They settled in one of
the glorious drawing rooms, where Meg and Lucy consumed tea and cakes and shared idle gossip.

"You wouldn't believe it," Lucy said. "One of the
housemaids was missing for the better part of two hours
last week before we got the notion to check the silver
closet. Turns out she'd been accidentally locked inside."
Lucy clucked her tongue. "The door has a most unfortunate tendency to stick."

"That's positively outrageous," Meg replied with a
laugh, trying to ignore the nerves bubbling in her stomach as if she'd drunk too much champagne.

"Isn't it, though?" Lucy took a sip of her heavily sugared tea. "I've asked one of the footmen to repair it, but
he's had little luck. We're afraid we'll have to replace
the entire contraption. None of the housemaids will go
near the thing. I cannot blame them."

Meg took a deep breath. She pressed her shaking
knees together.

One. Two. Three. "Your Grace," she began.

"No, no. We'll have none of that, Meg." Lucy gave
Meg a sharp glance. The two had long ago established
the informality with which they addressed each other.
Meg had forgotten due to nerves. She nodded and gave

Lucy a tentative smile while bringing her shaking tea-cup to her lips. "Yes, of course, Lucy. There's something I need to ask you."

A catlike grin popped to the duchess's lips. She moved closer to the edge of her seat and leaned slightly toward Meg. "Ooh, what is it? You know I adore it whenever anyone asks for my assistance."

Meg closed her eyes briefly and took another forti-fying deep breath before she launched into her tale.

"And so you see," Meg finished after relating her en-tire story—minus the part about what had happened between her and Hart the night before Sarah's wedding. "I am greatly in need of your help, and time is of the essence."

The duchess stood and paced. Meg anxiously watched her from the settee. Lucy took another turn about the room and tapped her cheek.

"To begin with." Lucy came to a stop in front of Meg, "I applaud you for coming to me first. As you may know, I've helped many people, but so few of them have *asked* to be helped. Such a pity. It's a credit to you that you're wise enough to know when you're up against seemingly insurmountable odds and require skilled assistance." Lucy grinned at her.

"Do you truly think you can help me, Lucy?" Meg asked breathlessly. She had leaned forward so far she'd nearly toppled off the settee. Her knee was bouncing, her teacup was jittering on its saucer in her hand, and she felt as if she might cast up her accounts at any moment.

Lucy resumed both her pacing and her cheek tapping. "It won't be easy. You're dealing with a serious imbal-ance in station, a long-standing family feud, and a highly unfortunate lack of dowry."

Meg worried her bottom lip. She set the teacup on the table beside her so the telltale jittering would stop. "Yes. I know. I am prepared to—"

"However," Lucy interrupted, still tapping her cheek, "you are adorable. You are clever, and you are determined. Not to mention." Lucy paused, and the catlike smile resumed its spot on her lips. "You have *me* helping you. There are two questions I must ask you. Two exceedingly important questions."

Meg held her breath. If Lucy would only agree to help her, she'd do anything, try anything, say anything. "What are they?" Meg asked, her stays biting into her too-full lungs.

"First." Lucy turned to face her and folded her arms over her chest. "I must know why you love him. Or at least why you think you do."

Meg blinked rapidly. She had not been expecting such a question. Why did she love Hart? She just did. It was a fact, like how the sun rose every morning and set every evening. No one had ever asked *why* before. Sarah was the only other person who knew Meg's feelings and Sarah had certainly never questioned them. Sarah loved him, too. She understood.

Meg cleared her throat. "Well, let's see. He's handsome, he's charming, he's witty, he's friendly, he's good at absolutely everything he does."

"Yes, those are all true, dear, but there must be something deeper."

Deeper? Deeper? "He's impossibly good to his sister, he treats his servants like treasured friends, and I've never known him to pass by a beggar without tossing along whatever coins are in his pocket." She sighed. Who wouldn't love Hart Highgate?

"All outstanding qualities," Lucy agreed. "But there must be some reason why you fell in love with him. Out of all the men you've ever met. Why *him* precisely?"

Meg bit her lip. "I've loved him since I was sixteen," she offered lamely.

The duchess crossed her arms over her chest. "Yes, you said as much, dear, but I still need to know *why*."

"Does it truly make a difference?" Meg searched Lucy's face. She'd heard Lucy could be difficult to work with in such circumstances, but she certainly hadn't been expecting to be quizzed so thoroughly.

Lucy shook her head back and forth slowly. "Oh my dear. It makes all the difference in the world. We love others for many reasons, but if you love Hart merely because he is handsome, rich, and dashing—and believe me, he is all three of those things, I agree—you will not have the type of solid foundation that *true* love is based upon. I am a romantic at heart but I only wish to help people who are in love for the *right* reasons. You must understand."

Meg took yet another deep breath. She searched her memory, all the way back to when she was sixteen. She bit her lip and met Lucy's piecing gaze. "Very well. I actually do know why I love him. I've always known. But if I tell you, you must promise not to tell anyone." The idea of sharing this story with Lucy felt awkward . . . uncomfortable even.

The duchess shook her head emphatically, and one of her black curls popped loose from her chignon and bounced along her forehead. "I would never laugh at love." She said the words so solemnly, Meg believed her.

"Very well." Meg folded her hands in her lap and gazed at the coffered ceiling, contemplating where to begin.

"When I was sixteen, Hart accompanied Sarah on a visit to my father's house one day. They were on their way elsewhere and I'm certain Hart must have been bored senseless by being forced to stop and pay a call on his sister's little friend. But he sat in the drawing room and acted polite while I did my best to impress him with my tea-serving skills and my vocabulary."

Lucy smothered a grin. "You continue to be adorable. What happened?"

"I was the veriest silly thing," Meg admitted, her face heating at the memory. "Red spots on my face, blushing too much, giggling far too often, that sort of thing."

"And Hart was kind to you?" Lucy prompted, sympathy clearly written across her fine features.

Meg swallowed hard. It was not a memory she liked to dwell on. She'd long ago stuffed it inside her journal and otherwise attempted to forget it. "My mother discovered that Sarah and Hart were in the drawing room with me. Father was supposed to be there with us, but he was still in bed after a night of gambling."

"Egad." Lucy knew all about Father's gambling. Everyone did, but they never admitted it in polite company.

"That's not unusual for Father," Meg replied, shame making her voice thin.

"Go on, dear," Lucy said kindly, reaching down and patting her hand.

"Mother stormed into the drawing room and ordered Sarah and Hart to leave. I was so embarrassed I wanted to expire. It was soon after our parents' falling-out, you see, but until that day I hadn't realized they were *that* angry with one another."

"The rumor is that your father owes Sarah's father a gambling debt," Lucy said quietly. "Is that true?"

Meg swallowed and nodded. "I've heard the same thing but only through gossip. My parents never told me the details. I only knew I wanted to die from shame that day. Mother said she wouldn't have the Earl of Highfield's rich, entitled little brats in her home."

"No!" Lucy gasped.

"I'm afraid it's true." Even after all these years, the memory brought an avalanche of shame. She busied herself with another sip of tea, hoping the cup might hide her cheeks, which were doubtlessly red. "I have every reason to suspect that Mother had been drinking as well that particular afternoon."

"What happened next?" Lucy asked, searching Meg's face.

"Hart and Sarah stood to leave, of course. It was clear they both felt awfully sorry for me."

"And Hart did something?" Lucy asked, taking a seat next to Meg and patting her hand again.

"It wasn't until they were nearly out the drawing room door that Mother turned to me and said, 'Don't think they actually enjoy your company, Margaret. They're only here to lord over you and show you how much finer their clothing is. How much more costly their fancy carriage is. You are not good enough for the likes of them and you never will be.'"

"No!" Lucy's face was red with anger now. Her nostrils flared and her pupils dilated.

"Yes," Meg breathed. As long as she lived she'd never forget what happened next. "Hart turned back, and, completely ignoring my mother, he looked me in the eye and said, 'Don't listen to her, Meg. She's an unhappy person. You'll always be good enough for us.' Mother scoffed at that and Hart turned to her and said, 'Madame, say what you will about my sister and me, we can take it from your venomous lips, but if I ever again hear you say anything as awful to your daughter as I have just witnessed, I will make you wish you hadn't.'"

"He didn't," Lucy breathed, pressing a hand to her chest.

"Yes, he did." Meg had loved him for it ever since. He'd never paid much attention to her before or since, but in that moment he'd been her hero. The only person in the world who had ever stood up for her. Her mother constantly berated her, blamed her for not finding a husband, not being pretty enough or smart enough.

But something had changed in Meg in that moment that Hart had stood up for her. She'd actually believed it. Believed that she was good enough and that she was worth something. When Hart stood up for her, she'd realized. She was good enough. She was worth something. Sarah, of course, had apologized and squeezed Meg's hand and left quickly with tears in her eyes, but Hart's words rang in her memory forever.

"Very well," Lucy said, dabbing at her suspiciously wet eyes with a handkerchief she'd produced from her pocket. "I can see you've got reason to love him. I love him a little, too, for doing that."

Meg swallowed again and shook her head to clear the unshed tears from her eyes. "What is the second question?" she asked, ready to change the subject.

"Second question?" Lucy echoed, her eyes clouded with confusion.

"You said you had two questions to ask me about Hart."

"Oh yes, thank you for reminding me, dear. The second question is simply, what does Hart think of you?

Have you any reason to suspect he might return your admiration?"

Meg's shoulders slumped. She set down her teacup once more and furrowed her brow. What *did* Hart think of her? "I've no idea. You would have to ask him." More blinking. She squared her shoulders, determined to keep her emotions under control.

"You have no clue? No inkling?"

Meg splayed her hands wide, her worn reticule bobbing around her wrist. "I assume he thinks I'm Sarah's friend. These days he rarely seems to notice me at all . . . except . . ." Oh no. She hadn't meant to say that last word aloud.

Lucy, of course, pounced. The woman resembled a cat in more ways than one. "Except . . . ?" She eyed Meg down the length of her patrician nose.

Meg worried her bottom lip again. There was no help for it. She was going to have to tell the duchess. She wanted to sink through the settee and pull the fine Persian carpet over her head. "Except for the one time that . . ."

Lucy slowly raised her brows and tilted her head to the side, staring at Meg. "Except for the one time that . . . ?"

Meg scrunched up her nose. She squeezed her eyes shut and covered them with her gloved fingers. "Except for the time that he kissed me."

CHAPTER FOUR

"Pardon!" Lucy nearly shouted, her voice reaching an octave Meg hadn't heard before.

"Shhh!" Meg pulled her hands away from her face and gave Lucy an imploring, be-quiet glare.

Lucy plunked her hands on her hips but thankfully lowered her voice. She dropped to the floor next to the settee and knelt in front of Meg. "Except for the time that *he kissed you*?"

Meg nodded so vigorously that two of her blond ringlets bounced free from their pins. She hastily tucked them behind her ear. "Yes, yes. But it wasn't at all how you think. He didn't know it was me."

If it was possible for the duchess's fascinating eyes to get any wider, they surely did. For a few moments Lucy merely hovered there, her mouth opening and closing, no words emerging. Finally, she said, "My dear girl. You have done the impossible. You have rendered *me* speechless."

Meg pressed her palms to her cheeks. "Does this mean you cannot help me?"

"On the contrary," Lucy replied. "If the man has already defended you from what sounds like a hideous mother *and* kissed you, I'd say we're off to a fine start indeed."

"No," Meg said. "I told you, it wasn't like that. He didn't know he was kissing *me*."

Lucy stood and dropped back down to sit beside Meg. "Yes, about that. I'm going to need to hear that story, dear. Immediately if you don't mind."

Meg swallowed and took a deep breath. She smoothed two fingers over an eyebrow. "Very well, but I must ask you to keep it to yourself. I haven't told this to anyone . . . including Sarah."

"Cross my heart," Lucy replied, doing so and nodding, her eyes sparkling with anticipation.

Meg settled back against the settee and readjusted her skirts. It was a pity the gown was so old and stained she'd been forced to dye it pink. Long ago it had been white and lovely. She shook her head. She'd never been one to dwell upon her reduced circumstances. "It all happened the night before Sarah's wedding."

"Yes." Lucy had turned to her. Her eyes were trained on Meg's face in rapt attention.

"I decided I needed to speak to Hart, to see if he thought we should do something to . . . stop the wedding or to try to convince Sarah not to marry the Marquess of Branford."

Lucy nodded. "Yes. I recall how desperate we all were that day. It was so obvious that Sarah and Berkeley were meant to be together instead."

Meg nodded. "It was awful. As each minute ticked by, I felt more helpless."

Lucy squeezed Meg's hand. "Oh my dear, Berkeley and Sarah needed to come to that realization on their own."

Meg squeezed Lucy's hand, too. "I know that now, of course, but at the time I felt as if my dearest friend was drowning and I was merely watching from the bank, doing nothing to help."

"You're a good friend," Lucy said, patting Meg's hand. "Go on. So you decided to enlist Hart to help you?"

Meg nodded. "Yes. Sarah wouldn't listen to either of us individually, but I thought perhaps *together* we might convince her."

Lucy's eyes widened even further. "Surely you didn't go to his apartments?"

Meg shook her head, and the pesky curls popped out again. She brushed them away once more. "No! Of course not. That would be a certain scandal."

Lucy's face flooded with relief. "My point entirely, dear." She placed a hand over her heart and expelled her breath. "Where did you meet then?"

Meg's cheeks heated. She'd been a complete fool that night, but she might as well out with it. Besides, the duchess had seen and heard plenty of scandalous things. Meg's little story was probably not much in comparison. "I sent Hart a note. I asked him to meet me in the park next to Father's house, after dark. I told my parents and my maid that my head ached and I intended to go to bed early. Instead I sneaked outside."

Lucy gasped and squeezed Meg's wrist this time.

"Dear, that's horribly unsafe. You could have been accosted, robbed, murdered even."

Meg swallowed. "I know, but my parents live on the park and I asked Hart to meet me nearby. It truly wasn't far, only next door, really. That's why I thought . . ."

Lucy's brow furrowed. She eyed Meg warily. "Thought *what*, dear?"

Meg closed her eyes and allowed the words to rush from her lips. "That's why I thought he'd know who sent the note when I signed it only with my initials."

"MT?" Lucy expelled her breath and rubbed the tip of her nose with two fingers. "Oh." A moment ticked by. "Dear."

"Oh yes," Meg echoed. "I didn't want to sign my name for fear someone would find the note and it would cause a scandal."

Lucy poked at her curls with her finger. "Yes, asking a bachelor to meet you in the park at night isn't exactly prudent for one's reputation. Not that I am judging."

Meg took a deep breath. "So there I was hiding in the dark, and . . ."

The memory struck Meg then, captured her, and she was back in the park next to her father's house with her arms wrapped around herself, shivering in the night breeze, the smell of jasmine and freshly chopped grass surrounding her. Even though it was summer, it had been unusually cold that evening and she'd left home without her pelisse. She would never forget a moment of it.

"Are you there?" Hart's familiar deep voice sounded through the hedge, a voice she'd memorized, a voice that never failed to send gooseflesh skittering up her arms.

"I'm here," she'd breathed and for a moment, one heart-stoppingly wonderful moment, she'd pretended he was coming to meet her because they were lovers, affianced and unable to stay away from each other, eager to be in the other's arms. So it had shocked her beyond measure when Hart had stepped behind the hedge where she was waiting, pulled her straight into his strong, warm, muscled arms, and lowered his mouth to hers. The kiss lasted for only a few moments but it might as well have been an hour. Hart's firm lips molded hers to his and his tongue boldly pushed its way inside her mouth.

It must have been the tiny squeak of surprise or perhaps her taste, perhaps her height, but he soon knew his mistake. He pulled away. Setting her a respectable distance from him he said, "I beg your pardon." His breathing sounded ragged.

"Hart?" she'd murmured, knowing full well it was him. She knew him from his stance, his scent, his voice. Simultaneously, her heart sank as she realized he had thought he was meeting a lover. Just not her. *Dear God, who did he think MT was? Jealousy flooded through her, but she didn't have time to dwell upon the feeling because Hart immediately grabbed her hand and pulled her out under a beam of moonlight where he promptly exclaimed, "Meg!"*

"Yes?"

He dropped her hand.

She rubbed her wrist where his fingers had been, longing for his touch again. "Who did you think I—?" She hated how small her voice sounded.

His eyes were wide with surprise. "What are you doing here?" His voice was sharp, almost accusatory.

Tears sprang to her eyes and Meg swallowed. "I sent you a note."

"You sent—" He rubbed his palm across his forehead, mussing his black hair. His emerald eyes glowed in the moonlight. This was decidedly not how she'd envisioned her first kiss, but ah, it had been with Hart as she'd always dreamed it would be. For goodness' sake, if she'd known sending him an ambiguous note would result in a rendezvous in the park and a scorching kiss, she would have sent the note ages ago.

"Miss Timmons, I sincerely apologize for my untoward behavior. I didn't know it was you." Hart seemed nervous, which meant he was probably calculating the likelihood of her telling anyone about what had just happened, and his being dragged unceremoniously to the altar. Just like the Annabelle Cardiff disaster. Meg wanted him, of course, but not *that* way.

"Don't worry," she hastened to assure him. "It's my fault. I should have signed the note with my entire name."

"Why did you send me a note in the first place?" His voice still had an edge to it.

"Because . . ." Suddenly she felt utterly silly. Suddenly she had no idea whether Hart would even agree with her that Sarah and Branford were an awful match. Suddenly Meg wished she'd never sent that note. Suddenly tears stung her eyes again.

"I'm sorry. I didn't think." Her voice was embarrassingly high and tight. Oh, why did she always have to act like such a ninny in his presence? Why couldn't she be calm, collected, sophisticated?

"It's all right," Hart replied. He stepped forward and rubbed her shoulders. The gooseflesh spread like wildfire. "You're freezing." He stepped back, pulled off his *coat in one fluid motion, and slipped it around her shoulders. It was large, warm, and smelled like him. She sniffed it longingly, never wanting to let it go.*

"Calm down," he said. "Tell me what's wrong."

"It's Sarah." *Meg pulled the coat even tighter.*

Hart's eyes went wide with alarm. He searched Meg's face. "What is it? Is Sarah all right?"

"Yes. Yes. Of course." *Meg nodded, clutching the coat around her shoulders and rubbing her cheek against the expensive fabric.* "She's fine. I mean to say, she will be fine. I hope. It's just . . . Lord Branford. She doesn't love him. She cannot marry him. She loves Lord Berkeley. I know it."

Hart continued to stroke Meg's arms, which was ever so distracting, even with the fabric of the coat between them. He sighed and looked at the ground. His jaw was tight. "I agree with you, but—"

Meg forced herself to forget the scent of Hart's coat enveloping her and to concentrate on why she'd come. "I think Sarah is ruining her life to make your parents happy."

Hart nodded. "I agree."

"She's going to be miserable," *Meg continued.*

Hart's jaw was tight, as if set in stone. "I agree."

It faintly pierced Meg's consciousness that Hart was agreeing with her, but he didn't appear ready to spring into action. "What are we going to do?" *she asked, searching his face.*

Hart's hands dropped from her shoulders. He clenched his long fingers into fists and put them on his hips. "Absolutely nothing."

Meg shook her head. She must have heard him incorrectly. "Nothing?"

"That's right." He stood there in the moonlight, his feet braced apart, a determined look on his handsome face.

Meg started toward him and then forced herself to stop. "What? Why? You just agreed with me."

Hart nodded slowly. "And I'll continue to agree with you, but I've already spoken to Sarah and her mind is made up."

"Oh." Meg bit her lip. "But don't you think, if we both—"

"No." His voice was calm, resolute, echoing through the still night air.

"Why?" she asked quietly. She had to ask. It hadn't occurred to her that Hart wouldn't want to interfere.

Hart paced away from her and slid his hands inside his pockets. He looked out across the hedgerows behind them. "Because I know my sister and you do, too. She's stubborn. I think she's less likely to listen to us if we push harder."

Meg shivered and nodded. He had a point. "You told her what you thought?"

"Yes, and I suspect you already have, too."

"Yes," Meg admitted. Hart was right. Sarah didn't like to be told what to do. The more they tried to convince her she was wrong, the more stubborn she would become.

Hart turned back to face her. "Don't you see? That's all we can do. All that's left is to hope for the best."

"Do you really think so?" Meg shamelessly wanted to prolong her time in his company.

"I know so," Hart replied. "Now let me get you home."

Hart had escorted her back to the ivy-covered wooden door that led from the park to her father's property, and while they'd shared an awkward moment in Hart's father's coach the next day after Sarah had fled her wedding, they'd managed to avoid each other for months.

Meg finished recounting the entire tale.

"Hmm," Lucy said. "Now that is something. I'd say it's entirely promising."

Meg blinked. "How is it promising?"

"Mostly the part about him avoiding you afterward," Lucy replied brightly, pouring herself another cup of tea and reaching for the sugar bowl.

Meg's brow remained tightly furrowed. "I don't see how *that's* promising."

Lucy stirred the small silver spoon around and around the cup. "Of course it's promising. If it hadn't affected him, he wouldn't have cared one way or the other."

Meg had no time to reply to *that* ludicrous pronouncement before Lucy said, "Now let's get to business. Please say you'll allow me to give you a gown for the Hodges' ball tomorrow night." The Hodges were hosting the first ball of the Season, and Meg intended to attend with Lucy and Sarah as her chaperones.

"You know I won't." Meg stared at her slippers to avoid Lucy's gaze.

"I know you say you don't want to take any—as you call it—charity." Lucy rolled her eyes.

"Precisely," Meg replied with a resolute nod, her hands folded in her lap. She'd never once accepted a handout from anyone and she was exceedingly proud of that. She refused to pretend she was anything other than what she was: a penniless wallflower. If she was going to be mocked by members of the *ton*, it would be because of what she truly was, not because she was using her well-to-do friends for favors and putting on airs.

"But it would make *me* so happy to have a gown fitted for you," Lucy prodded. "Doesn't that count for anything?"

"Unfortunately, no. Because it would make *me* decidedly unhappy." Meg couldn't fathom it. It wasn't about being too proud to take charity. Her worst fear was being pitied. One of the reasons she loved Sarah so dearly was because Sarah didn't pity her. Sarah never mentioned the vast difference in their stations. Meg knew Lucy didn't intend to make her feel bad, but pointing out the inadequacy of her wardrobe wouldn't change Meg's mind. "Hart is well aware of my circumstances," Meg said. "Dressing me in fancy clothing won't make a difference."

"Perhaps," Lucy replied. "But he may *notice* you a bit more and so might other gentlemen, dear. Which might make Hart take even *more* notice. I've said it before and I'll repeat it, men *adore* competition, whether it be over horses, cards, or—sorry to say it—ladies."

Meg plucked at the strings of her reticule. The one she'd already had to patch on more than one occasion. She and Lucy would never agree. Meg needed to change the subject. "We're not even certain Hart will be at the Hodges' ball. He doesn't usually attend such events."

"Nonsense," Lucy retorted, taking a sip of her tea. "He's looking for a wife this Season. Dull as they may be, *ton* balls are the only sensible place for a man of Hart's station to find a suitable wife."

Meg bit her lip. "What if he already has someone in mind?"

Lucy flourished her free hand in the air. "We'll have to change his mind."

"What if he doesn't look twice at me?" Meg breathed.

"We'll have to force him to notice you." Lucy winked at her.

Meg worried the reticule string. "What if he notices and isn't interested?"

Lucy nodded sagely. "We'll have to make you exceedingly interesting."

Meg couldn't help the small smile that popped to her lips. "Do you have an answer for everything, Lucy?"

"Yes," Lucy retorted without hesitating, taking another sip of tea.

The butler arrived then and announced Lady Sarah Berkeley. After he left to fetch the lady in question, Meg turned to Lucy with wide eyes. "Sarah's here?"

"Yes," Lucy replied. "I invited her because I suspected I'd need reinforcements in this argument with you about the clothing. Sarah and I have been plotting for days to get you to change your mind and allow us to help you with your wardrobe."

Meg's heart hammered in her chest. "You cannot mention any of this to her. About Hart I mean."

"Of course I won't," Lucy answered, her smallest finger in the air. "You swore me to secrecy, did you not? But Sarah knows you're looking for a husband, even if she doesn't know you're specifically looking toward Hart. Rest assured. I don't tell secrets, I devise plots, and speaking of plots, we must get to planning yours, dear."

Moments later, the door to the drawing room opened and Sarah came floating through it. The brunette viscountess with green eyes so like her brother's made her way to the settee where Meg sat. "So good to see you both," Sarah said brightly, plucking off her gloves.

"There you are, Lady Berkeley," Lucy said. "Thank you for joining us. I was just telling our Meg, here, that to attract a proper husband this Season she must allow us to help her with her clothing. Don't you agree?"

Sarah sank to the settee next to Meg. "I'd love it if Meggie would allow me to purchase some new gowns for her, but I understand if she doesn't want to accept our help."

"It's charity," Meg groaned.

"It's not charity, it's fun," Lucy replied, a disgruntled look on her pretty face.

"I don't see how I could possibly have fun if I felt indebted to either of you," Meg replied, glancing between the two ladies.

Lucy tapped her finger along her cheek. "My dear, you have been wearing the same gowns for the last three years now, correct?"

"Yes," Meg said, blushing slightly.

"What if I told you the new gowns are only a loan?" Lucy asked. "You may pay me back one day when you're happily married and have all the money you could ever want."

Meg opened her mouth to retort, but Lucy continued. "How in heaven's name do you expect anything to change this Season? If you want different results, you must do things differently."

Meg opened her mouth yet again, and Lucy interrupted again. "Just try it once. One gown. One time. One ball. See if anything is different. I promise you, your circumstances will change."

The duchess was making sense. A *loan* wouldn't be

so horrible. Meg's resolution began to crumble. How perfectly lovely it would be to wear a new gown. She eyed Sarah. "What do you think?"

Sarah squeezed Meg's hand. "I think you've got nothing to lose by trying. Let us make you into a princess, Meggie. You're certain to attract a gentleman's attention."

Behind Sarah's head, Lucy gave Meg a knowing smile. "Hopefully, the *right* gentleman."

CHAPTER FIVE

"Keep your eye on the receiving line. Your future wife may appear at any moment."

Hart nearly rolled his eyes at his sister's statement. If he could have, he would have whistled and stuck his hands in his pockets. That was how uninterested he was at the Hodges' ball. Boring. That's what this *ton* event business was. Excruciatingly boring and here he was . . . trapped.

He'd been to the refreshment table and been chased out of Lord Hodge's study by his own father who scolded him and informed him he wasn't about to find his future countess in the *study* of all places. He'd even taken a stroll through the Hodges' prizewinning gardens. None of it had been the least interesting.

There was not nearly enough brandy here and apparently, according to Sarah, *ton* hostesses looked askance at guests who downed glass after glass of liquor. Who knew? Hart had surrendered to his sister, asking Sarah to point out the most eligible, pleasant, least-concerned-with-wealth-and-titles ladies of her acquaintance. Sarah had done just that, but Hart was still . . . bored.

Lady Carina Hardwater was too quiet. In the time he'd spent in her company, nearly half an hour, she'd uttered perhaps three words and all three were related to the weather. On the other hand, Miss Banks talked *far* too much about topics *far* too uninteresting. In the mere quarter of an hour he'd spent in *her* esteemed company, he'd learned all about a riding accident she'd experienced as a child, her fondness for hot chocolate, and the fact that she preferred the color yellow above all others. Meanwhile, Lady Isabella Jones had a decided frown upon her face, clearly indicating to Hart that she was wholly uninterested in his company. They hadn't spent even five minutes in each other's company before she feigned an attack of the nerves, turned on her heel, and nearly galloped off to her mother's side, peeping at him from behind her fan every once in a while as if he were an ogre.

Less than three hours into his first ball of the Season, Hart quickly realized that finding a bride would *not* be as simple a task as he'd hoped.

He groaned and took another halfhearted glance around the room. Perhaps there was something the matter with him. Perhaps he didn't possess the same qualities other gentlemen did. Perhaps the social custom of finding a wife was something at which he would fail. A vision of Annabelle flashed through his mind. Annabelle had just made her debut six years ago when she'd attempted to trap him into marriage. At the age of three and twenty, his father had ordered him to find a wife. When Hart hadn't taken any steps to do so, his father had threatened to suspend his allowance. Like a fool, Hart had actually believed the old man. The threat had sent him into a round of attending *ton* balls.

He enjoyed the company of women. Always had. The business of finding a wife couldn't be *that* awful. His father had spent most of Hart's teenage years warning him about the consequences of choosing the wrong bride. Hart was prepared to make a good decision. Then he met Annabelle.

She was gorgeous. Blond, blue-eyed, sweet, shy. She'd batted her eyelashes and laughed at all his jokes. He'd been smitten, no doubt about it. He'd taken her riding in the park. He'd introduced her to his parents. He certainly had *contemplated* marriage, but something about her kept him from offering. Day after day he put it off, despite his father's increased frustration. It had been the best decision Hart had ever made.

He shuddered. Looking back, Annabelle did remind him of his mother: cold, calculating, and manipulative. The same woman who'd been willing to take Sarah back after her scandalous journey to Scotland, and lied to her betrothed about where she'd been. His mother had no compunction when it came to securing the most advantageous match for herself or her offspring.

After more than a month went by with no proposal, Annabelle had turned calculating. At a party, she'd begged Hart to take her out to the gardens. Once outside, she'd convinced him to take her deep into the maze grove. When he'd reluctantly complied, her closest friend had just happened to come upon them, threatening to sound the alarm and tell everyone they'd been caught in a compromising position. Neither girl had been a good enough actress to accomplish their plot, however, and he'd told them both that if they insisted upon continuing with their scheme, Annabelle would be ruined and he would not stand up for her. Thank God she'd believed him.

It made him nauseated to think about it. Annabelle's trap sounded jarringly close to the horror story his father told him about how his mother came to be the countess. After coming so close to marrying the exact wrong woman for the exact wrong reasons, Hart had promised himself never to make that same mistake again. He'd called his father's bluff, using the money he won racing horses to supplement his allowance until his father had relented in disgust and reinstated it. Meanwhile, Hart guarded both his heart and his company.

He scanned the ballroom. Ladies in pastel ball gowns fluttered their fans in front of their faces while gentlemen in peacock-like attire strutted around in front of them. The infamous London Marriage Mart. Why was this so difficult? So fraught with peril? It shouldn't be. It should be simple, easy, natural even. Was that how it had been with Sarah and Berkeley?

He'd never heard the details of what had happened when Berkeley found Sarah living in his hunting lodge in Scotland. They clearly adored each other. Though he'd never admit it aloud, Hart wanted that.

He'd never had a problem garnering the attention of ladies, but not the kind he would wish to marry. Until recently he'd been engaged in a pleasant affair with a tempting widow.

Lady Maria Tempest was the exact sort of woman he'd gravitated toward since the debacle with Annabelle. Jaded, knowledgeable, decadent, confident, Maria liked to give and receive pleasure with no strings attached. It had been Maria, he believed, who'd sent him the note the night before Sarah's wedding. At first he'd been horrified, worried that perhaps Meg Timmons would cry and run off, causing an incident that would result in an attempt to wring a proposal out of him, yet again.

In that case, Hart most likely would have had no choice but to do the right thing and offer for her. He'd been the one to grab her, pull her into his arms, and passionately kiss her, after all. But it turned out, unlike Annabelle, Meg was a capital sort of girl. She had quickly made it clear that she held him in no way responsible for the mistake, which was sporting of her, given the fact that she had been the one to send him a message asking him to meet in a clandestine location. In hindsight, it had been wise of the girl, given that of all the young women in London, Meg Timmons would be the very *last* one he might marry.

He'd admitted to himself later, however, that the kiss they'd shared in the gardens had been nothing less than . . . surprising. Hot, passionate, full of longing. He'd looked twice when he'd realized he'd been kissing Meg and not Maria. Try as he might, he'd been unable to forget the kiss.

Hart rubbed his forehead, dispelling all thoughts of his sister's closest friend. The fact remained that he was in need of a wife. In want of one, actually, and this particular ball on this particular night was sorely lacking in eligible candidates. He stifled a yawn while his sister shook her head at him. Sarah had been the belle of the Season two years ago when she'd made her debut. She'd promptly received an offer from the Marquess of Branford and then run off to Scotland to hide from that same offer, which was where she'd, ahem, *met* Berkeley. Not everyone could be so fortunate as to literally stumble upon (her chaperone had broken her ankle in the stumble) true love.

"You're not even trying," Sarah scolded. Her hands were planted on her hips. Her slipper tapped the marble floor.

"Yes I am," Hart replied, trying and failing to stifle a second yawn. "I let Lady Isabella scowl at me for at least ten minutes. I listened to Miss Banks prattle on for what felt like days. I even—"

A commotion by the doorway caught his attention, and Hart turned to look. The Duchess of Claringdon had arrived, dressed in her signature emerald green.

Next to her stood a vision in gold. The woman's straight blond hair was pulled atop her head. A strand of rubies encased the thin column of her throat. A lovely golden gown that reminded Hart of a Roman goddess covered her ample bosom, then fell down her slim body, sparkling like a waterfall with the sun shot through it. From so far away, Hart couldn't make out the color of her eyes, but they glowed with mirth as she laughed at something the duchess said. He couldn't take his gaze off her. She seemed *vaguely* familiar. He elbowed Sarah and nodded toward the door.

"Who is that?"

"The Duchess of Claringdon," Sarah replied absently.

"No, not the duchess. I meant that *gorgeous* creature with her."

Sarah let out a loud sigh. "Oh, Hart. You dolt. *That* is Meg."

CHAPTER SIX

Lucy Hunt was not one to waste time. No sooner had the butler announced their names than the duchess had swept Meg into a group of her friends to keep her safely cocooned while the whole of the Hodges' ball conjectured as to whether it was possible for Meg Timmons to have suddenly come up in the world.

Meg's heart hammered against her chest. She couldn't help but feel like both a fool and a fake. She'd spent the day at Lucy's town house, where a veritable team of seamstresses worked to concoct the most glorious gown Meg had ever seen. Then Lucy's maid had set about straightening Meg's confounded ringlets with a hot iron and applying a bit of rouge to her lips and cheeks. Finally, Lucy had emerged from her private bedchamber with a strand of rubies so breathtaking Meg doubted they were real. Lucy had handed them to Meg as if they were nothing more than a bauble, saying, "These were a gift from a Spanish princess."

Lucy had insisted Meg wear the priceless jewels and while she had to admit the effect was striking, she couldn't keep from worrying whether the necklace would somehow slip off or go missing. As a result, she touched it obsessively while simultaneously wondering how Lucy had come to know a Spanish princess.

"I cannot pay for them if they are misplaced," Meg must have said half a dozen times in the coach on the ride to the ball. Lucy had merely laughed, waved her hand in the air, and said, "They're only rubies, dear." Oh, to be wealthy.

Neither Mother nor Father was here. Lucy had taken over official chaperone duties from Meg's mother for the evening. When Meg asked Lucy about it, she'd got another hand flourish and a vague, "Leave everything to me." That also made Meg nervous. The duchess hadn't confided in her about her plans. But she reminded herself, she had asked for Lucy's help, and to continue to question her benefactress would be the height of rudeness.

Meg had given herself a silent talking-to in the coach, one that relied heavily upon attempting to remain calm and enjoy herself. But now that she was here, standing in the middle of the ballroom, glimmering conspicuously like a bar of gold, with all eyes fastened on her, she wanted nothing so much as to turn and run. She wasn't used to being seen, being watched, being the center of attention.

She greeted the duchess's good friends Cassandra, Lady Swifdon, the countess, and her husband, the earl, Lord Julian. Lucy had recently shared the news with Sarah and Meg that the countess was expecting a baby, though she wasn't far along and still able to go out in

Society. The couple was good looking and clearly devoted to each other. The earl stayed close to his beautiful blond wife and hovered near her, solicitously inquiring after her health every so often. Meg's heart ached as she watched them. Their obvious mutual adoration was what she hoped for with Hart.

Next Meg greeted Mr. and Mrs. Upton, the future Earl and Countess of Upbridge. Garrett was Lucy's cousin and her father's heir. Jane had dark, watchful eyes that blinked at Meg from behind silver-rimmed spectacles and a reticule weighed down by at least two books. Meg soon learned that Jane was possessed of a biting wit and Garrett of a good-humored nature. They were as devoted a couple as Cassandra and Julian were.

All of the men soon excused themselves to find amusements and drinks in the study, leaving the women standing together in the ballroom. Meg worried her bottom lip, convinced that Lucy's plan would not work.

"You look breathtaking," Cassandra said, smiling warmly at Meg.

"Agreed," Jane added, also smiling at Meg.

Meg returned both ladies' smiles. Lucy had probably asked her friends to say such nice things. Meg had never in her life been described as breathtaking. According to her mother she was too short, too thin, had too many curls in her hair, and looked too much like her father. Regardless, it was kind of Lucy's friends to bestow compliments.

Meg hadn't got up the nerve to glance around the ballroom to see if Hart was there. She desperately wanted to ask one of the other ladies if they'd seen him, but she wasn't that bold. She didn't have to wait long, however, because Sarah came hurrying up to their group.

"Meg," Sarah said after she'd properly greeted everyone. She stood back, and her gaze swept over Meg. "You look perfectly splendid." Tears shimmered in Sarah's eyes.

"Doesn't she look stunning?" Lucy asked. "Of course I can take no credit for it. I merely employed the proper people to make this happen." Lucy flourished a hand from Meg's head to her feet.

"Oh, Meg," Sarah continued. "I'm so pleased you allowed Lucy to help you. I've no doubt you'll catch the interest of some nice gentleman. Why, you should have seen Hart's face." Sarah laughed. "He didn't recognize you at first."

Meg's breath caught in her throat. Was it true? Did she really look so different that Hart didn't recognize her? When she'd seen herself in the looking glass at Lucy's house, all she'd seen was her same old self blinking back at her from inside a gown she didn't belong in, wearing a pair of slippers that slightly squeezed her feet. She felt like a child playing dress-up in her mother's clothes. But if Hart had noticed . . .

Could it be that Lucy was right? Did clothing and hair and rouge truly make a difference? It was on the tip of her tongue to ask Sarah where Hart was when Lucy interjected, "Perfect. That is precisely what we need."

"What?" Sarah asked, blinking at Lucy.

"Yes. What?" Meg echoed, once again worried Lucy would reveal to Sarah her plan to attract Hart.

A slow smile spread across Lucy's face. "An exceedingly eligible gentleman to show interest in our Meg here, of course." Lucy nodded to Sarah. "Hart is the perfect candidate. Please go ask him immediately to ask Meg to dance."

"No!" Meg nearly shouted before clapping her gloved hand over her mouth. On second thought, perhaps that had been rude. The gloves were new, provided by Lucy, of course—and Meg pulled the glove away from her face, worried she'd stained it with rouge.

Lucy turned her head and gave Meg a private what-are-you-doing look, distracting her from her study of the glove. "Whyever not, dear?"

Meg's cheeks heated. "It's just that . . . I mean Hart would not . . . He's not . . ." How could she possibly explain it to someone like Lucy Hunt? Meg wanted Hart, but not out of *pity* of all things. Asking Sarah to convince him to dance with her was the equivalent of yet another unwanted favor, and *that* would be both embarrassing and ghastly.

"I'm afraid Meg's right," Sarah replied. "Mother and Father are here and are keeping a close eye on Hart. Unfortunately, our lovely Meg is the very last lady they would approve of him dancing with."

"They approve of your friendship, don't they?" Lucy retorted.

Sarah laughed. "Hardly. They *tolerate* our friendship, but only because Meg insisted to our parents when they had their falling-out that she didn't care what had transpired between them, she refused to lose her closest friend as a result."

Lucy's eyes widened, and regarded Meg with respect in their depths. "Well done of you, Miss Timmons. I'm impressed."

Meg gave Lucy a tentative smile. Sarah's parents had allowed Meg into their home, but she'd never been truly welcomed there.

"Don't let her fool you," Sarah said, squeezing Meg's hand and smiling at her. "Our Meggie has a spine of steel."

"I've recently learned as much," Lucy said with a sigh.

This time Meg gave Lucy a what-are-you-doing look. If Lucy forgot herself and revealed their plan to Sarah, Meg would never forgive the duchess. Sarah had told Meg often enough that Hart would break her heart.

Lucy flourished a hand in the air and addressed Sarah again. "Regardless of your parents' silly concerns, Hart is one of the only remaining bachelors I know. Most of my friends have been properly married recently. Frankly, your loving husband, Berkeley, used to be the one I'd ask to do such things, but you've snapped him right off the marriage mart." Lucy winked at Sarah. "Besides, it's only a dance, for heaven's sake. Surely your parents can abide one dance. We'll wait right here while you speak to your brother."

Meg closed her eyes, wanting the floor to open and swallow her. This was not how she'd envisioned this evening. In her mind's eye, she'd pictured herself floating into the ballroom wearing this gorgeous gown, Hart seeing her and losing his breath, rushing to her side to ask her to dance posthaste, and falling in love with her that very evening. Of course, she'd known that wasn't likely, but it was also a far cry from Sarah cajoling her brother into asking Meg to dance.

"Lucy, I simply don't think Hart will agree," Sarah began. "He's on the hunt for a wife these days and is spending his time looking for one." Sarah paused and gave Meg a sympathetic smile.

"Has he found anyone yet?" Lucy asked while Meg held her breath and said a brief prayer to the heavens that the answer would be no.

"No," Sarah said.

Meg expelled her breath.

"He seems wholly uninterested in everyone here," Sarah continued, shaking her head.

"Perfect," Lucy replied. "Then perhaps a turn around the room with Meg will give him a new perspective."

Meg wanted to elbow Lucy in the ribs, but she remained frozen in her spot, a calm smile (the exact opposite of how she felt) plastered on her face.

"What if I cannot get him to agree?" Sarah tossed Meg another sympathetic look. This time it included a telling wince.

Lucy crossed her arms over her chest and tapped her fingertips against the opposite elbows. "Oh come now, dear. You are a younger sister. I suspect you know the *precise* way to persuade your brother to do something you think he might otherwise decline."

That appeared to stump Sarah. She knitted her dark brows together and tapped her slippered foot against the parquet floor. "He tends to do the opposite of what Father tells him to do."

"Excellent," Lucy exclaimed, while Meg fumbled in her reticule for her fan. It had become exceedingly hot in the ballroom, and she had no doubt this was going to end in tragedy like a sad Shakespearean play. *Hamlet*? *Macbeth*? Perhaps *King Lear*.

Meg was still contemplating tragedies when Lucy cleared her throat. "Go and tell your brother you overheard your father say how desperately he hopes to *never* see Hart dancing with Meg."

CHAPTER SEVEN

Sarah was midway through her explanation of why Hart should ask Meg Timmons to dance when Hart made up his mind that he would do exactly that. There were several reasons for his decision. First, Sarah had never asked for his help before, and elevating the status of her friend in the marriage mart was not too great a favor to ask. He would do anything for his sister.

Second, his father would hate it, as Sarah had just finished pointing out. Riling his father might be the only entertainment Hart claimed at this mind-numbingly boring event.

Third, Hart was going to ask Miss Timmons to dance because he wanted to. Although she was exceedingly ineligible for him to *marry*, she was the only young lady who'd impressed him enough to ask for a dance.

Fourth, he was intrigued by the notion that Sarah apparently thought his reputation so great he could somehow turn an infamous wallflower into a sought-after dance partner.

Fifth, he couldn't stop remembering the kiss they'd shared in the park. Had the passion he'd felt from the little miss been a figment of his imagination? What sort of dance partner would she be? Laughing and entertaining? Coy and flirtatious? Or quiet and shy, which had been his assumption about her all these years until that kiss.

He'd learned that night how much she truly cared for Sarah. She'd put herself in danger in more ways than one, and she'd done it because she was concerned about Sarah's future. Clearly, Miss Timmons was good at heart. Was there more to his sister's friend that he'd yet to learn? Hart decided to find out. It was time to stop avoiding Meg Timmons.

Meg soon discovered that a new gold ball gown, straightened hair, and some rouge, did, in fact, serve to elevate her from the status of wallflower. A discovery that was a bit disconcerting to her. Being lonely and ignored had always held a sad sort of comfort. She'd attempted to resume her usual position on the outskirts of the ball. Only this time she had company in the form of the dashing Duchess of Claringdon whose lovely, popular friends kept stopping by to greet her. One did not simply hide in the corner when one was accompanied by Lucy Hunt.

As a result, Meg had made the acquaintance of the Viscount and Viscountess of Cavendish, Lord Owen Monroe and his lovely wife, Alexandra, and Sir and Lady Cavendish, the viscount's twin brother, Cade, and his wife, Danielle. These glittering, gorgeous people were nothing but kind to Meg, and after some time had passed, she took a perverse sort of pleasure in her newfound popularity.

Still, it was shocking when she'd wandered off into the corner to greet her friend Helen, another wallflower, and turned around to see none other than Hart standing before her. Her mouth went dry, and she might have made something akin to a squeaking noise. She wasn't entirely certain.

Seeing him made her gasp and her gasp resulted in a hideously timed bout of hiccups. So it was when Hart Highgate, the man she'd dreamed about for years, finally asked her to dance at a *ton* ball, Meg grasped at the unfamiliar rubies at her neck and replied with a stilted, "Oh . . . I . . . Yes . . . Hic. I should like that very . . . hic . . . much."

Hart wore black breeches, a startlingly white superfine shirtfront, and an expertly tied white cravat with an emerald-green waistcoat and black evening coat. He looked—as he always did—as if he'd stepped out of a fashionable men's periodical. While she knew he was only standing in front of her because Sarah had somehow convinced him to ask her to dance, Meg reminded herself that when one's dreams came to life, one shouldn't question the means by which they were delivered. She did, however, glance behind her to ensure he was talking to *her* and not, say, the wall.

Once it was firmly established that he had indeed asked *her* to dance, Hart bowed to Meg and led her to the dance floor. That was the moment when she became overwhelmed by the irrational fear that she had completely forgotten how to dance. She hadn't done it in years, after all, being a first-order wallflower. That atop the ridiculous hiccups and this was certain to end in disaster. Had Shakespeare ever included hiccups in his tragedies? Juliet with a bout of the hiccups, for instance, may well have made the whole tale slightly less awful.

"I apologize in advance," Meg said, "if I—hic—step upon your feet—hic—fall, or—hic—trip you."

She expected him to be horrified by her candor and by her hiccups but instead he . . . laughed. "Not one for dancing?" he asked, his voice smooth and deep. He smelled like a mixture of starch and some sort of spicy, clean cologne. The same scent his coat had held when she'd worn it in the park last year. She'd never forget it. She wanted to breathe him in forever.

"I quite enjoy—hic—dancing," she clarified. "I'm just not entirely certain I—hic—recall how to properly do so given my—hic—immortal status as a—hic—wallflower."

He smiled at that, and she could tell by the way the sides of his mouth curled up that he was trying to keep from laughing more at her hiccups. Oh, perfect. She was ridiculous to him. Perhaps this was more like Shakespeare's *Comedy of Errors*. Tripping him would decide it for certain.

"I believe it's like riding a horse," he said. "One never forgets. You see, you're dancing quite well."

She glanced down at her own feet, amazed that he was right. She was indeed dancing as if she knew precisely what she was about. "How do you like that? Hic." She looked back up at him with wide eyes and smiled. "I am. Hic."

"I don't mean to be impolite," he said, leaning down and whispering to her in a conspiratorial voice. The brush of his breath against her ear sent gooseflesh skittering down her neck. She immediately decided to fake being hard of hearing in order to get him to whisper everything he said into her ear. "But are you, by chance, suffering from a bout of the hiccups?"

Her face was no doubt bright pink when she replied, "Yes. Yes, in fact, I am." Honesty was always the best policy, was it not? Besides, there was not much use in denying it. Hiccups were hardly hidable.

Another smothered laugh from him, during which he pressed his firm lips together. His green eyes twinkled. "I'm sorry to hear that."

She sighed. "Yes, well, it only—hic—makes the ignominy of the fact that—hic—my first dance in years is with a gentleman whose sister—hic—had to convince him to ask me, all the more—hic—excruciatingly embarrassing. Hic. But I still hold out hope that I won't also trip."

Hart's brow furrowed. "What's that?"

"I only mean that the glamorous—hic—beautiful ladies you would normally ask to dance of your own—hic—volition would no doubt never do anything as common as—hic—be overcome with a bout of hiccups."

This time he laughed and shook his head, watching her as if she were a marvel or some inexplicable being like a mermaid or a unicorn. "First," he replied, "my sister may have suggested it, but in all my years she has never been able to convince me to do anything I did not choose to do, and second, you happen to be the most beautiful lady here tonight."

"Pardon?" She blinked and glanced behind herself for the second time. This time she was *certain* he was talking about someone else. Surely, he couldn't mean . . . *her.*

"It's true," he replied. "Why do you seem surprised?"

He had a way of looking at her that made her feel as if she were the only woman in the room. "You know I'm Meg Timmons, don't you?"

His tongue flicked out to lick his lips, and he pressed them together, obviously to keep from laughing. "I know who you are, Meg."

She narrowed her eyes on him. "Were you—hic—quite serious? When you said I'm the most—hic—beautiful lady here, I mean? Hic." She glanced around. "Did Lucy Hunt put you up to— " She snapped her mouth shut. Stupid, naive Meg. Of course he was saying flattering things. That's what men did at balls while dancing with young ladies. They flirted and bestowed compliments and said things they did not mean. She simply had no experience with such flirtations. She was horribly green. She blushed. She must say something equally nonchalant and airy.

"I thank you, my lord, for taking pity—hic—on a flower of the wall variety such as myself. I daresay dancing is quite—hic—as much fun—hic—as I remember it."

"Is it?" His lips twitched.

"I think so. I cannot be certain as in the past I mostly danced—hic—with my tutor. It is infinitely more diverting with a—hic—gentleman at a ball. My tutor was elderly and had trouble with his hip. He also—hic—tired easily and danced with a cane." No doubt he was the least expensive tutor to be had.

"Your dancing tutor danced with a cane?" Hart pressed his lips together.

"I'm afraid so. He also seemed to be inebriated most

of the time." Meg sighed. Poor Mr. Barton. She wasn't entirely certain her mother hadn't paid him in brandy.

"Sounds a bit like my valet," Hart replied. "But I'm glad to hear you prefer dancing with me. I'd hate to be less diverting than a drunken old tutor who uses a cane."

"Oh no. I only meant . . . Hic." Lovely, now she'd gone and insulted him. She really should speak less. It would help with the hiccuping problem, too.

"It's all right. I understand."

"No. No. I should have said that it's infinitely more diverting to—hic—dance with a handsome gentleman, who—" Oh dear Lord. Had she just called him handsome? To his face? This was worse than tripping. Perhaps she could fake a trip to distract him.

"You think I'm handsome?" His grin was legendary.

She winced and scrunched up her nose. "Yes," she squeaked. "Hic. Frankly, my lord, I didn't think your handsomeness was ever in question."

He gave her another knee-weakening smile. "Do you know what?"

Yes. You're exceedingly handsome. "What?"

"I've heard there is a cure for hiccups."

"Is that so? Hic." Good. Talk about the hiccups. No more talk about the handsomeness.

He leaned down and whispered in her ear again. More gooseflesh skittered down her neck. "Yes, and if you'll come outside with me, I'll show you."

CHAPTER EIGHT

There had been times in her life when Meg desperately wished for a bout of hiccups to subside. Tonight, however, she had never, ever been so grateful for a prolonged case of them. Hiccups were lovely. Hiccups were magnificent. Hiccups were glorious, given the fact that they had procured an offer for additional contact with Hart and an invitation to go outside with him. Alone. Huzzah for hiccups!

Meg briefly prayed that the hiccups would not cure themselves before she had a chance to take Hart up on his offer. Shamefully, she briefly considered whether she could believably *fake* a prolonged bout of hiccups if necessary. Fortunately, she did not have to make that awful choice. By the time Hart escorted her outside over the terrace, and out into the gardens to a secluded spot, she was still very much . . . hiccuping.

He positioned her in front of him, a tall hedge behind

him, blocking them from view of the terrace and the house. She watched him, wide-eyed and exceedingly curious. The only remedy she'd ever heard for hiccups involved swallowing a spoonful of sugar upside down. She tried that nonsense before and it had not worked. She also highly doubted Hart was hiding a spoonful of sugar in his waistcoat.

"Ready?" he asked, glancing behind them as if to ensure no one would see what he was about to do.

"I suppose so . . . hic." What exactly involved so much secrecy? Especially when it came to hiccups cures.

Hart grabbed her by her upper arms, pulled her close, and of all unexpected things . . . kissed her!

His warm fingers dug slightly into her skin but she didn't mind. She was much more interested in the feel of his lips moving against hers and the pure shock. Was this a dream? Perhaps Hart had suffered a head injury and didn't realize who he was snogging in the gardens. Sarah hadn't *mentioned* a head injury but perhaps—

Meg pulled herself away from him and stepped back, prepared to ask after his poor head. She touched her fingers to her burning lips and simply stared at him.

"I beg your . . ." Wait. She didn't beg his anything. Indeed *he* should be the one to beg any pardons. At the very least, she needed to be reassured he'd *meant* to do it, sans head injury.

"Are your hiccups gone?" he asked with a wide smile on his handsome face.

"Are my . . . ?" She waited. No hic. She waited some more. Still no hic. She counted ten. Then twenty. Nary a hic. "Yes. I do believe they are gone," she announced, dumbfounded.

"It worked, then?" He was still grinning and looked nothing if not proud of himself.

"What worked?"

"My remedy for hiccups."

Meg closed her eyes and cupped her hand behind her ear. "Pardon? Are you . . . do you mean to say that your remedy for curing hiccups is . . . kissing?" No doubt about it. She was no longer in a Shakespearean tragedy. Definitely *Comedy of Errors*.

Hart laughed so loud he had to clap his hand over his mouth and glance around to ensure the sound hadn't drawn an audience. "No," he said, "not at all."

She blinked at him. The man was making no sense. Perhaps a head injury had occurred after all. She considered asking him if he'd been listening when she stated her name as Meg Timmons.

"The remedy is surprise," he explained.

More blinking. "Surprise?"

"Yes. I surprised you, didn't I?"

No. The man had *astonished* her. "That is one word for it."

His face fell. "Please tell me I didn't offend you, Meg. Normally, I have a strict policy against escorting young women out to gardens. However, in our case . . . I thought . . . given the fact that somehow that it wasn't the first time that we've . . ." He trailed off, evidently reacting to the look on her face, which Meg wanted to believe was nonchalant and practiced but was probably more a mixture between horrified and near-to-crying.

Why, oh why, couldn't she be a sophisticate? Why couldn't she pretend to shrug this off the way other ladies of Hart's acquaintance might if he'd played a similar prank on them? But he had called her Meg in the most heartbreakingly vulnerable tone she'd ever heard from him, and *that* had been her undoing. Not to mention, her belly was still aflutter.

The kiss had been dream-worthy and, well, she simply wasn't the type of young lady who could quickly recover from such things. She perceived that she had better do her best to laugh this off as quickly as possible so Hart stopped looking at her as if she were a wounded deer, if she ever had any hope of getting another kiss from him—pretend or otherwise.

"Yes, yes, of course," she said, forcing a smile to her lips and plucking at the rubies at her throat. "I remember. It was in the park, wasn't it?"

His mouth drew into a frown. "Yes, the night before Sarah's wedding."

"Of course. Of course. My, but *that* was a silly misunderstanding, wasn't it?" Was that nonchalant enough?

He stared at her as if she'd lost her mind.

Oh for heaven's sake. She was being *beyond* nonchalant now. She'd moved into downright insulting territory, calling his kiss silly. She must sound like a fool. It was official. She was rubbish at pretending to be sophisticated.

Hart's voice was quiet. "I'm terribly sorry if I've offended you, Meg, either that night in the park or tonight."

"No. No. No. Not at all," Meg replied in a high-pitched trill, but it was too late. Hart felt like a complete and utter arse. Her hiccups were gone but he'd clearly upset her. She'd looked on the verge of tears a few moments ago. Of course she would. She was a gently reared English girl with little experience, not one of his jaded widow friends who took such things in stride.

Worse, he'd offended this poor young woman, not once, but twice, by kissing her of all unwelcome things. *Twice!* He was worse than a cad. He was a scoundrel. He wouldn't blame her if she slapped him.

Wait. No. That wasn't the worst part. The worst part was that while he'd used the excuse of surprising her out of hiccups, if he were honest with himself, he'd admit he'd really kissed her because he *wanted* to, which was selfish and awful of him.

But she looked like a goddess and was even more beautiful up close. She had a tiny smattering of freckles along the bridge of her nose and the tops of her cheeks. She had the darkest black eyelashes that framed her extraordinary bright-green eyes shot with speckles of gold. She had a tiny scar just above her left eye and she smelled like strawberries. How in the hell had he never noticed her beauty all of these years when she'd been traipsing along with his sister? How had he never noticed the strawberries? He knew why . . . it was *because* she'd been traipsing along with his sister. She'd always been there, right under his nose.

Hart grabbed both of Meg's gloved hands, held them, and squeezed. "I'm sorry, Meg. Truly. What can I do it make it up to you?"

The color leached from her face. "Oh, it was nothing, really. A joke. A lark. I understand completely. No need to make *anything* up to me. You did cure me of my hiccups. Thank you for that."

The color was slowly returning to her face, a fetching shade of pink. She was such an innocent. So guileless and pure and completely undeserving of his profligate influence. Sarah would probably slap him if she got wind of this. But he didn't have time to draw a request out of Meg. He had to get her back to the party quickly or there would be ugly gossip. He'd been rash bringing her out here to begin with, but he'd already known after their encounter in the park that he could trust her to remain silent.

"I know." He let go of her hands and snapped his fingers. "I'll come to the next three balls and dance with you."

"Pardon?" Her gold-flecked green eyes widened, and her plump bottom lip fell open.

"Sarah told me you're on the hunt for a husband."

The pink in Meg's cheeks deepened. He wanted to reach out and stroke his thumb across her soft skin, to brush that spot just beneath her eye. He wanted to take her bottom lip between his teeth and—"I'll help you. I'll dance with you and get my friends to do so as well." His friends were rogues, too, but they were well-connected rogues.

"Oh, that is not necessary—" She shook her head rapidly and backed away from him, her slippers making scratching noises in the gravel.

He frowned. "Unless you think it won't help you."

She froze. Her eyes were wide as the wheels on his new phaeton. "Are you jesting? I've been the queen of the wallflowers for years. Any attention from you and your friends would be more than helpful."

"It's settled then." He grinned at her. "Now you must get back. You go around to the doors on the right. I'll wait a few minutes and come back through the doors on the left."

Meg stopped and stared into his eyes for a moment before turning to leave. Reluctant to see her go, he couldn't resist calling after her softly. "I'll see you tomorrow night at the Kinleys' ball."

CHAPTER NINE

"My dear Miss Timmons," Lucy Hunt said the next afternoon from her place on the settee in Meg's father's embarrassingly worn drawing room. The wallpaper was patched, the carpet threadbare, a brown water stain glared hideously from the ceiling, and most of the accoutrements that had once graced the room had been sold to pay Father's debts, leaving the space sparse and tattered.

"Yes?" Meg did her best to keep her hands steady as she poured tea for a duchess with twice-used leaves out of a chipped china pot. Lucy had arrived the minute calling hours had begun, surprising Meg and sending the entire household, which was unaccustomed to such esteemed guests, into a frenzy. A maid was sent scurrying to purchase sugar lumps, which they normally never indulged in.

"Do you intend to tell me where you and Hart got off to last night for the better part of ten minutes?" Lucy lifted her chin and stared at Meg.

Meg gulped and opened her mouth to reply, but Lucy continued, "Because while I was busily telling everyone you were in the ladies' retiring room, lying through my teeth like a good chaperone should, I happen to know you were outside in the gardens somewhere, alone with him."

Meg sighed. Honesty was the best policy. She spent a moment fumbling with the teapot's lid before admitting, "Hart took me out there to cure my hiccups."

"And?" Lucy drew out the word dramatically, her eyebrows conspicuously raised.

"And it worked." Meg pushed the silver bowl containing the precious sugar lumps closer to Lucy.

Lucy ignored the offering and arched a dark brow. "What, may I ask, was the cure?"

Oh dear. Honesty. Honesty. Honesty. Meg finished pouring the tea, set the pot on the tarnished silver salver, and took a seat across from the duchess. She left her teacup sitting on the salver. "He kissed me."

To Lucy's credit, she didn't even blink. In fact, her face remained completely blank. "Are you telling me that the dance I orchestrated last night turned into a full-blown kiss in the span of a few moments?"

"Yes, but it wasn't exactly like *that*." Meg splayed her hands wide as if to explain.

Lucy cocked her head to the side. "I'm sorry. Didn't you say he kissed you?"

"Yes," Meg admitted, lacing her fingers together and setting her hands in her lap. She was tempted to indulge by taking a lump of the forbidden sugar, but her mother would scold her unmercifully, if she dared.

"Then it was *exactly* like *that*," Lucy declared, taking a sip of curiously sugarless tea.

"By the by, I didn't particularly like that you forced Sarah into convincing Hart to dance with me. I don't want to be pitied, Lucy."

Lucy nudged at a dark curl with her free hand. "The man kissed you. It doesn't sound as if he pities you one bit. Besides, regardless of my methods, which are admittedly often messy and unconventional, you got what you wanted, didn't you? A dance with Hart."

Meg leaned forward. "Yes, but—"

"Look, dear, it's a fact. Sometimes you need to make a thing happen before it is wanted."

Meg furrowed her brow. "Pardon?"

Lucy shrugged one shoulder. "Sometimes a thing *becomes* wanted due to its having happened."

Meg leaned forward and picked up her teacup. "With all due respect, Your Grace, that sounds insane."

"Does it, dear? For example, when I first met my husband, Derek, I wanted him to go away immediately, but he wouldn't go. He was convinced he needed to marry Cass out of some misguided sense of honor to Julian, whom we all thought was dead at the time, but that is not the point. The point is, Derek wouldn't leave, and the more time I spent in his company, the more I realized I wanted him for myself. Which made everything horribly complicated but that, also, is not the point at the moment."

Meg pressed a fingertip to her temple, determined not to lose track of *her* point. "I don't want Hart forced into anything."

"A dance hardly hurt him, dear. Not to mention, he obviously enjoyed it if he kissed you afterward." Lucy winked at her, her eyes twinkling.

Meg set her cup back on the salver and lifted the

sugar bowl in her hands. She offered it to Lucy. "He was only trying to cure me of hiccups."

"Ridiculous. I've never heard of that particular remedy. I certainly wouldn't kiss, say, Lord Cranberry if he began to hiccup. I must commend Hart on his ingenuity, however. It was quite a good ruse to steal a kiss." Lucy hesitated for just a moment before waving away the sugar.

Perhaps Lucy was right. Would Hart have kissed anyone else who had hiccups? "I want to be clear," Meg said. "I've asked for your help, but I want Hart to fall in love with me and ask me to marry him *willingly*."

Lucy rolled her eyes. "Dear, what do you expect me to do? Truss him up like a hare and deliver him to you upon an altar? Even *I* don't have that sort of power or influence." Lucy narrowed her eyes thoughtfully. "Although I admit I had not considered such a scheme, and it does have a certain efficiency about it, doesn't it?"

The look on the duchess's face was positively frightening, as if she were truly considering it. "Lucy, you wouldn't—"

Lucy waved a hand in the air, dismissing the thought. "Let's concentrate on the details. After he kissed you, did he say or do anything else promising?"

Meg blushed. "In apology, he did offer to dance with me at the next three balls. To help me find a husband."

Lucy grinned from ear to ear. "Excellent. Why didn't you tell me that earlier, dear? It's precisely what we need of him."

Meg pressed the balls of her hands to her eyes. "What do you mean? I don't want Hart to help me find a husband. I want him to *be* my husband."

Lucy took another sip of sugarless tea and winced.

Meg eyed the sugar bowl. If the duchess didn't use the stuff, perhaps they could return it and get their money back.

Lucy cleared her throat. "I mean him showing an interest in you has already helped, has it not? After your dance with him last night, did you or didn't you receive two other offers to dance from other gentlemen?"

"It's true, but—"

"But what, dear? This is what you've been waiting for after all these years. Didn't I tell you your circumstances would change if you did things differently? You're finally getting the attention you deserve." Lucy set down her teacup and rubbed her hands together with obvious glee. "At some point, I must get permission from your parents to act as your chaperone, but for now it sounds as if we need to get you another gown . . . or three."

CHAPTER TEN

By God, Hart actually found himself looking forward to the next ball, a turn of events he never would have guessed a short twenty-four hours ago. After the Hodges' ball last night, he'd gone home, dismissed his valet who could barely stand, climbed into bed, and tossed and turned. He couldn't sleep, thinking about Meg Timmons of all people. He'd even had an entirely indecent dream about her, her petal-pink lips, her gorgeous thick blond hair, and her sparkling bright-green eyes. In the span of one day, she'd gone from his sister's friend to a woman he couldn't stop thinking about. How the devil had *that* happened?

She was funny and unexpected. The first time he'd kissed her he'd half expected her to demand marriage. The second time he'd seen her struggle with her confusion and do her best to shrug it off. She wasn't one for histrionics or drama. He'd learned that about her that night in the park. Unlike his mother, Meg hadn't shrieked or carried on. She hadn't called for smelling salts or raised her voice in an attempt to convince him she was right.

Meg was intelligent and perceptive, quietly explaining why she thought Sarah should not marry the marquess. Even when Hart had disagreed with her on how to oppose the match, she'd evenly accepted his position. He liked a woman who was calm and reasonable. He was *surprised* by a woman who was calm and reasonable.

For a moment last night after their kiss, he'd seen her cool reserve slip. She had been not just surprised, but *affected*, and that's when he'd realized he'd been a cad. Hence his offer to help her tonight, and perhaps the reason why he was *looking forward* to attending a *ton* ball. Not only that, but he'd gone to his favorite gaming hell last night to rouse his most respectable friends. First he beat them all soundly at faro, then demanded they help him as payment. Besides, they all owed him a favor or three and he bloody well would call in the favors for Meg's sake.

It was only because *ton* events were so exceedingly dull. Since he had to be there in his own quest for a wife, concentrating on helping Meg was something to pass the time. That was all it was.

Truly.

And so it was that the popular and charming Duke of Harlborough, Earl of Norcross, and Viscount Wenterley all danced with Meg Timmons at the second ball of the Season. She was already a smashing success before Hart even had a chance to ask her to dance, himself.

"Is your dance card too full for an old friend, then?" he asked, coming to stand next to her near the back of the room. Her cheeks were pink and she was breathless from the reel she'd just finished with Wenterley. She wore a bright-turquoise gown with matching pearls at her neck and ears. Her hair was straightened once more and she looked like a goddess again. She still smelled like strawberries. He'd always liked strawberries.

She turned to him, a smile on her face. It was nice to see her smile. Where was she getting these gowns? Her father was penniless, everyone knew that. He suspected the Duchess of Claringdon and his sister had a hand in it. Apparently, they were doing their best to help Miss Timmons find a husband. Why did that thought make him uncomfortable?

"Never too full for you, my lord," Meg answered brightly, her small white teeth flashing.

Hart straightened his cravat. "I take it you approve of the chaps I sent your way, then."

She folded her gloved hands together in front of her. "I cannot tell you how grateful I am. I—"

"No." He put up a hand. "No thanks are necessary. I owe you a favor."

Her gaze shifted to the floor. "One you've repaid with interest. I'll be indebted to you forever."

She lifted her head and their gazes met. Hart didn't want to look away. The kiss they'd shared burned in his memory. Both kisses, actually. His confounded body hardened in response.

Their gazes swung away from each other when Lucy Hunt marched up with a man hovering at her side. "Meg, dear, allow me to introduce you to Sir Michael Winford."

Ah, his suspicion about the duchess helping Meg had been correct. Hart narrowed his eyes on the man. Tall but still nearly two inches shorter than Hart, Sir Winford was a decent-looking chap, he supposed, if one preferred thin, pale, blond sorts.

Meg curtsied to Sir Winford. "A pleasure."

"No, Miss Timmons, the pleasure is all mine," the knight replied with an overly familiar smile that made Hart narrow his eyes further.

Lucy glanced at Hart as if she'd only just noticed him standing there. "Oh, Lord Highgate, do you know Sir Winford?"

"No," Hart replied tightly. "We've not met."

The two men exchanged pleasantries before Lucy interjected, "I believe Sir Winford was about to ask Miss Timmons to dance."

"*I* was about to ask Miss Timmons to dance," Hart replied, his jaw clenched.

Lucy's smile was full of teeth and obviously fake. "Will you excuse us for one moment, Sir Winford?"

"By all means, Your Grace." Winford bowed to the duchess.

"Lord Highgate, might I have a word?" Still smiling like a loon, Lucy pulled Hart aside. They made their way to the nearest wall, several paces from where Meg and Sir Winford remained. Lucy's smile faded as soon as she turned to Hart. "Surely you see the logic in allowing Meg to dance with a man who might actually *offer* for her, my lord."

Hart clenched his jaw more tightly. Damn. He couldn't argue with her. "I do, indeed, Your Grace."

"Good then, it's settled." She turned and nodded in Lord Winford's direction, another ridiculous smile plastered to her face.

Hart watched over Lucy's shoulder as Sir Winford offered his arm to Meg and escorted her to the floor. A footman walked by carrying a tray full of brandy glasses. Hart grabbed one, his eyes still trained on the couple heading off to dance. Meg glanced back. Was that a reluctant look she gave him? Was she wishing she'd been able to accept his offer instead? Or was Hart a fool to think it?

He remained standing next to the duchess, clutching his brandy glass tightly as he watched Meg and Winford twirl around the floor. Why in the devil's name did it bother him so much that she wasn't dancing with him instead? He'd only come here tonight to dance with her, and roust his friends to do the same, in an effort to assist her in finding an eligible match. Sir Winford was obviously such a match.

Hart had done his duty. He should get back to his affairs, namely finding his own blasted wife. He was about to excuse himself when Lucy Hunt sighed and said, "They look good together, don't they?"

"Who?" Hart tossed back the rest of his brandy.

"Miss Timmons and Sir Winford, of course."

Hart glared at the dancing couple. "I suppose."

"She's had a hard time of it, you know," Lucy continued, her arms crossed as she stared at the couples on the dance floor.

"I do know. I've met her mother." Why did Hart want to crush his brandy glass in his fist? What was happening? He was normally lighthearted and jesting. Looking for fun and finding it. Anger was a foreign emotion to him.

"She's a gem. It's *such* a pity we live in a Society that so highly values things like *dowries* over people's dispositions."

"It's the world we live in," Hart ground out. Why was the Duchess of Claringdon lecturing him on how wrong Society was?

"Still . . . it's a pity." Another sigh from Lucy. "It seems Sir Winford, however, may be willing to overlook such a thing. Wise of him. I do so admire wisdom in a man."

"Sir Winford was recently made a knight over some business dealings he procured for the Crown. He's hardly good *ton*." Hart clenched his teeth. "Marrying into the Timmons family would be a step up for him. Even with their scandal."

"It would be indeed," Lucy agreed, her nose lifting ever so slightly as if she smelled something that didn't agree with her.

Was it Hart's imagination or was Lucy Hunt side-eyeing him?

"He's quite wealthy in his own right, however, and hardly needs a paltry *dowry* when choosing a bride." Lucy sneered the word *dowry* as if it were something awful.

Hart returned her side-eyed glare. "As you well know, Your Grace, there are many dowries that are far from paltry."

"Yes, but when one is already vastly wealthy, what does a dowry matter, *really*?"

Hart snorted. "Try telling that to my father." Had he suffered a head injury? Was he truly speaking to a duchess about whether dowries mattered? They both knew they mattered a great deal to people in their world. What the devil was Lucy Hunt getting at?

"Or my father, for that matter," Lucy agreed with yet another sigh. "I'm merely making the point that those of us with brains in our heads should know better than to choose the person we intend to spend the rest of our days with based upon something as inconsequential as a dowry."

"Seems to me your husband was quite wealthy and in possession of the title of *duke* when you married him," Hart countered, giving her a tight smile.

That didn't even give the duchess pause. "A mere co-incidence, I assure you. I seem to recall Sarah telling me after she ran out of the church and you followed her to the coach, she said your mother and father would never forgive her for slighting a marquess for a viscount and you said, 'Who cares if they forgive you?'"

Hart narrowed his eyes on the duchess. How the hell did the duchess know about *that*? And why in God's name was she bringing it up now? "Indeed I did," he replied. "But Berkeley is a viscount and vastly wealthy to boot."

"Meg is one of the kindest, sweetest, most gracious young ladies I've ever encountered and she shouldn't be penalized for having a drunken lout who's awful at gambling for a father."

"Agreed, and I suspect someone like Sir Winford agrees as well."

Lucy Hunt opened her mouth to make a retort but Hart stopped her. There was no point in continuing this inane conversation. "You've reminded me. I must get back to Sarah. She's promised to point out the suitable ladies who are as pleasant and *easygoing* as their dowries are large. If you'll excuse me, Your Grace."

As Hart walked away, he heard the distinctive sound of the Duchess of Claringdon sighing yet *again*. She may even have stamped her foot.

CHAPTER ELEVEN

Meg took a deep breath. She and Lucy had discussed this in detail, but nerves were getting the better of her now that the time had come. She was sitting in the breakfast room with her parents, who rarely spoke to each other, even at meals. She pushed the eggs around her plate, counted three, and lifted her head to look at her mother.

Her mother was gorgeous, or would have been if anger hadn't settled into every line of her face. Meg could only suspect the reason for her mother's unhappiness was because her husband had gambled away every bit of security they had. Father went out drinking and playing hazards nearly every night. Mother had long ago given up attempting to stop him.

Meg's childhood had been marred by frightening screaming matches between her parents on more occasions than she cared to recall. She had huddled beneath her blankets in bed but their voices had carried, far enough for her to understand what they fought about. Father couldn't stop gambling and Mother couldn't forgive him for it.

Meg didn't blame her mother for being angry with her father, but Meg had seen her father come home with red-rimmed eyes and regret on his face. Something had been clear to her always: Her father wanted to stop but was unable to.

Still halfheartedly pushing the eggs around her plate with her fork, Meg glanced over at her father. He'd always been fun loving and quick to smile and joke and pat her on the head when she'd been small. He was handsome, her father, exceedingly so, blond with bright green eyes, though the years and the stress and the drinking hadn't been kind. He had wrinkles near his eyes, but the laugh lines at the corners of his mouth reminded her of the man he once had been.

She tried to imagine her parents when they were young. They must have been in love at one point, or so Meg chose to believe. Was there any love left between them? Had it ever been there to begin with? She couldn't quite imagine them laughing together or holding hands the way she'd seen Sarah and Christian do. She wanted Sarah's type of marriage, to a man she both loved and respected, and Lucy was going to help her get it.

"Mother." Meg forced herself to speak before she lost her nerve. "There's something I wanted to ask you, ask both of you."

Her father didn't so much as glance up from his paper. It was yesterday's paper, brought home from whatever club or gaming hell he'd frequented last night. She wondered if he'd even heard her. Probably not.

"What's that?" Mother asked, taking a drink from a teacup that Meg suspected was laced with brandy.

Meg straightened her shoulders and cleared her throat. "The Duchess of Claringdon has asked if I may be her . . . sort of . . . ward."

Her mother's head snapped up, and a scowl covered her face. "Ward? What do you mean, ward? What sort of nonsense is that?"

Her father glanced up from the paper. His eyes narrowed on Meg. "You don't require another family, Margaret. What in the devil's name are you talking about?"

It was ironic that the only thing her parents seemed to agree on was making her life more difficult. Meg took another deep breath. "I wouldn't be a ward . . . exactly," she continued, cursing herself for bungling this important conversation. She shouldn't have used the word *ward*. "Her Grace would simply, you know, oversee my clothing and be my chaperone and . . ."

"She's already spent far too much time with you as it is," Mother snorted. "I've no idea why such an important lady as the duchess would take an interest in you of all people." Mother downed more tea.

"I don't think you should get your hopes up, Margaret," Father replied, turning his gaze back to his paper. "A rich lady like that might take an interest in a wallflower from time to time but she'll bore quickly and soon be on to the next amusement."

Meg squeezed the napkin in her lap. She'd expected such insults, was prepared for them. "We're friends, Father. The duchess has agreed to provide me with gowns and I intend to pay her back once I marry well and—"

"Marry well?" Her mother's voice dripped with incredulity. "What makes you think you'll marry well?" Her voice took a biting tone. "Your father's put an end to that. Even a duchess's fine clothing can't make up for the fact that you haven't any dowry. I doubt the duchess has offered to provide you with one."

Her father gave her mother a withering glare and returned his attention to his paper.

"Of course not," Meg replied. "That would be inappropriate, but she's offered to help and I'd like to accept her offer. It's very kind of her." Meg blew out a breath, prepared to make her final argument. "Besides, my prospects cannot possibly be any worse with her help."

Her mother's scowl intensified, but she lifted her brows and shrugged. "I suppose you have a point."

"What exactly *are* your marital prospects this Season, Margaret?" Father asked from behind his paper.

This was it. Her opportunity to mention Hart. To see if her parents had thawed toward his family in any way, to determine if there was hope.

"Sarah's brother, Hart, has been helping me. He's come to a few of the balls and danced with me. I've garnered some attention as a result." Of course her parents would already know this if they'd been paying any attention.

The paper snapped against the table, rattling the silverware. "Hart Highgate? Highfield's heir?" Father sneered.

"Yes," Meg said, forcing herself to meet her father's gaze. Nothing but anger covered his features. The kindness had vanished from his eyes.

"That young man is just like his father, cares nothing about anyone other than himself," Father continued.

"You're one to talk, Charles." Mother's eyes narrowed to slits.

Meg jumped in before they had a chance to go at each other. "He's been helping me. He's been quite kind."

"The Highgates aren't kind," Mother interjected. "They're pompous and self-centered and—"

It was no use. Meg needed to return their attention to the matter at hand. "Do I have your permission to allow the duchess to help me?"

"Do whatever you like," Father said from behind the paper. "But stay away from that Highgate lad. He's a scoundrel."

"Again, you're one to talk." Mother set down her teacup, braced her elbows on the table, and steepled her fingers, staring at Meg across the dulled wooden surface of the table. "So, you're willing to go into debt to a duchess on the small chance you might find some man willing to take you on as a burden for life?"

Meg's gaze reverted to her mother's eyes. She swallowed the painful lump in her throat. Why did her mother hate her so much? "I told you. I intend to repay her."

Her mother's sharp crack of laughter filled the room. "Isn't that what your father says, every time he takes on a new debt? You're more like him than not, Margaret."

"I've had enough of you for one day, Catherine." Her father stood, tossed the paper onto the table, and stalked from the room.

Meg watched him go. She didn't care. The two of them could argue all day as long as they allowed Lucy to continue to help her and be her chaperone. Her father had already provided his permission.

"There are men who might be willing to marry me, Mother. Not everyone puts all their attention on a dowry."

Mother shrugged one shoulder. "I suppose you're right. I suppose your father's name is still good for *something*. Some no-name fool might come sniffing around you after all if the duchess puts enough baubles on you."

Meg clenched her jaw. She would let that go, too, like all the other insults her mother had heaped upon her over the years.

"I need your permission, Mother," she said in a tight voice.

Her mother picked up her teacup again and took another sip. "Fine, I'll allow the duchess to be your so-called chaperone, but don't come sobbing to me when she tosses you over for another ward with more potential."

"Thank you," Meg managed to choke out. She was just about to push back her chair and ask to be excused when another thought struck her. While she was being brave she might as well ask one more question.

"Mother?" she ventured.

Her mother cradled the teacup in her hands. "Yes."

Meg swallowed. She'd wanted to ask this question for years. She had to blurt it out before she lost her nerve. "What exactly happened between our family and Sarah's family?"

Her mother's nostrils were pinched. She shook her head and rolled her eyes. Then she leaned forward and lowered her voice. "Do you *really* want to know, Margaret?"

"Yes." Excitement bubbling in her chest, Meg leaned forward, too. Was this really it? Would her mother truly tell her?

"Then ask your useless father." Mother stood, threw her napkin to her chair, and marched from the room.

CHAPTER TWELVE

"Lucy, I still don't understand why you thought it was a good idea to send Hart away last night and allow Sir Winford the dance instead."

They stood on the sidelines of the Cranberrys' ball. Meg was dressed in a gorgeous light-green satin gown with cap sleeves and a low V in the back. The gown had embroidered white flowers along the bodice and an empire waist. Lucy's team of dressmakers had worked all day to invent the gorgeous creation after Meg had sent Lucy a note informing her of her parents' permission. Meg had reiterated that she insisted upon paying Lucy back one day.

Lucy had purchased Meg a new set of kid gloves and some bright-white satin slippers. The seamstresses had made her an adorable matching reticule with tiny white rosebuds scattered across it. After adding some diamond earbobs and a silver-and-diamond necklace, also borrowed from Lucy, Meg looked and felt like the veriest princess. She well knew it was all a show, an act staged by Lucy Hunt, but one that appeared to be working.

After her dances last night with Hart's friends, Meg had become downright sought-after. A steady stream of people stopped to greet her this evening, an occurrence that would have been unheard of last Season. The combination of new gowns and preferred dancing partners had changed her circumstances overnight. Ah, what power a duchess and a viscount wielded. It was truly fascinating.

"Dear, we've been over this," Lucy replied. "If Hart had won the dance, he wouldn't have had a chance to *miss* dancing with you, nor would I have had a moment to discuss with him how entirely silly choosing a bride over a dowry is. You must trust me."

"I do trust you, Lucy, but—"

"You hated to miss a dance with Hart. I completely understand. We must make choices for the good of our cause and not for a moment's pleasure, however."

Meg squeezed the diamond earbobs to ensure they remained securely in place. Then she shook her head. "You should have been a general, Lucy. Your talents are completely wasted in the ballroom."

Lucy smoothed one dark brow. "Derek tells me that quite often. He says Waterloo would have been won before the Prussians arrived if I'd been there. But I disagree with you . . . my talents are not entirely wasted in the ballroom."

"No?"

"No. As evidenced by the fact that both Sir Winford and Lord Highgate are on their way toward you. Do *not* look!"

Meg did her best to keep her eyes on her champagne

flute and pretend she didn't know the two men were making their way toward her from opposite directions in the crowd. She desperately hoped Hart would get there first. She took one rebellious little step in his direction.

She breathed a sigh of relief when Hart appeared at her side. He wore black superfine evening attire with a perfectly starched white shirtfront and cravat. An emerald winked from a pin in his cravat. "Miss Timmons." He bowed to her. "You look as breathtaking as ever."

"You don't have to dance with me tonight, Hart," Meg said, hoping desperately that he wanted to dance with her regardless.

"Nonsense. I promised you three nights of dancing and I am a gentleman of my word."

"Sir Winford is on his way over," Lucy pointed out, sipping from her own champagne flute, probably to hide her catlike smile.

"Sir Winford will have to wait," Hart ground out. "This dance is *mine*."

Meg pressed her lips together to keep from smiling and handed her glass to Lucy, who eagerly took it. "If you insist."

"I do," Hart replied, bowing.

Hart offered his arm and they left for the dance floor before Lord Winford made it through the crowd.

A waltz began and Hart pulled Meg into his arms. "Are you disappointed to be dancing with me and not Sir Winford?"

Meg contemplated the question. The Meg of a week ago would have immediately said, *No!* Blurted it even. This Meg had been in Lucy Hunt's company for the last several days and knew better than to be so unsophisticated.

"Sir Winford seems quite nice," she said instead. Her voice was perfectly even and calm, but her mind raced with worry. What if Hart decided Sir Winford was a good choice for her? What if he encouraged the match? Sarah had already done so on numerous occasions. The truth was, under any other circumstances Sir Winford *would* be an excellent choice for a husband. He was titled, wealthy, and handsome. Somewhere in his mid-thirties, he was far from an old man. He seemed witty and pleasant. It was a deuced inconvenience, perhaps, that she was madly in love with Hart.

"I don't know him," Hart said. Was it her imagination or had he squeezed her hands slightly when he said it?

Meg concentrated on keeping her tone light. "He owns an estate in Devon, a town house on Leicester Square, and a great many horses, from what I understand."

"Told you all that in a span of a dance, did he?" Hart had the faintest hint of a sneer in his voice.

"No." Meg shook her head. "Lucy's been researching him."

Hart's brows lifted. "Lucy approves of him, then?"

"She likes that he's not worried about my lack of dowry."

"That is commendable." Hart's jaw remained tight.

Meg glanced at her slippers. At least she was dancing properly this evening. She had yet to step on his feet. Thank God for small favors. "Hart, I . . . have you and your friends to thank for my sudden change in circumstance and . . ."

Hart stared into the crowd over Meg's head. "Seems

you have the duchess to thank as well. I imagine your jewels and gowns have something to do with her."

Meg blushed and hoped neither of the earbobs was missing. "It's true."

He lowered his gaze to hers. "You look beautiful, Meg. You should never have had to wear rags."

A lump formed in Meg's throat. She tossed her head. Was he remembering that day when she was sixteen and he'd stood up for her as she was? "I resisted Lucy quite a bit before agreeing to wear the gowns she's had made for me."

Hart searched her face. "Why?"

"I don't . . ." Meg glanced away into the crowd. The lump grew larger. "I've never wanted to be pitied."

"Pitied?" Hart's brow furrowed. "Is that what you think? Let me assure you, no one is pitying you."

Meg forced herself to stare at his black-clad shoulder. His familiar scent enveloped her senses. The lump in her throat was so large, she was nearly choking on it. "But no one looked twice at me before I began wearing these gowns, before you danced with me."

He leaned down slightly to catch her eye. His breath caressed her ear when he spoke. "Sometimes it takes a bit of polish to get fools to see a diamond in the rough."

Meg pressed her lips together. She met his gaze. "Is that what I am? A diamond in the rough?"

His eyes scanned her face. Her décolletage? "You're a diamond, without question."

She barely had time to contemplate that loaded statement when he asked, "No hiccups tonight?"

She smiled and shook her head. "Nary a one."

"A pity." His grin was downright roguish.

By God, was he *flirting* with her? She'd never been

flirted with by a handsome, young gentleman. By any gentleman, for that matter. She needed to think of something equally flirtatious with which to reply. "I can fake a bout of hiccups if you'd like." Oh dear Lord, had she actually said that? Aloud? She was a complete hoyden.

"No need," Hart replied, the roguish grin still on his face. "There are other reasons to go out into the gardens. Like, say, a walk."

Butterflies winged through her belly. This was the type of moment she'd dreamed about for years. *Years.* Her journal brimmed with such dream-worthy exchanges. "Are you offering, kind sir?"

He straightened to his full height, and the side of his mouth ticked up into a half smile. "I am indeed."

"What about Sir Winford?" she ventured.

"Sir Winford is not invited."

The music came to a stop and Hart let go of her hands and lifted his arm in an offer of escort.

Meg's fingers shook as she settled them on his warm sleeve. "By all means, lead the way."

CHAPTER THIRTEEN

Five minutes later, Hart was strolling down the foot-paths in the Cranberrys' garden, with Meg next to him. She had sneaked past Lucy and Sir Winford, who were obviously looking for her. Hart and Meg had decided to break apart and exit the house from different sides. Meg made her way out of the French doors on the right of the patio and Hart met her outside. He'd gone into Lord Cranberry's study and left through a similar set of doors there.

Hart glanced down at Meg, still marveling at the beauty he'd only noticed recently. By God, he needed to pay more attention to things. To people. While he watched out of the corner of his eye, the cool night air lifted the ringlets at her temples. She'd had her hair straightened, but the tiny curls remained. He was tempted to reach out and touch them. Instead he kept his hands innocently folded behind his back as they strolled down the graveled path. Tiny twinkling candles lit their way, and the scent of jasmine floated in the air. If he didn't know any better, he'd think the scene was entirely . . . romantic. *Not* that he noticed such things. Ever.

"How is Goliath?" Meg began, breaking the silence between them.

Hart stopped and stared at her. He furrowed his brow. "You know the name of my horse?"

Meg didn't look at him. She cleared her throat and continued slowly walking. "I'm certain Sarah mentioned it a time or two."

Hart resumed walking next to her. The gravel crunched beneath his feet. "Goliath has just recovered from a slight injury. Found a pebble in his shoe."

"He's a gorgeous animal," Meg said softly.

Hart's brow remained steadfastly furrowed. "You've seen him?"

The hint of a smile touched Meg's pink lips. "Of course I've seen him. Don't you remember the race outside of town last autumn? I was there when you were injured."

"Yes, of course. It was a miracle Goliath escaped without injury. Wish I could say the same for my phaeton." Hart scratched the back of his neck. It was also a miracle he hadn't bloody well broken his own neck. Drinking and racing did not mix.

"But you purchased a new one already, didn't you?" Meg's reticule bounced along the back of her gown as she stepped along the gravel.

Hart blinked. "Yes, I have." Apparently, Meg knew more about him than he realized.

"Any plans to purchase more horses? I know how much you adore them."

"Do you?" He stopped again to stare at her. How did

she know that about him? How had he been so blind to her all these years?

"Ye . . . yes." Her voice shook slightly.

"What is it that *you* adore, Meg?" He had no idea why he'd asked that question. It had been as much a surprise to him when it came out of his mouth as it obviously was to her. She blushed beautifully and glanced away from him. She fingered a rose on the bush next to the path. "Oh, that doesn't matter."

"Yes it does," he prodded. "I'd truly like to know." Meg knew how much his horses and racing meant to him, but he had no idea what she liked. "Tell me."

She shrugged and gave a halfhearted laugh. "Your sister is quite important to me. I love her."

"Yes, Sarah is the best person in our family, by far." Meg smiled at that.

"What else?" he prompted.

"My books, my home, my . . . writing."

He pushed a boot through the gravel. "You write?"

One small hand fluttered in the air. "Oh, nothing important. Only a bit in a journal every now and then."

Ignoring the voice in his head that was willing him to stop, Hart continued to kick at the gravel. "What sort of things do you write about?"

She shook her head and plucked one of the small pink roses from the hedge. She brought it to her lips, closed her eyes, and inhaled. Hart had never before wished he were a rose petal. First time for everything.

"I write about things that happen in my life," Meg replied, her eyes opening again. Allowing the hand holding the rose to fall to her side, she twisted the stem with her gloved fingers.

"What sorts of things?" he forced himself to ask, trying to ignore the virulence with which he wanted to kiss her.

"The dates of the servants' birthdays, ideas for running a house on a slight income, the name of my friend's brother's horse." She glanced up at him and smiled. "Silly things," she murmured.

"Those things don't sound silly to me," he replied, still absently kicking at the gravel. Meg thought about things, saw things, remembered them. How many ladies knew the servants' birthdays? How many worried about running their households with little money? She was no silly miss. She might not talk much, but she was listening. And she cared about other people.

"May I ask you something?" she said, surprising him.

"Of course," Hart answered, forcing himself to stop pushing his idiotic boot through the gravel like an untried lad nervously talking to the first pretty female he'd encountered.

Meg pushed a small curl behind her ear. "Do you . . . do you know how much money my father owes your father? The reason they had a falling-out, I mean."

Hart turned to search her face. It was shadowed in the darkness, but the light of the candles illuminated enough of it for him to see the serious look on her face. "You don't know?"

"I've never heard the amount, no. Is it quite a lot?" Meg winced.

Hart resumed walking, looking straight ahead this time. "I'm not certain." Did she truly not know? He scrubbed a hand through his hair. On second thought, he supposed it stood to reason. Sarah didn't know, either.

He'd made certain of that. He doubted either of Meg's parents would be quick to share the details with their daughter.

Meg resumed walking beside him. "Sarah and I have speculated upon it of course."

She wanted him to say more, Hart could tell. He searched his mind for a properly vague reply. It would only hurt her to know the truth, and he didn't want to hurt her. "It doesn't matter, does it? It's been at least five years."

"Something like that," Meg murmured, still twirling the flower between her fingers.

"I doubt they will ever mend their rift, Meg." Perhaps she was asking because she held out hope. Perhaps she was counting on the fact that one day she and her closest friend's parents would be friendly again. False hope was a dangerous thing.

Meg had opened her mouth and was about to say something else when Lucy Hunt's voice came floating over the hedges. "Meg, come quickly. It's your father. He's had an attack!"

CHAPTER FOURTEEN

Pure terror pulsing through her heart, Meg tossed away the rose, lifted her skirts, and raced back to the house. She didn't know Hart had followed her until she arrived on the terrace with him behind her. Lucy was there, a worried expression on her face. "A footman came from your house looking for us," the duchess explained. "We must leave immediately."

"Is he . . . alive?" Meg managed to choke out of her dry, swollen throat.

"Yes, I believe so," Lucy replied, clutching Meg's arm.

Trembling, Meg turned to Hart. "I'm sorry. I must go."

"Of course," Hart replied. "Please tell me if there's anything I can do to help. Do you have a ride home?"

"Sir Winford has already gone to call for our carriage," Lucy replied.

Meg barely registered the disgruntled look on Hart's face. She was trying to control her rapid breathing. Father? Father was ill? He had acted hideously this morning, but the idea of her father (she could hardly bring herself to think it) *dying* made her hot and cold all over.

Meg flew through the ballroom on Lucy's heels, ignoring the partygoers who watched their flight. Lucy had assured her she'd already paid their respects to Lord and Lady Cranberry and thanked them for their hospitality. The two ladies entered the corridor on the other side of the ballroom, quickly made their way toward the foyer, and exited through the front door. Sir Winford stood outside near the carriage line. Just as Lucy had said, he'd ensured the duchess's coach was brought around. The conveyance was waiting for them in the street when they arrived.

"Thank you, Sir Winford." Meg barely glanced at the knight before allowing one of the grooms to help her into the coach beside Lucy. They were on their way in a matter of moments.

Less than a quarter hour later, Meg was kneeling at her father's bedside, clutching his cold hand. Her mother sat in a chair on the opposite side of the room, glaring at her husband as if he'd got sick on purpose.

Lucy had ensured that Meg's father was resting abed before taking herself off, assuring Meg that if she needed anything night or day, she had only to send a note. Lucy also promised to call for her husband's private physician to evaluate Meg's father. Meg was ever so grateful.

"Oh, Papa," Meg said, rubbing her father's hand. "I was so worried. Are you all right?"

Her father lifted his opposite hand and patted her on the head. "Yes, Margaret, I'm fine now."

"What happened?" Meg asked, searching his familiar face.

"I had an awful pain in my chest. My arm seized. I fell to the floor. It was all quite terrifying."

"I can only imagine." Meg's eyes filled with tears. Her father was reckless, irresponsible, and often thoughtless, but he had always loved her. "Have you any idea what happened to cause it?"

"Oh, he knows *exactly* what caused it," Meg's mother intoned from her throne across the room. "Tell her, Charles." Her voice was a sneer.

Meg searched her father's face again. "What? What is it?"

Her father took a long, deep breath. He patted her head again. "Margaret, dear, I must . . . that is to say *we* must . . . I've decided we must move to the Continent. Immediately."

"What?" Meg nearly shouted. Lifting herself from her knees, she stood next to the bed. "Why?" She continued to squeeze her father's hand. "What does that have to do with your illness?"

"Tell her, Charles," Mother prompted, her dark eyes narrowing.

"Tell me what?" Meg searched her father's pale face. She'd got her curls from him, and her green eyes. She'd also got her love of life. Despite his circumstances, Father had always been ebullient and happy. Perhaps it had been what made him not care that he owed so much money. Yes. He was reckless, her father. A trait she had decidedly not inherited. But she loved him despite his faults.

"My dear Margaret," her father said, letting his hand fall to the bedspread. "I was paid a visit tonight by two gentlemen who . . ." She could tell her father was searching for the right words.

"They were *hardly gentlemen*, Charles," her mother scoffed.

"Yes, well, they, ahem, threatened me," her father continued, clearing his throat. "You see, I owe them both a great deal of money and they want it back."

"Oh, Father, no!" Meg squeezed her father's hand tightly. "They threatened to hurt you?"

"Yes," her father replied. "They did. If I don't come up with ten thousand pounds in three weeks' time, that is."

"That's what caused your episode?" Meg asked.

"I'm afraid so," Father replied, nodding.

"And we must leave our home and all our friends and possessions, such as they are, to run like bandits in the night from these men." Mother's knuckles were white from clutching the wooden arms of the chair so tightly.

"No." Meg shook her head frantically. "There must be another way." Ten thousand pounds was a fortune. There was no way her father would be able to come up with a sum as great as that in such a short amount of time. They would be forced to move to the Continent. It stood to reason, of course. The Continent was where men went who owed more money than they could ever afford to repay. Meg had never considered it. She'd never contemplated that Father might make such a decision. Not now. Not when she was finally getting her chance with Hart.

"We must go," Father said. "We've no other choice, I'm afraid. We leave in a fortnight."

A fortnight? So soon? Her future dimmed before her eyes. There was little chance she could make Hart fall in love with her in the span of a fortnight. Or even wring an offer from Sir Winford. She wouldn't marry for money and she'd die before she'd admit to either man that she was leaving so her father could hide from creditors. There would be gossip enough as it was.

She would end up a spinster somewhere in Europe, remembering her few cherished dances with the man she'd once loved. And Sarah? Meg couldn't even contemplate being ripped away from her dearest friend. Would she ever even see Sarah again? Meg's eyes filled with tears, but she forced them away. She had to be brave for her father's sake.

"Where will we go, Father?" she asked in a shaking voice.

"I've heard Spain is quite nice," Father replied.

"He's heard Spain is quite cheap," Mother mumbled, her hands still gripping the arms of the chair.

Meg swallowed. Spain? So far away. No. She could not go to Spain. She must think of some way to stay. Meg let go of her father's hand and turned to face her mother. "What if the Duchess of Claringdon agrees to take me in for the remainder of the Season?"

"Have you gone mad?" Mother scoffed, rolling her eyes. "The duchess may have taken an interest in you for the time being, but I hardly think she has any desire to have you move into her fine mansion. You're thinking far too highly of yourself, Margaret. Dressing you up and allowing you to borrow some baubles is one thing. Moving into her home is entirely different."

Meg's mind raced. There must be another way. "Fine. What if Sarah and Lord Berkeley agree to sponsor me for the rest of the Season?"

"Absolutely not! We won't allow you to be a charity case for the likes of that Highgate girl." Pure venom dripped from her mother's voice.

Meg swallowed hard. Tears of frustration burned the backs of her eyes. She clenched her fists at her sides. Her mother was right. Meg hadn't even asked Lucy if she would agree to such a thing before she'd offered it as a solution. Lucy couldn't possibly want the subject of such an ugly scandal residing under her roof, and it had been beyond presumptuous of Meg to suggest it. There had been no hope her parents would allow her to stay with Sarah. She was being selfish, not thinking of her poor father.

"I advise you to accept it as I have." Mother stood and walked stiffly toward the bedchamber door. "We're leaving for the Continent in a fortnight, and you're coming with us."

CHAPTER FIFTEEN

The third ball was the Morgans', and this time Meg wore a gown of light peach satin with silver embroidered dots and another charming matching reticule, all courtesy of Lucy, of course. When the duchess arrived at Meg's father's town house to escort her to the ball, Meg's mother was standing in the foyer next to Meg, waiting for her.

"Good evening, my lady," the duchess said to Meg's mother, while Meg watched worriedly from her spot near the door.

"Good evening, Your Grace." Her mother curtsied, and for a moment Meg believed that her mother might actually be civil and act normally for a change.

"I hope you don't mind my carting Meg off to the Morgans' ball. It's certain to be a lovely evening," Lucy said.

"By all means." Mother's tone was angry, and Meg sucked in her breath when she heard it. "Best of luck attempting to get this spinster daughter of ours married, even with all the fancy clothing you've dressed her in. You only have one more fortnight, by the by." Mother gave Lucy a tight smile, turned, and left the room.

"Two weeks?" Lucy asked Meg, a frown wrinkling her brow.

"I'll tell you later," Meg replied, slipping on the gorgeous silver pelisse Lucy had brought for her.

"Seems your mother is fine with placing you in my care," Lucy said as they made their way down the steps toward the duchess's coach. "You never told me, did they have any objections?"

"Not many," Meg replied. "I made the argument that I couldn't possibly do any worse. Besides, Mother hasn't offered to escort me to any events this Season. I suspect she feels guilty. She's usually half in her cups by now."

"Your mother is quite something," Lucy said magnanimously as the groomsmen helped both ladies into the fine carriage.

"That's one way to describe her," Meg replied with a small laugh. She dreaded telling Lucy about her move to Spain. She'd already asked the duchess to do the impossible, help her catch the eye of the last man in the kingdom who could marry her. Now she would have to explain why they had only two short weeks to accomplish the task.

"How's your father's health, dear?" Lucy asked as their coach rumbled along the muddy cobbled streets toward the Morgans' town house. "Dr. Thomas said he'd had a mild attack of the nerves."

"Yes." Meg's skin heated. She didn't want to admit the reason for her father's attack, but she had to be honest if Lucy was going to continue to help her. "It was brought on by a great deal of worry."

"Worry?" Lucy clucked her tongue. "I've always found worry to be a complete waste of time."

Meg couldn't muster a smile for her benefactress. She merely nodded weakly.

"What's wrong, dear?" Lucy fumbled in her reticule for something.

Meg took a deep breath. She might as well get this over with. "Father's had some trouble with creditors. He informed us last night that we're moving to the Continent in a fortnight."

Lucy didn't so much as look up from the search of her reticule. "That's unsporting of him."

Meg furrowed her brow. "I don't think you heard me. I said I'm leaving the country in a fortnight's time."

"I heard you, dear." Lucy finished her search, plucking out a vial of perfume. "I brought this for you. It smells like passionflower. Lady Danielle Cavendish has convinced us all of the importance of a good French perfume. Delilah Montebank is especially enamored of the idea, even at the ripe old age of fourteen."

Meg took the vial but blinked at Lucy. "You heard me and you're not concerned?"

"Should I be?" Lucy blinked back.

Meg groaned and let her forehead drop onto her free hand. Lucy could be positively maddening.

"It does make our plans a bit more pressing, dear, I'll give you that, but it hardly changes anything," Lucy said. "Sir Winford appears to be on the verge of an offer. Now dab some passionflower behind your ears and let's get to work."

"But I don't *want* to marry Sir Winford," Meg moaned, glaring at the small vial of perfume.

"Of course you don't, dear, but you do want his offer." Lucy gestured to the vial and Meg reluctantly pulled off her gloves, plucked off the stopper, and dabbed a bit of the perfume behind both ears as directed.

"Why do I want his offer?" Meg asked. The passion-flower smelled lovely. It filled the coach with its rich scent.

"Because an offer will force Hart's hand."

"What? How?" Meg placed the stopper on the vial and handed it back to Lucy, who dropped it unceremoniously into her reticule.

"I've seen the way he's spoken to you over the last few nights, dear. He's undeniably attracted to you. He's just so annoyingly determined to stick to conventions. You saw his face when I mentioned that Sir Winford was bringing the coach around."

"That hardly means—"

"Allow me to finish, dear. Once Hart realizes you're off the market, or could be, he'll have to take a long hard look at himself."

"You truly think an offer from Sir Winford will wring an offer from Hart?" Meg tugged on her glove once more. "It seems like a dangerous gamble."

Lucy's different-colored eyes sparkled. "I think there is only one way to find out. Remember, I've seen this sort of thing play out once or twice before."

"But this is the last night. The last ball Hart agreed to come to and dance with me."

"Yes," Lucy agreed. "The three nights of balls are over, and with your father's ridiculous pronouncement we have even less time than before. We must make our next move immediately."

"What is our next move?" Meg asked, shifting to sit on the edge of her seat, half frightened to hear the answer.

"I shall host a small dinner party tomorrow night, with featured guests, you, Sir Winford, and Hart."

CHAPTER SIXTEEN

The Morgans' ballroom was crowded with guests, but Meg had little trouble finding Hart. His height made him stand out. He wore his black superfine evening attire with a sapphire waistcoat and startlingly white cravat. His hair brushed his collar, his breeches clearly defined his, ahem, assets, and as always his eyes glowed like emeralds. Lucy had made it clear that Meg was to wait from him to come to her, and so she tapped her silver slipper against the marble floor while pretending not to notice the most handsome man in the room was heading her way.

Hart strolled up to Meg and bowed to her. "Care to dance, my lady?"

Meg's heart did a little flip. It would never get old, hearing him ask her to dance. The *my lady* part was especially swoon-worthy, and yet this might be the last time—ever—that she danced with him. She must enjoy and remember every moment of it.

"You seem sad," Hart said as a waltz began to play.

Meg nodded slowly. There was no use denying it. "The truth is . . . I am sad."

"Sad? Why? You look beautiful, you seem to have your choice of gentlemen to dance with, and you happen to be dancing with the most handsome of the lot." He gave her a devilish grin. "What possible reason do you have to be sad?"

He leaned down to catch her eye. She'd been staring into his cravat, trying not to cry. He sounded so caring. She wanted to ask him to love her, right then and there. Wanted to beg him, really. The thought of Lucy having her own attack of the nerves over it put a stop to that. Furthermore, Meg didn't think a needy plea would be particularly effective. No. She must remain subtle. Sophisticated. No matter how much she disliked pretending.

She took a long, deep breath. Could she tell him this news without tears springing to her eyes? Could she tell him she was leaving? She bit the inside of her cheek. She was being such a ninny. "I'm—"

Sir Winford tapped Hart upon the shoulder. "The duchess sent me," the knight announced with a broad smile.

"Of course she did," Hart ground out.

Meg quickly swiped away her tears and plastered a fake smile on her face for Sir Winford while Hart stepped aside and allowed the knight to take Meg's hands.

"Good evening, Miss Timmons," Hart said in a perfectly even, calm voice. "I do hope you feel better." He turned on his heel and strode away.

Hart slid the empty brandy glass onto the tray of a passing footman and grabbed a full snifter from the same tray. By God, this night was not going the way he'd planned. How he'd planned, he'd no idea. But not like *this*. He was in the devil's own mood. He'd intended to help Meg in the marriage mart. He'd intended to dance with her a few times and perhaps elevate her reputation. Instead he found himself angry with Sir Winford for cutting in while he himself was completely uninterested in finding another dancing partner. The episode had put him in a foul mood. He was never in a foul mood.

"You look as if you're about to beat someone with your fists, dear brother," Sarah said, approaching him warily, a flute of champagne in her gloved hand.

Hart took another gulp of brandy. "I might."

Sarah arched a brow. "Truly? Do tell. Who is the unlucky gentleman?"

It was on the tip of Hart's tongue to say *Winford,* but that would elicit a slew of unwanted questions from his only sibling. "It's nothing. I merely have a devil of a head."

Sarah took a dainty sip of champagne. "Again? Wouldn't have anything to do with the fact that you're at a *ton* ball, would it?"

"I believe it might." Hart took a deep breath. He might as well focus his energy on something he actually had control over. Meg Timmons and her marital prospects were none of his concern. Even if he did happen to have the rose she'd tossed away in the garden last night pressed between the pages of a book on his nightstand. He refused to so much as consider why. He didn't know why. The moment she'd tossed it away, he'd immediately swooped down and grabbed it, tucking it gingerly into his waistcoat pocket as he'd raced behind Meg toward Lucy's voice.

"Any eligible prospects here tonight?" Hart forced himself to ask his sister.

Sarah glanced around. "Yes, actually. Lady Eugenia Eubanks is here."

Hmm. Lady Eugenia. Tall, blond, pretty, rich. If only he could muster any enthusiasm for that news. He grabbed another brandy from another tray. Perhaps if he had enough to drink, Lady Eugenia might seem more enticing to him.

"I've been considering all the names of friends and acquaintances, trying to come up with someone you might be more interested in," Sarah offered. "I do believe Lady Eugenia is a fine candidate."

"How are her teeth?" An image of Meg's small perfect teeth tugging at her bottom lip flashed through Hart's mind. Damn, it made him hard. He tossed back another gulp of brandy, trying to think of anything that might dull the lust he was feeling for Meg.

"Her teeth are quite even, if I remember correctly," Sarah replied with a laugh.

"Where is Lady Eugenia?" Hart asked, glancing about.

"Standing right over there looking for all the world as if she could use a dance partner," Sarah replied in a singsong voice.

"Introduce me then." Hart tossed back the final finger of brandy. "It's high time I found a wife."

CHAPTER SEVENTEEN

"There you are, son, I've been looking for you."

Hart glanced up and winced as his father strode into the room at Brooks's. It was barely past noon, far too early in the day to deal with his father. Hart was only two brandies in.

His father always strode into a room as if he owned the place. Hart wouldn't be surprised if his father had attempted to purchase the gentleman's club, but he hadn't heard as much. Without asking if he might take a seat, his father grabbed the chair next to his and settled himself into it.

"Good afternoon, my lord," Hart drawled. "To what do I owe the pleasure of your company?"

His father ordered a brandy from the same footman who'd supplied Hart with his last two, and rubbed his hands together in obvious glee. "I've heard you've taken an interest in Lady Eugenia Eubanks."

This was precisely what Hart had been hoping to

avoid, but the *ton* was full of gossips. Namely, his own sister. "Who told you that?"

"Does it matter?"

"Sarah told you."

"Is it true or not?"

Hart groaned and rubbed a hand across his face. Yes. Last night, he'd forced himself to dance and flirt with Lady Eugenia. It had been mildly amusing. She was exactly the type of young woman his father would approve of. Father would like nothing better than to hear the announcement of his betrothal. It was far too premature for that. He'd only danced with her twice last night, for heaven's sake. Lady Eugenia didn't strike him as the calculating sort, but it was far too early to tell, and his father's glee reminded him far too much of his experience with Annabelle.

"I spent some time with her last evening if that's what you're asking," Hart admitted.

"Excellent. A fine choice."

"There has been no choice yet."

His father took the brandy from the footman. "No. No, of course not."

Hart eyed the older man. His father had been handsome in his day. His dark hair was now liberally streaked with silver. His green eyes were a bit dulled, but his physique was still impressive, tall and broad. He hadn't begun to lose his waistline the way so many of his peers had. The man kept himself fit. He rode his horses often, and his mistresses more often.

His father had been hardened by his marriage. His wife's infidelities had spawned his own. He'd gone from drinking and complaining, to trying to one-up his wife. But they were discreet. He'd give them that. His parents were united on one point and one point only. They detested scandal.

"I told you I intend to take a wife, but there is no rush, Father. The Season has barely begun."

"Yes, of course. I couldn't agree more. But I've been asking around about Lady Eugenia. She'd make a fine choice. Large dowry. Good family. No scandal. She has her share of wealthy, titled suitors. Obviously isn't after you for those things."

"Aren't all women after me for those things? Isn't that what you've always told me?"

"No woman is perfect, Hart. You'll have to pick one of them eventually."

"Sarah likes her."

"There," Father said in a booming voice. "You see."

Hart took a healthy swallow of brandy and winced. "Father, may I ask you something?"

"Of course."

Hart braced himself. "Other than her lack of dowry, would Meg Timmons be *entirely* unsuitable for me?"

His father's eyes bugged from his skull, and he nearly spit his drink. Hart suspected only decades of breeding kept him from it. "Meg Timmons? Have you lost your wits?"

Hart took another swig of brandy. "She's beautiful, healthy, from good *ton*."

"If you call Baron Tifton good *ton*," his father scoffed. "The man is a profligate. He owes money to half of London."

"You were once thick as thieves with the family. Or do you forget?"

"I haven't been in years, or do *you* forget?" His

father's face turned red with anger. "Meg Timmons is the last girl on earth I'd allow you to marry."

Father had been deep in his cups when he'd told Hart the real reason he and Meg's father had a falling-out, but the old man often forgot the things he said when he was deep in his cups. Things he had no business sharing with a teenage boy. Things Hart had never wanted to hear about his mother, his father, and their marriage. All the man had managed to teach his son was how to be wary of all women and how to drink himself to distraction. "I seem to recall you relenting on Sarah's choice of husband," Hart pointed out.

His father's face went redder still and his jaw hardened when he spoke. "I had no choice but to relent and allow Sarah to marry Berkeley. The man ruined her in a church full of people. Besides, while the Marquess of Branford would have been a much more esteemed title to have in the family, Berkeley at least is wealthy and titled, but I *will not stand* for the daughter of my sworn enemy to be a part of this family ever. Do I make myself clear?"

Hart tossed back the rest of his brandy. "Perfectly."

CHAPTER EIGHTEEN

Lucy Hunt's magnificent saffron-colored drawing room was crowded with London's best. Meg glanced around uneasily. Many of the room's occupants were people who had ignored her for years. Except for the duchess's friends like Lady Cassandra and Mrs. Upton, the partygoers seemed to eye her with suspicion, as if she were a servant who'd dressed up like a fine lady and pushed her way in. She was wearing a shimmering pink gown that was far too tight in the bodice and convinced her that she looked like a salmon, though Sarah and Lucy assured her she did not. Sarah stood at Meg's side, stalwart amid the private panic that had Meg's stomach tied in knots.

"Sir Winford has arrived." Sarah clasped Meg's hand and squeezed it. "He looks quite dashing tonight."

Meg dared a glance up. Sir Winford did indeed look handsome, as he did every night, but it wasn't Sir Winford who made her heart skip and her pulse race. Hart stood not twenty paces away talking to Lady Eugenia Eubanks, whom Lucy had invited at the last minute.

"Yes." Meg nodded blindly. "Sir Winford looks quite well."

"He would make a fine candidate for a husband," Sarah said for perhaps the dozenth time in the last two days.

"He would indeed," Meg agreed numbly, trying not to stare at the back of Hart's dark head and trying not to wonder at what Lady Eugenia had said that made him laugh that way.

"And given your news . . . ," Sarah continued.

Sarah had been full of outrage over Meg's father's plans to move his family to the Continent. She'd invited Meg to stay with her for the remainder of the Season.

"Mother has refused, I'm afraid," Meg had replied. "And Lucy has already tried."

"Tried what?" Sarah had asked.

"She offered to allow me to live with her, to be my chaperone."

"Your parents refused an offer from a duchess?"

"Father seemed to agree with the plan, but Mother was adamantly against it."

Sarah planted her fists on her hips. "Your mother is awful. No offense, Meggie."

Meg sighed. "None taken."

"I simply cannot believe she'd want you to languish alone on the Continent instead of finishing out the Season here," Sarah said.

"Her exact words were, 'If you haven't found a husband yet, there's little chance of finding one now.' Then she proceeded to inform me how much a London Season cost and how Father couldn't afford to keep me here.

Even after Lucy offered to pay for all of my expenses. Mother is quite proud. I understand. I cannot blame her."

"Not too proud to run from your father's creditors." Sarah left off after she saw what must have been the miserable look on Meg's face. "I'm sorry, Meggie, truly I am, but your parents are being so . . . difficult."

"That's one word for it." Meg took another sip from her flute. Champagne was the only thing making her feel better this evening, especially after the arrival of Lady Eugenia. After her dance with Sir Winford last night, Meg had watched Hart dancing with Lady Eugenia. When he danced with the lady once more before the evening was over, Meg had decided she didn't care for Lady Eugenia. She was the exact sort of woman Hart should marry. One his father would approve of. One with a hefty dowry and a family untouched by scandal.

"Don't worry," Sarah said. "Lucy's informed me that we must step up our efforts."

Alarm clutched Meg's chest. "Step up our efforts at what?"

"With Sir Winford, of course."

"Oh yes, Sir Winford." Meg breathed a sigh of relief. She took another sip of champagne. "Of course."

"Who else did you think—?"

Meg was spared having to answer that question by the arrival of Sir Winford and Lucy's announcement to the entire room that it was time to go in to dinner.

"Miss Timmons," Sir Winford said. "Her Grace asked me to escort you into the dining room. If you don't mind."

Meg pasted a smile on her face. "Thank you, Sir Winford."

"I'll just go in search of my husband, then." Sarah scanned the room for Lord Berkeley.

The couples lined up together side by side in the drawing room. Meg and Sir Winford were near the back of the line due to their status, which meant, given his height, Meg had a clear view of Hart's head and shoulders next to Lady Eugenia several paces in front of them. Meg cleared her throat, lifted her chin, and smiled widely at Sir Winford. Sarah had confirmed that Hart had decided to court Lady Eugenia. That news somehow made Lucy think she should invite Lady Eugenia to this dinner party. Meg failed to see how Lady Eugenia's presence was helpful to their cause.

Perhaps Meg was a fool chasing Hart. Though he'd danced with her a few times and kissed her twice quite accidentally, not romantically, and he'd seemed to enjoy her company upon occasion, that hardly meant he would toss aside his years of breeding and duty to marry someone so far beneath him with no dowry. Hart's parents expected a solid political and social alliance from his future wife, not the impoverished daughter of their sworn enemy.

Which was why Meg had determined this afternoon she would do her best to get to know Sir Winford. He seemed kind and pleasant. He was exactly the sort of man she *should* be thrilled to garner attention from. She was a wretched ingrate to be so inhospitable toward him. Besides, she owed the duchess a considerable sum for her gowns and slippers and reticules.

Though she knew Lucy would never force her to repay the debt, Meg had made a promise and she intended to keep it. Unlike her father, to Meg, a debt owed was a debt she must pay. Sir Winford had more than enough money to pay the debt. While it made her stomach turn to think of marrying for money, it was better than being banished to Spain. Sir Winford was pleasant and intelligent. Perhaps she could learn to love him. Vowing to try, she smiled at the knight more brightly as he escorted her in to dinner.

Meg resolved to avoid so much as looking in Hart's direction during the dinner party.

It was a good resolve, too, until she entered the dining room and discovered she was seated directly across from him. The duchess had informed her guests this was to be an informal party, in which everyone might converse not only with the people sitting to their right and left, but also with those across from them. There was Lady Eugenia, sitting next to Hart, across from Sir Winford. Bother.

The wine was poured and the first course of squash soup was being served when Hart addressed Sir Winford. "Miss Timmons tells me you've an interest in horses, Winford."

Sir Winford tugged at his lapels. "Yes, yes, indeed. I cannot pass up a race. Won the steeplechase in Devon last month." This last part he said with a proud sideways look at Meg.

Hart's jaw hardened. "Really? I won the steeplechase in Surrey a fortnight ago. We should race sometime."

"Oh indeed. Sounds like a jolly good time."

"Name the place and the time," Hart replied with a calculated smile.

Alarm bells sounded in Meg's head. Was this really happening? Was Hart truly challenging Sir Winford to a race? He sounded positively competitive. Wasn't he always? Especially when it came to horses? Surely, it had nothing to do with *her*.

Sir Winford looked taken aback. "Hampstead Heath, Thursday afternoon?"

"Perfect." Hart took another long draught of wine.

"I should love to come and watch the race. It sounds like terrific fun," Lady Eugenia purred. Meg had never cared for cats. Except for Lucy.

Meg clutched at the velvet seat of her chair. She didn't think it sounded like terrific fun at all. It sounded much more like a disaster in the making.

Sir Winford turned to her with a hopeful look in his blue eyes. "Miss Timmons, won't you come and watch, too? For my sake? I'm certain to win if I have you in my corner."

"I wouldn't be so certain about that, Winford." Hart tossed back half of his wineglass and narrowed his eyes on the knight.

"Hart, do you truly think another race is a good idea?" came Sarah's voice from a few seats down the table.

Hart's smile was tinged with roguishness. "My sister hates for me to race." This he directed toward Lady Eugenia, whom Meg wanted to kick.

"Only because you've nearly killed yourself half a dozen times," Sarah replied sweetly.

Hart rolled his eyes. "Yes, and I'm much better at racing as a result."

"Nonsense." Lucy clapped her hands. "I think a good race is just what is needed to break up the doldrums of the Season. Let's all go watch and make a party of it on Thursday afternoon."

Excited murmurs filled the room as Meg lifted her

gaze to Hart's and tried to . . . tried to what? Smile? Give him a reassuring nod? What if he broke his neck this time and died racing a man she'd brought into his social circle? She'd never forgive herself. However, if the fool wanted to break his neck while trying to impress Lady Eugenia, that was his affair. Meg had no intention of watching it play out.

"I cannot make it Thursday afternoon," she said. "I must oversee packing. I'm moving to the Continent in a fortnight."

CHAPTER NINETEEN

Hart's spoon clattered to his bowl. A dollop of soup splashed across his pristine white shirt. "Blast," he called out before grabbing his napkin to wipe it away.

"Nonsense," Lucy said again, this time directed toward Meg, completely ignoring Hart's troubles with his soupy shirt. "I'll send some servants to help you pack. You'll be ready in a twinkle. Meanwhile, you'll come with us to Hampstead Heath. Besides, there's always the possibility that you might become *engaged* before you have a chance to leave." Lucy grinned from ear to ear.

A footman had rushed forward to help Hart clean his shirt. "No, leave it." Hart said, waving away the man.

"Some silver polish will get out the stain," Lucy said. "My mother's housekeeper taught me that. You'll be quite amazed. Henry," she added to one of the footmen, "will you please fetch the polish from the silver closet?"

"I'll do it!" Meg called out. She had her napkin off her lap and stood before anyone had a chance to notice.

"I need a bit of fresh air and I know where the silver closet is." Running out of the room seemed by far the best choice at the moment. It would spare her from having to explain her statement about moving to Sir Winford, who looked poised on the brink of asking a great many questions. More important, it would spare her from having to explain Lucy's loaded statement about a marriage proposal to . . . anyone.

"Nonsense," Lucy said for the third time. "Henry here can easily—"

"No, no. You see, I'm already on my way. I'll be right back." Meg was already hurrying toward the door. No doubt all of Lucy's fine friends would think she'd lost her mind, but she couldn't sit there in the stately room across from Hart and Lady Eugenia and talk about either her leaving or the race. For some reason it felt . . . excruciating.

Meg planned to find the silver polish and send back a maid with both the polish and her regrets. She was done with Lucy's plotting tonight. Why, oh why, had the duchess invited Lady Eugenia? To sit across from the gorgeous blonde, knowing she was exactly who Hart was looking for in a wife, dowry and all. Definitely too much. Meg had got in over her head. She would send a note to Sir Winford tomorrow saying she had left tonight with a megrim and asking him to call upon her at his first opportunity. She would *not* be attending the race at Hampstead Heath.

Meg picked up her salmony skirts and swam down the cool corridor toward the silver closet. The small room was at the back of the house across from the servants' stairwell to the kitchens. She'd noted it on a tour of the house Lucy had once given her. It was to be Meg's sanctuary tonight.

Moments later, she arrived in front of the closet. She tried the door handle. Confound it. Of course it was locked. She hadn't thought about *that* possibility before she'd rashly rushed from the dining room. She needed the key.

Conveniently, Mr. Hughes, the butler, materialized moments later. "Miss Timmons," he said, bowing. "Her Grace indicated you might be in need of this." He presented the key to the closet upon a silver salver. A small smile popped to Meg's lips. Everything in a duke's household was grand, apparently, and the servants thought of everything.

"Thank you very much." Meg pulled the heavy key from the salver and turned toward the door. "Do you know exactly where the silver polish is located?" she asked the butler. But the man was gone, as if he'd vanished through the walls.

Meg slid the heavy key into the lock and twisted. It was stuck. Lucy had mentioned that the door was problematic, hadn't she? Meg jiggled it once, twice, and then kicked it with her slipper. It opened. Thank heavens. She'd hate to have to slink back to the dining room and admit she hadn't even been able to open the door.

She stepped inside the dark room, hoping the silver polish was readily apparent using only the light from the corridor. It was not. There was no help for it. She'd have to light a candle. Luckily one sat in a holder on the bureau near the door, a flintlock beside it. She lit the candle and held it aloft, searching the rows of shelves for the polish.

Still not readily apparent. Bother.

Not being particularly tall didn't help, either. There was a small set of movable wooden steps to her left. She set the candle on the bureau, bent over, and pushed the steps toward a large closed cabinet against the back wall. If she could get up high enough to open the doors to the cabinet, perhaps she would find the elusive polish.

She climbed up and reached for the latch on the cabinet's doors. She was forced to stretch far above her head. Her gown and stays compressed her chest and she momentarily felt as if she might faint. Why exactly had she thought this was a good idea? If she had any sense, she would simply inform one of the maids that her mistress required silver polish in the dining room and call for her coach to be brought around. But she had promised to locate the blasted polish and locate it she would.

She reached farther, straining, straining more. A loud ripping noise ensued and cool air rushed across her chest. Her gown had ripped clear down the bodice just as the door slammed shut and the candle blew out from the force of it.

"Blast it. No!" She clutched at the front of her gown.

First things first. She'd have to get down and relight the candle to assess the damage to her gown. The bodice was certainly ripped open and gaping away from her chest, but how bad was it? More important, how indecent? It felt *quite* indecent. There was no way she could return to the dining room now.

She carefully made her way down the steps. Using her hands to feel her way toward the bureau, she located the candle, but curiously, there was no flintlock. She patted all around next to the candle where the flintlock had been. Nothing. Had it fallen to the floor? Bother. Bother.

Very well. She would open the door to let in a bit of light and hope no one wandering by noticed the state of her bodice. In the pitch-black darkness, she felt her way over the bureau toward the door. She smoothed her hand down the wood until she located the door's handle. She turned it. Locked. She turned harder. Still locked. She pulled with all her might. It didn't budge.

She expelled her breath and clenched her fist in her thoroughly ripped bodice. God help her, she was locked in the abominable silver closet.

CHAPTER TWENTY

Hart shifted uncomfortably in his seat. He didn't care about his blasted wet shirt. Or the light-yellow stain that was already setting in. Instead, a quartet of other thoughts possessed his mind. The first was the reason for his clumsiness to begin with. Meg's statement that she was leaving town. In a fortnight. What the devil could she possibly mean? Why would she be moving to the Continent?

His second thought centered on the reason why Meg had been gone for the better part of a quarter hour. How long did it take to find silver polish?

Then there was her reaction to the race. She'd looked stricken when he'd challenged Sir Winford. Did she wish he hadn't? Surely, Meg had to know he was an excellent racer. His accident last autumn had been a fluke. Or was her concern for that fop Winford? She was obviously trying to secure an offer of marriage from the man. Lucy had made that clear enough. Perhaps

Hart shouldn't have challenged Winford, but racing was his passion and the knight had so cavalierly indicated his prowess in the matter. Not to mention how the man was settled on his last nerve. Which was Hart's fourth distracting thought. Was Sir Winford on the verge of a proposal to Meg? Would she accept? She'd be a fool not to.

Why did the thought of Meg marrying Winford make Hart want to put his fist through the nearest wall? It wasn't as if she was suitable for *him*. His father's words burned through Hart's brain. "Meg Timmons is the last girl on earth I'd allow you to marry." What the hell did his father care? The man had been manipulative Hart's entire life. Playing people like chess pieces, ordering them about. He treated his son like the most prized piece of them all, and he demanded obedience. That's all Hart had ever been good for. Breeding stock. A dumb, beautiful, useless animal meant to be paired with another dumb, beautiful, useless animal for the sake of producing more useless progeny.

Hart glanced over at Lady Eugenia. She was lovely and accomplished and witty. She said all the right things and did all the right things. She had a hefty dowry. She was bloody perfect. He should offer for her immediately.

Yet she wasn't the one he wanted to see him win the race with Sir Winford. It was Meg. But why? Why did it matter to him? He owed her, he reminded himself. At least he *had* owed her. The reasoning for exactly what he owed her and why was blurry at best, but he had definitely behaved inappropriately with her more than once and she hadn't deserved it. His debt was paid, wasn't it? He should allow her her courtship with Winford. Challenging the knight to a race was probably not his most clever idea. He'd surely beat the man soundly and possibly ruin Meg's chances for happiness. But he couldn't convince himself to withdraw.

"The steamed halibut looks delicious," Lady Eugenia said pleasantly as the footmen delivered the next course.

Hart glanced up from his plate to see the butler stride into the room, lean over, and whisper something to Lucy Hunt. Lucy whispered back, and the man bowed and left the room. Had they been speaking about Meg? It would be rude to ask.

Hart concentrated on his halibut and making polite conversation with Lady Eugenia while Sarah smiled and nodded at him approvingly, but Meg's absence made it increasingly difficult for him to answer Lady Eugenia's questions with even a modicum of interest.

Finally, Lucy cleared her throat. "Lord Highgate, hasn't Miss Timmons returned yet? She must come back soon or your shirt is surely ruined. Then she'll have missed this lovely course for nothing."

"I'm happy to go in search of her, Your Grace," Sir Winford boomed, pulling his napkin from his lap and pushing back his chair.

Hart growled.

"Thank you, Sir Winford," Lucy began. "But I daresay Lord Highgate should go in search of her since she was on a mission to save his shirt to begin with." She turned her gaze to Hart and took a sip of wine. "Wouldn't you agree, Lord Highgate?"

Hart frowned and narrowed his eyes on Lucy. Why hadn't she asked the butler to find Miss Timmons? But Hart wasn't about to argue. His heart raced. The truth was it was nothing but fortuitous that Lucy had chosen *him* to go in search of her. He wouldn't be forced to sit any longer waiting and wondering.

Sir Winford opened his mouth to speak but Lucy's lioness glare stopped him. The knight reluctantly replaced the napkin on his lap and settled back into his seat.

"My pleasure." Hart stood, bowed, excused himself to Lady Eugenia and the others, and tossed his napkin to the seat of his chair. A footman rushed forward to fold it. "Though I'm not entirely certain I am aware of the location of your silver closet . . . if you'll point me in the correct direction."

Lucy nodded regally. "It's down the corridor, to the right, all the way to the back near the servants' staircase."

"Right." Hart bowed to her. "I'll be back shortly."

"Thank you, my lord," Lucy said as he left the room.

Once outside the dining room, Hart strode down the corridor. Following the duchess's instructions, he located the silver closet. The key was in the lock and the door was closed. He tried the handle. It didn't budge. He turned the lock and tried the handle once more. It was stuck. "Meg?" he called.

Her muffled voice sounded through the thick wood. "Hart? Is that you?"

"Yes." He pushed harder against the door, this time using his shoulder.

"Hart, don't come in here, I've ripped my—"

The door flew open and Hart nearly fell into the room from the weight of his shoulder against the door.

The closet was in darkness, but he made out the shadowy figure of Meg, a glimmering bit of pink a few paces away.

"Why is it dark in here? Are you quite all right?"

"Don't come any closer," she squeaked.

"What? Why?" He stepped into the room.

"No! Don't let the door—" Meg lunged toward it, a shadow in the darkness.

She was too late. The door slammed closed.

He'd stepped quickly to the side. "Why?"

"Because it will—" She jiggled the handle and sighed "—lock."

Hart turned toward the door and grabbed the handle again. By God, she was right. The door had not only closed, it had locked. What in the devil's name?

"I've been trying for the last ten minutes to get out of here."

"I see that," he said simply. "May I ask why you're waiting in the dark?"

"Oh, because I prefer it, obviously." Her voice dripped sarcasm.

He rubbed his fingers through his hair. "Tell me what happened."

"I was standing on the stairs looking for the polish when the door slammed shut and blew out the candle. The flintlock appears to have gone missing."

"There is a candle and a flintlock in here?" Instinctively, he turned to look before realizing *that* was a fruitless effort. He couldn't even see his own hand in front of his face.

"Yes. Somewhere," Meg replied.

"Then all we must do is locate it."

"Brilliant. I wish I'd thought of that."

Hart grinned in the darkness. "I never knew how witty you are." Miss Timmons confirmed again she wasn't the quiet little mouse he'd once assumed she was. He liked that. A lot.

"I suppose being locked in a silver closet in the dark with a ripped bodice doesn't exactly bring out the best in me."

"Pardon?" Had he heard her correctly?

"I said being locked in a silver closet isn't particularly my finest hour," she replied.

"No. The part about your bodice being, erm, ripped?"

"Oh yes. In addition to the door blowing shut, locking me in here, and divesting me of light, I managed to rip my gown while reaching for the silver polish."

"That is unfortunate." Hart's mind raced. What sort of state of undress were they speaking of? He could smell Meg's strawberry sweetness. Light. Ephemeral. Like her. His palms began to sweat. It had turned ungodly hot in the small space of a sudden.

"Quite unlucky," Meg echoed. "Therefore, if you are fortunate enough to find the flintlock and light the candle, I'd be ever so thankful if you would turn your back when you do so."

Hart chuckled.

"Is my misfortune amusing to you?" came her pert voice.

"Not at all. I'm merely considering the ridiculousness of all of this."

Two moments ticked by before Meg spoke, a decided laugh in her voice. "It is quite ridiculous, isn't it?"

Hart was already feeling his way across the top of a bureau, trying to locate the elusive flintlock. "Do you think the breeze caused by the door knocked the flintlock to the floor?"

"I got down on my hands and knees and felt around but wasn't able to find it. My next attempt was going to be to call for help. Your voice is louder. They're certain to hear you. Go ahead."

"Nonsense," Hart replied. "I'm not about to call for help like a ninny. I'm going to find this flintlock, light the candle, and open this blasted door."

"Are you calling me a ninny?" she asked, but the lightness in her voice remained. He could tell she found it amusing.

"No. I'm saying I don't need help from a servant to escape a silver closet."

"Very well, I'll wait here with my ripped bodice while you save the day. Please proceed."

Hart shook his head, even though she couldn't see him do it. He slowly lowered himself to the floor and on hands and knees scoured every inch of the floor of the silver closet while Meg quietly waited near the back of the small space.

"I don't understand it," he said, finally. He pushed himself up to sit on the floor, his back against the cabinet next to Meg. He drew up his knees. "I laid out the floor in a grid. I know I covered everywhere."

"As did I ten minutes before you."

"I touched every bit of space on the bureau, too."

"As did I," she said.

"It's not in here."

"My conclusion exactly."

"How can that be?" Hart asked.

"It's an excellent question and one I intend to pose to Lucy the moment I see her next, but for now, are you at all interested in calling for help?"

Hart sighed loud and long. He stood and made his

way carefully to the door. He grabbed the handle and pulled it as hard as he could. His shoulder wrenched but he pulled again. He took off his coat and tossed it atop the bureau. This time he put his back into it. He tugged, strained, and pulled with every ounce of strength he possessed. Still nothing. All he'd managed to do was work up a fine sweat. He swiped his wet hair away from his eyes. "Blast. Blast. Blast. Sorry," he said, remembering a lady was in the room.

"I don't blame you," Meg replied. "I said many similar things while trying to pry open that door. Let me know when you think it's time to call for help."

Hart sank back to the floor and propped up his knees, resting his arms atop them. He thumped his head back against the bureau behind him. Once. Twice. "Blast. There is only one problem with calling for help."

"What's that?" Meg's voice held a note of surprise.

"We've been in here together, alone, for at least ten minutes and your bodice is ripped. If we call for help we could do irreparable harm to your reputation."

CHAPTER TWENTY-ONE

There was no arguing with that logic. Meg bit her lip. It was true. Depending on who came to open the door, a scandal might well ensue.

"If Lucy comes, she won't tell. We can simply explain what happened." Meg desperately tried to think of the best possible outcome.

Hart's voice was grim. "If one of the servants comes, the entire household may know before the night is through."

"If the butler comes, I've no doubt he'll be discreet. He's a duke's butler after all," she countered.

"If it's one of the maids, however, she may have no such compunction. And what, pray tell, if it's one of the party guests?"

"Such as Sir Winford?" Meg asked, true panic beginning to set in. Hart was right. This was more than an unfortunate event. This was a potential disaster.

"Afraid your *engagement* might not happen?" Hart replied. His voice dripped sarcasm.

"Pardon?"

"What do you see in that man?"

"Sir Winford?" Meg could hardly believe her ears. Were they truly having this conversation?

"He doesn't seem particularly . . . manly to me," Hart continued.

Meg tried to quell the laughter in her voice. "Oh really? What do you consider manly?"

"I doubt he ever won the steeplechase in Devon," Hart mumbled.

"You're calling him a liar?"

"I have my doubts, that's all."

"Why do you care?" Meg's voice was matter-of-fact.

"I don't care for braggarts."

This entire conversation would be much easier if she could see him, tell from the look in his eyes what he was thinking. "Is that why you challenged him to a race?"

"Never could pass up a challenge."

"The race is a challenge? Is that it?" Why did he have to smell like that? Evergreen and soap. Just like his coat that fateful night in the gardens next to her father's house.

"Of course it's a challenge." Hart's voice was sharp, clipped.

"What do you care what I see in him?" She wanted to force him to admit to some bit of feeling, however small.

Silence ensued for a few moments before Hart said, "You could do a sight better in picking a husband."

That made Meg laugh.

"What's funny?" Hart's voice sounded bothered.

"That you think I could do better than Sir Winford."

"I only meant, he's not particularly well connected or—"

"You do realize I'm the biggest wallflower the *ton* has seen in years, don't you?"

"That's a bit of an exaggeration."

"It's not, really. I don't exaggerate. Never seen the need for it. The circumstances of my life have been horrible enough."

"Horrible?" His voice had changed completely. Now it was low, tense.

"My father is penniless and I have no dowry. You cannot pretend not to know the scandal surrounding my family. As a result, I've been unwanted and overlooked. If it weren't for your sister, I'd have spent the last years completely alone." She took a deep breath. "As it was, I've sat on the sidelines, ignored and . . . lonely."

Oh, why was she telling him all of this? She must sound like the biggest ninny in London. Was she truly explaining to one of the most popular men in town what it felt like to be lonely? Hart Highgate didn't even know what the word meant.

"I'm sorry, Meg." The true regret in his tone made tears spring to her eyes.

"It's nothing for you to be sorry about." Her voice was sharper than she'd meant it to be.

"But still, I . . . never thought about how it must have been for you. How . . . difficult." He took a deep breath. "You *want* to marry, then? Not because it's expected of you?" Confusion lay heavy in his voice.

That was a surprising question. "Yes, of course. You don't?"

A few silent moments ticked by. "I've tried to think about it as little as possible. The truth is, I've never considered before that it might actually be a choice someone made, not for duty or family, but actual desire. That's a novel concept to me."

Meg pushed her slipper along the floor. "I know," she whispered softly.

"How do you know?"

"I mean . . ." Meg's voice faltered. Why in the world had she blurted that out? Confound it. "Sarah and I have spoken about you, about your lack of desire to marry."

"You have?"

"Yes, you know, ladies talk." She did her best to sound nonchalant. Of late, however, that nonchalance did not come as easily as it once had.

"You and Sarah have spoken about me? I suppose it stands to reason." He was silent for a bit while Meg decided that she should remain quiet because she was obviously saying idiotic things here in the dark.

"*Why* do you want to marry?" Hart's words sliced through the darkness like a sharp knife through a fresh teacake.

Meg laughed again. His evergreen scent continued to fill the space, along with the tang of silver polish. She wished she could move away from his scent. All it did was make her want to . . . touch him. "What do you mean, why?"

"I'm quite serious," he said. "Why do you wish to marry? For your family's sake?"

"Not at all. I wish to marry because I want a husband and children and . . . love."

"Love? Are you serious?" A scoffing laugh followed.

"Blast. I hadn't meant to say that aloud. Pardon my language."

"Of course I'm serious. Haven't you ever wanted those things?"

Another moment of silence. "I've always known I must marry, but I cannot say I've wanted it. I'm resigned to the fact that it must happen. To secure the lineage."

Meg took a deep breath. She anticipated and dreaded his answer to her next question. "And you're . . . finally ready now?"

"Did Sarah tell you?"

"She mentioned it. And then there's the fact that I've never seen you pay anyone as much attention as you're paying Lady Eugenia."

"You've noticed whom I've paid attention to?"

"No. I . . ." Drat. Honesty was the best policy. "Very well. I suppose I have. Ladies tend to notice these things."

"Yes," he replied. "I've decided it's time."

She was quiet for several seconds. "Lady Eugenia is to be the lucky bride?" Confound it. Why did her voice have to shake?

"It would appear so."

At least he hadn't been able to manage enough enthusiasm to simply say yes. Wasn't *that* grasping at optimism?

"I almost married when I was younger." His voice took on a hard edge.

"I remember."

"You remember Annabelle?"

"Yes," Meg replied. "Why didn't you marry her?" The darkness was making her bold. She'd never summoned the courage to ask such a thing before.

"Because she tried to force me into it." Hart's voice was unmistakably angry. "I detest scheming women."

Meg gulped. Her discussions with Lucy marched through her mind. Guilt flooded her. She was scheming even now, wasn't she? "Force you? What do you mean?"

"Annabelle employed a friend to find us in a compromising situation she'd invented. We'd only been outside alone for a few minutes. I hadn't touched her. The entire thing was ludicrous. I learned that some young ladies will do nearly anything to secure a title and wealth."

"That is horrible."

Annabelle had left town, never to be heard from again. She had paid a steep price for her attempt at blackmail.

"Yes, well, that incident put me off marriage. That and my father's endorsement of the institution."

"After the Annabelle incident, I don't blame you."

A few moments ticked by in silence before Hart asked, "Are you truly leaving town?"

"Yes," Meg sighed, hearing the sadness in that sound, but not knowing what to say. What else was there? She was leaving the country and he was marrying Lady Eugenia.

"Why?"

There was no use denying it. Hart would find out soon enough. "My father has decided we must move to the Continent."

"Because?" Hart prompted.

Meg kept her cheek firmly between her teeth. She did not want to cry. "He owes quite a lot of money to a good many people."

"Ah. Of course."

"Apparently moving to the Continent is . . ." She couldn't finish the sentence.

"One way to outrun his debtors," Hart finished for her. "You're going too?" Hart spared her from a reply to the debtors comment.

She was not going to be able to say this without tears in her eyes. Despite the fact that he couldn't see her, she nodded. "Yes." She forced the word past her dry lips, ashamed at the quaver in her voice. At least he couldn't see her burning face.

"I'm sorry to hear that. Does Sarah know yet?"

"I told her this morning. Only Lucy hopes—" Oh, she couldn't finish that awful sentence, either . . . what Lucy had instructed her to say to Hart should this subject be broached.

"Lucy hopes Sir Winford will offer for you before you leave," Hart finished for her again.

Was the man a mind reader? More ridiculous nodding and then she said, "Yes."

"Is that what *you* want, Meg? To marry Winford?"

She turned her head toward Hart in the darkness with tears cooling her cheeks. Her throat was closed. She couldn't speak, couldn't get any words past the huge lump that had formed there.

"A marriage proposal would keep me here," she finally managed.

"I see."

She couldn't talk about Sir Winford anymore. All she wanted was get out of here and rush home and cry. Her skirts rustled as she stood. She brushed Hart's leg as she moved toward the door slowly, carefully, feeling her way. She tried to ignore the warmth of him and the scent of him. So near. So close. She could reach out and touch him . . . if she dared. Her body shook with pent-up longing.

Steeling her resolve, she made it to the door and stood and tugged at the handle again. "Lucy knows we're here. She'll come in search of us. We'll just have to hope she finds us and not some gossipy servant."

"Don't worry, Meg. Whatever happens, I'll stand up for you."

She snapped her head to the side. "What?" she asked breathlessly.

"If we're found by the wrong person and a scandal ensues, I will do the gentlemanly thing and stand up for you."

Her heart hammered in her chest. She couldn't breathe. Did he mean what she thought he meant? "What do you mean by 'stand up'?"

"Marry you, of course. If the scandal is great enough, I'd have to. We'd have no choice. It would be the right thing to do."

Meg had never prayed harder in her entire life. A fervent wish to the heavens that whoever found them would be an ally. She wanted Hart desperately, but she didn't want him forced into an unwanted marriage. *Never* that. She could not bear it.

She didn't have long to say her prayers before the door was wrenched open and the light from the corridor flooded their small prison.

CHAPTER TWENTY-TWO

"What in the world?" A female voice floated into the silver closet.

Hart blinked, adjusting his eyesight to the light.

It was Sarah's voice. Thank bloody Christ it was Sarah's voice. Was she alone?

"Sarah, is that you?" Hart stepped into the corridor. He had his answer. "Thank God you're alone."

Meg remained in the shadows. Sensibly, she wasn't about to leave the closet with her ripped bodice.

"What in heaven's name is going on here?" Sarah's face was a study in shock. "You were both in there in the dark? Alone? Meg, are you coming out?"

"No," Meg squeaked.

".What? Why not?" Sarah's voice rose in alarm.

Hart cleared his throat. "I will allow Miss Timmons to explain the situation. Being a gentleman, I must take myself off, but allow me to assure you that absolutely nothing untoward happened here. I'll return to the dining room and tell everyone I got lost on the way to the silver closet and never made it. I'll say you helped me locate Meg and she has a megrim and is leaving immediately." He glanced at Meg. "Meg can explain the rest."

"What? Why?" Sarah asked but Hart was already striding toward the dining room.

As he went, he considered what had happened in the silver closet. His throat had tightened when Meg told him she was lonely. Lonely. The word stuck in his chest like a knife. He'd never considered it. He'd known Meg was a wallflower. Everyone knew that. He'd give his right arm to be able to go to events and not be mobbed by marriage-minded misses looking to become the next Lady Highgate. He'd never considered it from her position. A young woman who was overlooked by everyone, due to her circumstances. He'd felt like an arse after bringing up her marital prospects. After she'd said she was lonely, he felt like an even bigger one.

Meg actually *wanted* to marry. She was looking for *love* of all things. It had both surprised him and softened him. Did she love Sir Winford? Was that possible? Hart didn't want to contemplate it. His gut ached.

He pasted a false smile on his face before opening the door to the dining room. "I never found the silver closet," he announced. "When Sarah came to look, she showed me where it was and we located Miss Timmons. She is fine but has been overcome by a megrim and Sarah is helping to call around her coach. I'm afraid she won't be joining us for the remainder of the evening."

He didn't mistake the obviously peeved look on Lucy Hunt's face.

* * *

"Come in, Sarah." Meg gestured with her hand from her safe spot inside the darkened silver closet. "But whatever you do, do *not* close that door behind you."

Sarah plucked a candlestick from a side table in the corridor and entered the closet. Five minutes later, Meg had explained the entire debacle to her. She left out the part where Hart had said he would stand up for her. She couldn't bear to think about that. By the time Meg had finished relating the story, her heart was pounding. Had the events of the evening truly happened to her? She'd come so close to causing a scandal. With Hart. That was the *last* thing she wanted.

"Don't worry. Don't worry." Sarah patted her shoulder. "I'll go and grab my shawl and call for your coach. We'll cover your bodice and I'll explain everything to Lucy and the others. Like Hart said, I'll tell them you weren't feeling well. There is nothing whatsoever to worry about."

Meg sighed a breath of relief. "Thank you, Sarah. I cannot tell you how much I appreciate it. I'll wait here."

Sarah paused, her hand on the doorjamb. "May I ask you something, Meggie?"

"Of course."

"The key was in the lock when I came. There was no reason for the door to be stuck. Lucy wouldn't by any chance be trying to help you win *Hart's* favor, would she?" A disapproving look shone in Sarah's eye.

Meg was relieved that she'd left out the part about Hart standing up for her. She, too, suspected Lucy was behind tonight's little drama. It was time to tell her closest friend the truth. She nodded slowly. "I'm afraid I've got in over my head, Sarah. I never expected Lucy to go to these lengths."

Sarah moved back into the closet, sighed, and shook her head. "I knew it. We *are* talking about the infamous Lucy Hunt, are we not?"

"I had no idea she'd conspire to lock me and Hart in a silver closet together!"

"I agree. It's a bit much even for Lucy. When I announced I would go in search of you two, she nearly tackled me trying to send Sir Winford instead. That's when I became suspicious. Well, I was somewhat suspicious before that, if the truth is told, as I've never heard of silver polish removing a soup stain from a shirt. Have you?"

"I've been a fool." Meg hung her head. "You know I've loved Hart for an age. I couldn't allow him to take a wife without at least *trying* to see if I stood any chance."

Sarah's eyes were filled with tears. "Oh, Meggie, I understand, truly I do. I'm sorry I haven't been more of a help to you. You know I've always been convinced he would break your heart. He's never been the type to treat a lady like a prize. I fear he'll take a wife, deposit her in the country, and go about his business with women like Lady Maria Tempest."

Meg gasped. "Maria Tempest? Is that who he's been with?"

"Until recently, I believe."

MT. Meg had her answer. Lady Maria was who Hart thought he was meeting that night. Maria Tempest was a gorgeous widow with raven hair and black eyes. Half the male members the *ton* chased after her.

"I know you've always had my best interest at heart, Sarah." Meg laid a hand on Sarah's arm. "But I cannot help but love him. He's just so handsome and noble. He was so kind to me that day my mother ordered you both from the house. When he smiled at me and said such nice things, it was all over. I've loved him ever since."

"I remember," Sarah said softly, tears rolling down her cheeks.

Meg pressed a hand to her chest. "I was so ashamed."

Sarah squeezed Meg's shoulder. "He's always been gallant to a female in distress, my brother. It's his long-term commitment to them I question. I've always believed Hart would obey our parents and choose a wife from his pick of the lot. Not that he doesn't adore defying Father, but I've believed he wasn't interested in who he takes to wife. After his awful experience with Annabelle, he's been resigned to his fate."

"I know. It's true."

"It's not because I wouldn't adore you for a sister-in-law, Meggie. You know I would, but I couldn't stand to see your heart broken. Hart is a rogue after all."

"I know it. I've always known. I wish it made a difference to me. I wish I could want Sir Winford. Truly, I do." Meg stepped forward and hugged her friend tightly. "Oh, Sarah. I could have been ruined. Hart could have been forced into marriage with me, which of course he doesn't want and I don't either, not that way, anyway" Meg groaned. "I should have known better than to ask for Lucy's help."

"Don't worry. No one will ever find out about this." A determined look shone in Sarah's eyes.

Meg planted both fists on her hips. "Thank you, Sarah, you're a true friend, and I intend to tell Lucy she is no longer employed as my matchmaker at my first opportunity."

CHAPTER TWENTY-THREE

The wind was high on Hampstead Heath as the racers and their audience gathered on Thursday afternoon. Although she hadn't yet had a chance to ask Lucy to stop matchmaking, Meg had arrived at Lucy's prompting. Well, not *only* Lucy's prompting. More specifically because Lucy had sent a coach to fetch her, and, true to her word, the duchess had also sent servants to Meg's parents' house to assist with the packing. A circumstance that had not pleased her mother. When Lucy swept into the foyer and asked for Meg to accompany her to the heath, Mother had had no choice but to allow her to go or risk offending the duchess.

The coach had taken Meg to Lucy's house, where she had yet another fabulous new gown waiting, this one of navy blue with white dots, a matching dark blue reticule, white kid gloves, and a navy-and-white-striped bonnet. Meg felt like a dressed-up doll yet again as she accompanied the duchess to Hampstead Heath, where either Hart or Sir Winford might break their necks. It would serve either or both of them right.

Sarah also accompanied the two. She and Meg had determined it would be the perfect time for Meg to ask Lucy to cease her matchmaking efforts. Meanwhile, Lucy's husband, Derek, and Sarah's husband, Christian, had accompanied Hart in Christian's coach.

"Who do you think will win, Lucy?" Meg asked as the coach jostled to a stop along the heath.

Lucy peered out the window at the bright, sunny afternoon. "My money is on Hart."

"Are you serious?" Sarah asked, looking nonplussed. Her voice was high with surprise.

"Entirely. I have fifty pounds on the matter." Lucy grinned.

"Have you ever seen Sir Winford ride?" Sarah asked.

"Of course not, but Hart is a superb rider and Goliath is certain to best whatever animal Winford brings." Lucy adjusted her bonnet. "Who *you* want to win is the more interesting question," she added to Meg, her different-colored eyes sparkling.

"It makes no difference to me. I only hope they both live through it." Meg crossed her arms over her chest and stared out the window.

"Liar." Lucy shook her finger at Meg. "You want Hart to win."

"He could use a bit of modesty," Meg replied, lifting her nose in the air.

"Give me an arrogant man over a modest one any day," Lucy said with a wink.

"Yes, well, Lucy, we want to tell you something," Sarah began, glancing at Meg who sat beside her. She settled her hands in her lap. "Meggie and I have been discussing her marital prospects."

Lucy blinked at them. "Yes?"

"It came to my attention the other evening at your dinner party, that you might have conspired to put Meg and Hart in a"—Sarah cleared her throat—"compromising position."

"Whatever do you mean?" Lucy continued to blink at Sarah innocently.

Sarah sat up even straighter. "Do I need to point out that any one of your servants should have been searching for silver polish before Meg was sent after it?"

"Meg volunteered!" Lucy interjected.

"You could have refused her," Sarah countered.

Lucy flourished a hand in the air. "Why in the world would I refuse her when it became immediately clear to me that the sticky silver closet door was the perfect excuse for Meg and Hart to be found together in a compromising position? Obviously."

"So you admit it?" A look of astonishment swept across Sarah's features.

"Of course I do. What is your point, dear?" Lucy sniffed.

"My point is that you're doing Meg a disservice," Sarah replied. "And I—"

"No, Sarah, allow me." Meg cleared her throat. It was high time she spoke for herself. "Lucy, I cannot tell you how much I appreciate everything you've done for me to date, but I see now that I've been going about it all wrong. Hart and I would make a terrible match. I would, however, appreciate your help in bringing Sir Winford to heel. I have resolved to stop trying to catch Hart."

"Yes," Sarah added. "It's a fruitless pursuit. It's cruel to poor Meg. My parents will disown Hart if he marries her. Most important, I think he'd make her a poor husband. He's charming as the day is long, but he's a complete rogue."

"My dear Sarah," Lucy replied, a perfectly serene look on her face. "I absolutely adore you, but you are woefully ignorant of how matchmakers work. We don't make matches based upon dowries and parents' preferences, as I hope you'll recall from your own match with Lord Berkeley. We make matches based on love and only love. Let me assure you, reformed rogues make the *very* best husbands. Besides, I seem to recall you being worried about your parents disowning you if you didn't marry the Marquess of Branford, and you appear to still be a member of the family." Finishing her little diatribe, Lucy sat with her hands folded primly in her lap, a catlike half smile on her lips.

Sarah sat in dumbfounded silence for several moments. "I'd never thought of it that way."

Meg glanced back and forth between the two ladies. Was Lucy actually changing *Sarah's* mind?

Lucy lifted a hand and smoothed one dark eyebrow. "Well, you'd best begin thinking of it that way, because as the bard said, love and only love makes the world go round. That's all I'm concerned with. I know Meg loves Hart and I have reason enough to believe Hart may love her back. He certainly is interested in her."

"How do you know that?" Sarah asked, glancing uncertainly at Meg.

"He's kissed her . . . twice," Lucy replied.

Sarah swiveled to face Meg, astonishment on her face. "What? Is that true?"

"Yes," Meg squeaked, her face heating.

"Why in the world haven't you told me?"

"It's not exactly like that," Meg replied.

"It's exactly like that," Lucy retorted. "I think they have an excellent chance at finding true love together."

Sarah leaned forward in her seat and searched Lucy's face. "Do you really think so?"

Meg continued to glance back and forth between them. Had the world gone mad? "Sarah, are you allowing her to talk you into this?"

"I want to hear what Lucy has to say," Sarah replied.

Meg fell back against the velvet squabs and covered her eyes with her hand.

"Do you truly think it's possible that Hart loves Meg back?" Sarah repeated.

"I do. I truly do," Lucy replied. "Now may I suggest that instead of thwarting your friend, you help her become your sister-in-law? She's already got quite the Romeo and Juliet plot to overcome, and I for one want to see this end in a happy marriage and laughter instead of poison and tears."

Sarah turned to Meg. She wrapped an arm around her shoulders. "Oh, Meggie, I've known you loved him forever. I never meant to be so thoughtless."

Meg couldn't help it. She sat up straight and let her hand drop away from her face, renewed hope coursing through her. "It's not your fault, Sarah. It's not as if he's always loved me back."

"No, but as Lucy says, perhaps he could. If given the right circumstances to get to know you."

"Precisely," Lucy said. "Which is why I've been trying to put them in each other's paths. This race is the perfect venue to do so yet again."

"But he'll be racing," Meg said. "Not paying attention to me."

"Both men are racing to impress you if I don't mistake my guess," Lucy replied.

"No, that cannot be true." Meg shook her head, afraid to believe, but desperately hoping Lucy was right.

"What if it's true, Meggie?" Sarah wore a hopeful smile as she tugged on her gloves.

"I'm certain it's true," Lucy said as the coach rolled to a stop on the heath. "Now, Sarah, let's join forces as ladies always should and go see to it that your brother falls madly in love with your closest friend."

CHAPTER TWENTY-FOUR

When they arrived at Hampstead Heath, Meg couldn't help but notice Lady Eugenia. The woman wore a pretty lavender-colored gown. Her light hair was hidden beneath her obviously costly bonnet, and she stood at Hart's side with a sunny smile on her face. Meg narrowed her eyes when the woman put her hand on Hart's arm and laughed at something he said. Harlot. Obviously.

"I'll jot off with Derek to set up the starting point," Lucy said.

Sarah turned to Meg. "I'll distract Lady Eugenia. You go greet Hart."

Meg turned to do just that, but Sir Winford came bustling up to them, leading his horse behind him.

"Miss Timmons, there you are. I was hoping you would come," the knight said, a wide smile on his face. He looked relieved to see her.

"We wouldn't miss it," Lucy replied, her expression pitying.

After they all greeted one another, Meg eyed Sir Winford's horse. Lucy was right: The animal, while quite fine, was no match for Goliath. "Are you feeling confident?" Meg asked him, after Lucy and Sarah excused themselves and trotted off across the field in different directions.

"Yes, indeed." Sir Winford patting his horse's flank. "Though I've heard Highgate can be reckless," he continued with a disapproving look on his face.

"Oh, he's not reckless, he's—" Meg stopped and coughed into her glove. It was better to leave off the rest of that sentence. Why should she defend Hart to Sir Winford?

"Will you give me a token, Miss Timmons? Something I can take with me during the race, to know I have your support?" Sir Winford began to reach for her hand but stopped himself.

Now probably wouldn't be the time to mention that Lucy had fifty quid riding on Hart. She glanced up into Sir Winford's bright blue eyes. The knight seemed so sincere, so kindhearted. Meg mentally kicked herself for the hundredth time. Why, oh why, couldn't she love someone as simple to love as Sir Winford would be? No, she had to love the most complicated man in the kingdom.

Meg glanced toward Hart only to see Lady Eugenia tying a lavender scarf to his sleeve. Meg clenched her jaw. "Yes, of course. I'll give you a token." She pulled her own dark blue scarf from her bonnet and tied it around Sir Winford's sleeve. "There. There you are."

Sir Winford smiled broadly, bowed to her, mounted his horse, and took off at a clip toward the starting point.

Meg tried not to look in Hart's direction again, pacing back and forth along the uneven ground. She was just about to go back and sit in the coach until the race began when the sound of horse hooves came trotting toward her.

She looked up to see Hart halt Goliath next to her. He wore tight riding breeches, black top boots, and a dark gray coat, and looked as if he'd been born to ride the magnificent steed.

He tipped his hat to her. "I wasn't certain I'd see you here today."

"Why is that?" She desperately hoped she sounded nonchalant. Why did the man have to look so good in riding breeches? Why hadn't she taken note of what Sir Winford was wearing?

"You mentioned something about needing to pack for your move."

"Oh yes. That." That was nonchalant, wasn't it?

"Are you still leaving?" he asked next.

She reached out and patted the horse's neck. "My father is leaving. I am obliged to go with him."

"Does that mean Sir Winford hasn't offered for you?"

That stung. Meg squared her shoulders. "Not yet," she flung back at him. She raised her chin. Lucy would be proud, but Meg only felt sick.

"You gave your scarf to him, though?" Hart's voice was tight. Why did he say it in a way that made her feel guilty?

Meg pushed her nose in the air. "You accepted Lady Eugenia's scarf."

"So I did." Hart's voice was curt and short. "May the best man win."

"Indeed."

Hart galloped off, leaving Meg thoroughly confused.

Had they just had a jealous exchange? She stared at his retreating form, blinking and wondering what to make of it.

Lucy and Sarah joined her soon after and the three of them locked arms and watched as the riders met. The two men gave each other short nods and spoke briefly, no doubt wishing each other luck. Derek Hunt stood to their far right, a pistol in his hand, ready to fire a shot in the air to indicate the start of the race.

"Where are they riding to?" Meg asked, biting at her lip. Her belly was filled with butterflies.

"Across the field, down the valley, around the church, and back," Lucy said.

Derek called to the riders to determine if they were ready. They both nodded. The duke raised the pistol aloft and fired. The riders' heels dug into the horses' sides and both animals took off at breakneck speed.

"Oh, I cannot watch." Meg extracted her arms from her friends' and lowered her head to stare at her slippers, which were partially hidden in the tall grass. The butterflies had not stopped their flight in her stomach. They made her queasy.

"I can't, either," Sarah said, her voice filled with worry. "At least I don't want to."

"Are you jesting? I'm going to watch the entire thing," Lucy nearly shouted with glee.

The party turned to watch as the riders galloped across the wide expanse of the moor and down the hill.

"What's happening?" Meg asked, still biting her lip and staring at the ground.

"Hart's horse is in the lead by at least one length," Lucy replied, clapping.

"I'd say two," Sarah added in an obviously proud voice.

"Oh dear." Meg wrung her hands. She dared a glance up. The riders had gone down the hill. She couldn't see them. "He's going to kill himself," Meg breathed, wrapping her shaking arms around her middle.

"Who?" Lucy asked. "Hart or Winford?"

"Hart, of course," Meg replied.

"Seems to me Lord Winford is the less skilled rider," Lucy replied.

"Hart loves that horse," Sarah added. "I just hope Goliath keeps him alive."

Many minutes later, the thundering of hooves signaled the riders' return. Meg dared another glance. The two men came over the hill toward the finish line. Hart was in the lead by at least three lengths. The horses' hooves thundered across the moor, kicking up bits of grass and mud as they went. As they topped the hill, a shocked cry shot through the small crowd. Meg held her breath and watched as Hart came riding hell-for-leather toward the finish with Sir Winford's riderless horse behind him. The knight had been thrown.

"Oh no!" Lucy exclaimed, her hand on her mouth.

Meg gasped. "Sir Winford!"

"Come with me," Sarah ordered. She grabbed Meg's hand and they rushed down the hill to find Sir Winford. Hart, who had looked back when he heard the crowd's gasps, was already slowing his mount. He turned in a wide circle and galloped back toward the fallen man. He reached him before Sarah and Meg did. Hart dismounted quickly and ran over to where Sir Winford lay. Hart knelt next to the knight, clearly checking for a pulse in his neck.

"He's alive," Hart called to the crowd, wiping mud from Sir Winford's face.

A relieved sigh murmured through the group. Winford's horse had slowed and Derek Hunt rounded him up.

Sarah and Meg rushed to Hart and Sir Winford. Out of breath from her run across the moor, Meg dropped to her knees, hovering over the knight. The man's leg was bent at an unnatural angle and he had a nasty bleeding bruise on the side of his forehead, but his eyes were open and he was blinking.

"Sir Winford, are you all right?" Meg searched his face. He was a dear man and she felt entirely responsible for this.

"I believe so. I just need to . . . rest a bit." The knight closed his eyes.

"Of course. Of course." Meg reached out and brushed the hair from Sir Winford's eyes. His hat had flown from his head and was lying on its side several paces away. Meg scrambled over to fetch it.

"Can we get you anything, Sir Winford?" Sarah asked.

Lucy came running up behind them. "Sir Winford, Derek has your horse and has given him to one of the grooms. He's bringing the coach around. We'll take you to the nearest doctor."

Meg came back slowly, turning the knight's hat over and over in her hands. She'd never forgive herself if Sir Winford was seriously injured.

"Thank you kindly, Your Grace," Sir Winford said, his eyes still closed. Ever the gentleman, even when his neck might be broken. Meg swallowed a cry. He looked so still and pale lying on the grass. She glanced at Hart, who was still bent over the knight.

"Can you feel your arms and legs?" Hart asked Sir Winford.

Sir Winford's boots moved and his fingers did, too. "I believe so." He winced as if he was in a great deal of pain.

Meg knelt next to the knight and untied her scarf from Sir Winford's sleeve. She pressed it to his forehead to stop the bleeding. "There, there." Her gaze met Hart's over Sir Winford's prone body. Hart looked . . . guilty.

Moments later Lucy's coach pulled to a stop nearby and all of the men, including Hart, Derek, and the grooms lifted Sir Winford carefully and placed him inside the coach. Meg and Sarah were helped in after him. Derek climbed atop to sit with the coachman and the conveyance headed for the doctor's house. As the coach rumbled over the heath, Meg fervently prayed for Sir Winford's health.

CHAPTER TWENTY-FIVE

Hart hadn't seen Meg since Thursday, the afternoon of the confounded race that he never should have suggested in the first place. Bloody awful idea. He'd known he was a far better horseman than Winford. Why did he always have to bloody well prove it? Why did he always feel the need to be so . . . competitive? The man's interest in Meg hadn't helped.

Now the poor blighter was laid up with a broken leg and a head injury and Hart had gone and made Meg Timmons's life worse. The one man she'd been expecting a declaration from, needed one from because she was leaving for the Continent soon, and Hart had gone and challenged the chap to a bloody race and the fool had hurt himself. Blast it.

Hart was a complete menace to Meg Timmons. He should stay far, far away from her. Which is why he was here, at another blasted ball, trying not to stare at Lady Elizabeth Forester's décolletage.

He couldn't remember a word Lady Elizabeth said, but Sarah had assured him she was eligible. This talking-to-women-at-*ton*-events-in-an-attempt-to-find-a-suitable-wife business was downright dull. No wonder he'd been avoiding it for years. He hadn't had a bit of fun at any of the parties except . . . except the time he'd spent with Meg. In fact, the most fun he'd had since all this had begun was being locked in the silver closet with her.

Thank Christ it had been Sarah who had found them. He intended to marry, but not at the wrong end of a scandal. He refused to consider the fact that for a few short moments before Sarah had opened the door to the silver closet, he'd actually been at peace with the notion of marrying Meg. His parents would hate it, of course, but he would be . . . well, it didn't matter what he would be, did it? The fact was that he'd have done the gentlemanly thing by marrying her. He supposed Meg would have a much better life with the calm, pleasant Sir Winford as a husband. That's what Sarah said she liked about Sir Winford. That he was *pleasant*. Not a word Hart would ever use to describe himself. Yes. It was all for the better that Sarah had been the one to open the silver closet door.

But why was it that the most fun he'd had all Season had been with the most ineligible lady of all? Life was bloody complicated, that's why. Their world worked in a certain way and the order of things like who should marry whom mustn't be disrupted by inconsequential things like who was more fun than whom.

Hadn't he always wanted to have the one thing he shouldn't have? Hadn't he always wanted to do the one thing he shouldn't do? That was his nature, and his nature was bloody wrong. He might be a rogue, but he would never do anything to dishonor Meg, despite his decent number of indecent thoughts about her lately. The fact remained that Meg should marry Sir Winford or someone of his ilk and Hart should marry Lady Eugenia or Lady Elizabeth or some other lady whose name probably began with an E.

It was inevitable. In fact, he might as well go ask Lady Eugenia for her hand now. She'd seemed willing enough, his father approved of her, and one suitable young lady was as good as the next. Yes, that was it. He tossed back his drink. It was time to stop this nonsense of thinking about Meg. He would go inform Sarah.

Meg was standing with Lucy, unhappily contemplating Hart's dance with Lady Elizabeth. She'd also been considering poor Sir Winford. According to the doctor they'd found near Hampstead Heath, he should remain abed for at least the next fortnight. Thereby ending any chance Meg had to secure an offer from him before she had to leave town. Perhaps they might continue their acquaintance via correspondence. Perhaps Sir Winford might offer for her via a letter to Spain. Hardly the romantic proposal she'd dreamed about as a girl.

Oh, it was probably for the best. She didn't love Sir Winford and never would. She'd realized that when she'd seen him lying on the grass, pale and unmoving. She'd been worried about him, but she didn't love him, and Sir Winford deserved better than that. He deserved a wife who adored him. Meg should go off to Spain and make the best of her new life. Spain would be lovely and bright and affordable and uncomplicated. Perhaps the Spaniards didn't care about things like outdated gowns and graying gloves.

Sarah came hurrying up. She wore a gorgeous ruby-colored gown, her dark hair piled high atop her head, and she had a decidedly worried look on her face.

"You look as if you've seen a ghost." Meg tried to shake off the uneasy feeling that had come over her the moment she'd seen Sarah's expression.

"You do look a bit pale, dear," Lucy agreed, searching Sarah's face.

Sarah wrung her hands. "It's bad news, I'm afraid. Quite bad."

"How bad?" Meg held her breath, bracing for news of her father suffering another attack or Sir Winford's health having taken a turn for the worse.

Sarah winced. "Hart just informed me that he intends to ask for Lady Eugenia's hand."

"What?" Lucy's eyes nearly bugged from her skull. "No!"

"When?" Meg breathed, doing her best to keep her voice steady. She could accept this news. It was for the best, after all. But she couldn't keep from feeling as if her chest were in a vise.

"Soon," Sarah replied.

"How soon?" Lucy prompted, already pacing back and forth and tapping her cheek.

"I don't know. I assume he'll want to speak to her father first," Sarah replied.

"You must discover exactly when he intends to do this," Lucy said.

"Very well, I'll find him and see if I can get more details." Sarah turned, lifted her skirts, and hurried off.

"We can manage this," Lucy said to Meg.

Meg slid down onto a robin's-egg blue silk upholstered chair that sat next to the wall. "No, Lucy, it's over."

"No, no." Lucy continued to pace. "It's not over. It's not over until he's legally married to someone else."

Meg hung her head. "He's going to ask her. She'll say yes, and they'll be legally married. It's all right. I've already decided it's for the best. I'm leaving for Spain soon and Hart should be married to someone of his station here in London."

Lucy stopped in front of Meg's chair. She leaned down, looped her arm through Meg's, and half lifted her from her seat. They paced together, their arms still linked. "Listen to me. You cannot be discouraged. It's not over until it's well and truly over. However, I do admit that this calls for immediate action."

Meg blinked at her. "Immediate action?"

"Yes. I simply cannot take another engagement and last-minute calling-off of a wedding. It nearly turned me gray when Christian and Sarah did it. Something tells me Sarah's brother is even more stubborn than she is."

"No, Lucy, no. It's over." Meg gave Lucy a stern stare.

"Hear me out, please." Lucy's eyes sparkled. "I have one final idea. If it doesn't work, then, and only then, will I admit defeat."

CHAPTER TWENTY-SIX

The Duchess of Claringdon's dinner parties were famously odd. On any given night one might find oneself with an eccentric group of people around the long cherry dining table in one of the finest town houses in Mayfair. Tonight's guest list was particularly odd, however, because it included . . . a child.

Hart had been introduced to one Lady Delilah Montebank, the fourteen-year-old cousin of Lady Daphne Cavendish, one of the duchess's closest friends. Lady Daphne and her husband, Rafe, the Viscount Spy, were seated at the table, along with Mr. and Mrs. Garrett Upton, Lady Cassandra and Lord Julian Swift, the duke and duchess, of course, and Meg, Sarah, Berkeley, and . . . Lady Delilah.

Lucy had declared the young woman one of the most witty and outlandish souls she'd ever met and told everyone that despite the fact that the girl had yet to make her debut, she was entitled to eat, wasn't she, and why couldn't she partake with them and keep them all company? All the other guests seemed to be in complete agreement and so Hart found himself sitting two chairs down from the precocious girl, half listening to her chatter, and wondering if Meg hated him for putting Sir Winford out of commission on the eve of her departure to the Continent.

Hart had intended to go to the Medfords' ball tonight and ask Lady Eugenia for her hand. But Sarah had insisted—rather vehemently—that he had already promised to come to the duchess's dinner party tonight. Hart hadn't recalled accepting any such invitation, but Sarah had been so adamant that he doubted his recollection. Then he discovered that Meg would be at the duchess's dinner party and *that* made up his mind. He hoped to have a moment alone with Meg sometime this evening. He wanted to ask if she'd been in contact with Sir Winford and if her father still intended for them to leave town soon. Surely if the man knew his daughter was about to receive an offer from an eligible gentleman, he would see the sense in delaying the family's departure. However, Meg's father had never been a particularly sensible man.

At any rate, Hart had decided to delay his own marriage proposal for one more night to meet his previous obligation to attend the duchess's dinner party. He was seated next to Meg, thankfully, and even more thankfully the duchess broached the subject he himself had been planning to.

"Meg, dear." Lucy waved her wineglass in the air as the footmen served the first course. "It's such a shame Sir Winford couldn't make it tonight. Have you had any word from him?"

THE RIGHT KIND OF ROGUE

Hart tried to concentrate on his cucumber soup, but he couldn't help but perk up at that question.

"His leg is broken, poor man." Meg took a dainty bite from her bowl.

"No!" Cassandra Swift said.

"I'm afraid it's true," Meg replied. Was it his imagination or was she not looking at him? She was angry with him for ruining her chances with Winford, wasn't she?

"Pity," he murmured.

Sarah cleared her throat. "If you two hadn't been racing like a couple of foolish lads—"

"Don't blame your brother," Jane Upton interjected. "He wasn't the one who came unseated. Nor did he cause Winford to fall. The man was entirely unfit for that horse."

Hart liked Mrs. Upton, liked her a great deal.

"I can still think it's a pity the man was injured, can't I?" Hart directed this question at his sister.

Sarah turned back toward Meg. "Did he say how long the doctor thinks he'll be abed?"

Meg took another dainty bite of soup. She swallowed and dabbed at her petal-pink lips with her napkin before replying. "At least a fortnight."

"More's the pity," Lucy said, taking another healthy swig of wine.

The dinner progressed with polite banter including discussion about the obligatory topics like the weather and politics. Lady Delilah gave a discourse on the proper care and feeding of a pet bird. Apparently, once she'd discovered there were pirates in her family—she outrageously insisted Cade Cavendish and his French wife, Danielle, were pirates—she'd decided a parrot must join the lot.

Hart could have sworn he heard Delilah telling Lucy she'd taught the bird naughty words and something about walking the plank. Hart shook his head. Lady Delilah was quite unique indeed. He couldn't blame Lucy for inviting her to dine with them.

Hart still wanted to speak with Meg alone. He wanted to tell her he was sorry for any part he had in injuring her beau. *He* didn't happen to care for Sir Winford, but that didn't mean Meg wasn't free to marry the man.

Just before Lucy declared the dinner at an end, she stood and made her way over to Meg. She leaned down and whispered in Meg's ear. Hart couldn't make out what she said, but Meg turned a shade paler and shook her head. Lucy said something more emphatic and Meg finally tossed down her napkin, stood, and excused herself. What was that about? Where was she going? He needed to speak with her.

After Meg left the room, Lucy clapped her hands. "Don't let's be formal tonight, everyone. I hate to miss my husband's company. Let's all go into the drawing room together and share drinks and laughter there."

Everyone agreed. Delilah was sent upstairs and the entire party, minus Meg, adjourned to the drawing room.

Hart was in a discussion with Berkeley and Sarah about how he needed to pay them a visit in Northumbria the next time they went to Berkeley's estate when Lucy strolled up to them.

"Highgate, may I speak with you for a moment?" the duchess asked, her voice slurred.

"Of course." They moved off to the side so they wouldn't be overheard.

Lucy had another glass of wine in her hand. "Won't

you be a dear and go fetch Miss Timmons? She's in the gardens."

Hart furrowed his brow. "In the gardens? Alone? What's she doing there?"

Lucy waved a hand in the air. "She's troubled."

Hart narrowed his eyes on the duchess. He had two thoughts. First, Lucy was a bit into her cups this evening. Second, regardless of why Meg might be in the gardens, he wanted to speak with her.

"Very well. I'll go."

CHAPTER TWENTY-SEVEN

Meg had been standing between two ten-foot hedges in the duchess's garden for the last ten minutes. She was doing absolutely nothing but worrying. When Lucy had declared her "one final idea" yesterday, Meg had wanted to argue with her, to insist that Lucy stop. Instead, Meg had heard herself ask, "What do you have in mind?" She'd told herself she shouldn't care, shouldn't continue this madness, but another part of her still held out the faintest hope. She should go to Spain and leave Hart alone. She was an awful, awful person.

Which was only proven by the fact that she'd allowed Lucy to stage this dinner party and had listened to the duchess when she'd insisted Meg leave the dining table and go out to the gardens. A pit had formed in Meg's stomach. Surely, Lucy didn't intend to do something as outlandish as the last time and lock her and Hart in a room together to be found in a compromising position. She'd refused Lucy at first, but the duchess said, "How in the world can I lock you in a *garden*? That makes no sense."

That logic had ultimately been the reason Meg relented, but each moment that ticked by had her more and more nervous. She suspected Lucy intended to send Hart out here to speak to her. Lucy wanted Meg to tell him she loved him. The duchess had said as much this morning when they'd been discussing tonight's party.

"Now is no time for timidity, Meg," Lucy had insisted. "The man is about to *propose* to another woman. If he has any feelings for you whatsoever, and I strongly suspect that he does, you have an obligation to tell him."

"But what if he refuses me, Lucy? What if he chooses Lady Eugenia's title and dowry over me?"

"Courage, my dear, courage. There is no way to know whom he will choose until you tell him the truth. And then you must face the future with courage."

Sarah had been there, a sad little look on her face. She knew what it would cost Meg to tell Hart the truth.

"What do you think, Sarah?" Meg had asked. "Do you think I should do it? Do you think I should tell Hart how I feel?"

"I know it will be difficult, Meggie," Sarah responded, "But at this point, I believe Lucy is right. It's the only chance you have. If he doesn't choose you, at least you'll know you did everything you could. You'll live the rest of your life knowing that."

Meg nodded. She'd thought about it all day and finally determined that her friends were right. She must tell Hart how she felt. He deserved to know how desperately she loved him before he betrothed himself to another woman. If he chose to do so regardless, at least she'd know she'd given love her best attempt.

This afternoon, the idea had sounded both brave and correct, but now, standing in the gardens, clutching at her own arms, anxiety filled every pore. Her courage appeared to have fled, because all she could think about was the pit in her stomach and the thought that roiled through her mind over and over: *What if he doesn't choose me*?

It didn't take long before she heard the steady crunch of boot steps over the gravel pathway coming toward her. "Meg?" came Hart's deep voice just before he rounded the hedge and found her standing there.

"Hart," she said inanely. There were a few twinkling candles spread throughout the path, but otherwise only the moon illuminated the gravel, the shiny dark-green leaves of the hedges, and Hart's ever-so-handsome face. He wore dark superfine trousers and a dark blue coat. His cravat was a startling white against the shadowy darkness, highlighting his perfect white teeth when he smiled.

"There you are," he said. "I was looking for you. Lucy thought perhaps you might be in trouble."

"Trouble?"

Hart stepped closer. He was only a pace or so away from her. She could smell his spicy cologne. She closed her eyes and breathed in the scent, trying to work up the courage to say what she needed to say. It was more difficult than she'd imagined with him standing here, tall and handsome and smelling good and looking at her with that charming smile.

She ran her hands up and down her chilled arms.

"You're cold?" he asked.

"A bit," she replied.

He pulled his coat from his shoulders, stepped forward, and hung it over hers. She pulled it close with both hands. This was so like the night in the gardens next to her father's house. But so much had changed since then.

"Thank you," she murmured.

"Meg, I want to tell you something," Hart began.

"Good because I want to tell you something, too." She had to be the first one to speak. She had a bad feeling he was about to tell her he planned to ask Lady Eugenia for her hand and if he did that, there was no way she could tell him she loved him.

"I'm sorry about what happened to Winford," Hart continued.

Had that been what he'd planned to say?

"It's not your fault—" She took a step toward him.

"Yes, it is. At least it feels as if it is." Hart paced away and scrubbed his hand through his hair. Then he turned back toward her. "It feels as if I've done nothing but cause you trouble ever since the Hodges' ball."

Meg blinked. "Caused me trouble? I don't understand."

"I kissed you, I locked myself in a silver closet with you, and then I caused serious injury to the man you hope to marry. The timing could not have been worse, with your father about to cart you off across the Continent."

"I still don't understand." Meg searched his face.

"I'm trying to say that I hope you'll forgive me for ruining your marital prospects."

"Ruining my—" Meg opened her mouth and closed it again. She had no idea how to answer that. It was so different from what she'd thought he might say she wasn't certain how to respond.

She pushed a slipper through the gravel and twisted her fingers together. "Oh, Hart, you haven't ruined my marital prospects."

"You won't have a chance to see Sir Winford again before you leave, will you?"

The last thing she wanted to talk about with Hart here in this romantic garden was Sir Winford. "He's broken his leg. He's not dead."

"You didn't answer the question. He won't be able to leave his bed until after you're gone, correct?"

"Yes, but—"

"That proves it," Hart replied. "I've officially ruined your martial prospects."

Meg took a deep breath. "Hart, there's something I must tell you. Something important."

"There's something else I must tell you, too. Some guilt I need to resolve myself of."

"Guilt?" She shook her head. "I told you, you haven't ruined my marital prospects. I—"

"Please," Hart said. "Let me finish. Because if I don't I may never be able to say this again."

All she could do was nod. He stepped forward, head and shoulders taller than she was. He pushed his hands beneath the coat, and ran his palms down the backs of her arms, pulling her toward him, and cupping her elbows. She sucked in her breath and held it.

"I feel guilt, Meg, not just because of my part in what happened to Sir Winford, but also because I can't stop thinking about you." He pulled her against his chest. "Like this." His mouth swooped down to capture hers. She opened for him and his tongue moved in to slide against hers. He was kissing her. Really, truly kissing her. The coat fell off her shoulders. His hands came up to cup her face. Her hands moved to his shirtfront, outlining the feel of his muscles beneath the fine fabric. He kissed the side of her mouth, her cheek, her ear. His tongue trailed its way down the side of her neck where he gently sucked. Then his mouth moved back up to tangle with hers again.

Meg was on fire. She'd never known kissing could be like this. When his hand moved up to cup her breast, she gasped again, but for an entirely different reason. Not surprise, but . . . delight.

"Meg," he murmured in her ear. She kissed him endlessly. Her hands traveled up his shirtfront to tug at his cravat. He helped her and soon his shirt was open and her gloves were off and she placed her palms against his hot chest and ran her fingers over his shoulders inside his shirt to feel the outline of strong, muscled arms.

Meanwhile his hands were busily undoing the back of her gown. His mouth moved down to her décolletage. His lips were on the top of her breast before she even realized it was exposed and she gasped for a third time when they covered her nipple and gently sucked.

Gravel crunched nearby and the hedge shook. They only had seconds to pull up their clothing and cover themselves before Delilah Montebank came racing around the side of the hedge, directly into their path. She stopped short and gasped when she saw them in their state of undress. Then she called out in a loud, clear voice that the entire household could no doubt hear, "Your Grace! I found them. And it's a scandal just like you said it would be!"

Within seconds half the dinner party came flying around the hedge as gasp after gasp filled the night air.

CHAPTER TWENTY-EIGHT

Hart broke away from Meg with an alacrity that frightened him. He pulled his shirt back up over his shoulders and leaned down to grab his coat, vaguely aware of Meg fumbling with her décolletage. She glanced at him, a stricken look on her face, just before Lucy and some of the other ladies bundled her off into the house. Hart was left with his sister, who watched him with a mixture of alarm and uneasiness. Hart ripped at his cravat and tied it. He paced around the small space, his boots crunching the gravel, anger filling him with every step.

Damn it. He'd been a fool. A complete and utter fool. He'd sat in that dining room and watched Lucy and Meg planning this and he'd walked directly into their trap. It was Annabelle all over again, only worse because he'd actually *trusted* Meg. He'd thought she was better.

"God damn it," he screamed to the night air.

"Hart, your language," Sarah said quietly.

"I doubt I could cause more of a scandal tonight if I tried. My language is hardly going to hurt." He paced away from his sister and just as quickly paced back. "I'm only going to ask you one question, Sarah, and I damn well deserve the truth."

Sarah's throat worked as she swallowed, but she nodded in agreement. "Go ahead."

"Did Lucy and Meg plan this? Did they send me out here to meet her on purpose? Did they send Delilah to find us?"

Sarah expelled a breath. "It's not like—"

"I said I deserve the *truth*!" Hart shouted so loudly his sister flinched. "You owe that to me. Was this thing planned?" He clenched his jaw so tightly it ached.

Sarah hung her head and stared at her slippers, her arms crossed over her chest. "Yes, but—"

"*Yes* was the only word I needed to hear."

"Hart, you must listen to me. There's more to—"

"I thought I could trust her. I'm an idiot, a fool. I have no one to blame but myself."

"No, it's not like Annabelle—"

"It's *exactly* like Annabelle. I even told Meg the story of what *happened* with Annabelle. Only Meg learned from it. She knew enough to send an entire *group* of people to find us."

"Hart, you're being unreasonable."

"Tell me, Sarah, how reasonable should I be when I discover I've been led into a trap? One my own *sister* was a part of?"

"Listen to me—" Sarah eyed him as if he were as unpredictable as a wild animal. At the moment, he felt that way.

"I can't even look at you right now." He shrugged on his coat and began to stride back toward the house.

"Where are you going?" Sarah called after him.

"I'm bloody well going to do what I have to . . . inform our parents and Meg's that we're betrothed."

CHAPTER TWENTY-NINE

"I'm going to retch." Meg paced back and forth in Lucy's drawing room, her hands pressed to her heated cheeks. Less than a quarter hour had passed. Less than a quarter hour in which Meg had pulled up her gown, Hart had straightened his shirt and retied his cravat, and the entire party had bustled back into the house.

Meg had barely a moment to glance at Hart's stone-like face before she'd been bundled off into the drawing room, Cassandra Swift's shawl wrapped around her shoulders. There was no mistaking it. Hart had been furious. Meg was going to cast up her accounts. She was certain of it.

Lucy took a deep breath. "Oh dear, please don't retch. Because if you retch, I will retch."

"If you both retch, I'm certain to retch," Cassandra said. "And I've been retching every morning for weeks. I cannot take any more retching."

"If all *three* of you retch, I cannot promise that I *won't* retch, even though I am not normally one to retch," Jane Upton added.

"No one is going to retch!" Sarah entered the room and shut the door behind her. She pressed her fingertips to her temples. "We must think about this logically. There has to be some way to fix this."

"Whatever do you mean, dear?" Lucy gave her a quizzical look. "Half of my dining room just saw your brother compromising Meg in the gardens. There is no way out of it. A marriage must take place."

Meg slumped to the settee. "What did Hart say, Sarah?"

"Not much, I'm afraid."

"He's angry?" Meg pressed a palm against her quaking belly.

Sarah pinched the bridge of her nose. "I'm afraid so."

"What does he have to be angry about?" Lucy asked.

"Oh, I don't know," Jane Upton replied. "Perhaps the fact that you clearly staged the entire scene, given that Delilah yelled it out in so many words."

"Yes, but I had no idea they'd be locked in an intimate embrace. I'd only hoped," Lucy replied. "How did you manage that, by the way, Meg? Brilliant!"

"Stop it! I didn't manage anything. It was entirely innocent until—" Meg's breathing was unsteady. If she didn't vomit, she was going to faint. She'd never been a fainter, but now seemed the perfect time to begin.

"I assume you told him you loved him and a passionate embrace was his reply. It seemed perfect to me," Lucy said.

"I never had a chance to tell him." Meg swallowed back bile.

"He kissed you for no reason?" Lucy asked, blinking.

Meg pressed her fingers to her temples. She couldn't think. Couldn't even remember how or why she and Hart had gone from discussing Sir Winford's broken leg to pulling off each other's clothing in the garden, but the moment Delilah's words echoed through the night air, Hart stiffened and pushed her away.

She'd seen his face, a mask of anger, and knew without a doubt that not only did he believe the entire thing had been planned, he believed she'd planned it. He had to. *That* was why she was going to retch.

"Lucy, how could you!" Meg stood and advanced upon the duchess. "I told you I didn't want him forced."

"Dear, I'm sorry. Truly I am. I should have been a bit more specific with my instructions to Delilah on precisely what to say when she happened upon you both, but you must know my intentions were good. Time is of the essence. The man was about to ask someone else to marry him."

"Couldn't you have waited until he had a chance to hear what I was going to say to him?" Meg pleaded.

Lucy turned pink. "Very well. I admit it. I was spying. I simply couldn't hear what you said. When I saw him take you in his arms and kiss you, I thought it had all gone according to plan, so I sent Delilah."

"If it was going so well, why didn't you assume he would ask to marry me?" Meg moaned. "Why did you need Delilah?"

"Extra protection, dear, is never a bad thing. Besides, I know how stubborn the man can be. He clearly cares for you. The scandal part was merely to ensure it went according to plan."

"Protection I didn't ask for and don't want. He's going to hate me now." Meg looked at Sarah. "Does he hate me, Sarah? Does he?"

"He didn't say that." The worried look on Sarah's face betrayed the fact that whatever he'd said to his sister, it wasn't good.

"Lucy, you've really done it this time." Jane Upton shook her head. "You've never known when to leave good enough alone."

"Good enough is never good enough when left alone," Lucy retorted, her nose in the air.

"Perhaps we should hold our judgment until we see how Hart feels," Cassandra offered quietly.

"Yes. Let's," Lucy agreed. "If I don't mistake my guess, a wedding shall result from this. A wedding between two people who love each other. Even if one of them won't yet admit it. That is never a mistake."

"It's a mistake if my husband hates me for it every day of his life," Meg groaned.

"He's not going to hate you . . . " But the duchess trailed off when she caught the look on Sarah's face. Lucy winced. "Just how bad is it?"

"It's bad. *Quite* bad." Sarah said. "Hart is going to speak with Mother and Father. Their reaction is certain to be anything but pleasant."

CHAPTER THIRTY

Meg's parents were waiting up for her two hours later when Lucy and Derek brought her home. Lucy had draped a cloak around Meg's shoulders to conceal her disheveled clothing. Lucy had employed one of her maids to put Meg's hair back into the semblance of a topknot, but Meg knew she must have looked supremely guilty when she trudged up the stairs to the front door and made her way inside. To their credit, Lucy and Derek remained by her side. She hadn't asked the duchess to come with her. Lucy had volunteered and insisted she help explain the matter to the baron and his wife.

The moment Meg stepped through the door her mother advanced on her.

"Margaret, what have you done?" Mother's voice was filled with disapproval. Obviously, Hart had already been here.

Her father stared at Meg in disgust, as if she were a bug.

"Let's all go into the drawing room and discuss this civilly," Lucy said.

They all marched into the drawing room and waited while the duchess lit a few candles.

Meg sat in a chair near the fireplace, her parents glaring at her from the settee. Lucy finished with the candles and came to stand behind Meg's chair, placing a hand on her shoulder. Derek stood on Meg's other side as if protection might be in order. Meg did feel comforted having them there.

"This may not have happened under the best circumstances," Lucy began. "But the fact is that your daughter is betrothed to a future earl. I should think you'd be pleased by that."

"Pleased?" Meg's mother's eyes nearly popped from her skull. "She's shamed us by behaving like a hoyden and is about to shackle us to a family we abhor. What in heaven's name is there to be pleased about?"

Meg searched her father's face. It was as stonelike as Hart's had been. "I cannot condone this marriage, Margaret."

"You have no choice," Derek Hunt interjected. "The damage has been done."

"That doesn't mean we have to like it," Meg's mother shot back, her voice dripping with anger. She turned her attention to Meg. "I should have known you were traipsing after Highgate. You brought him up more than once lately. I'm ashamed of you, Margaret."

Meg hung her head. She'd always hoped her parents would accept her wedding to Hart one day, *if* it happened, *if* he loved her, *if* he'd chosen her and had actually *asked* for her hand. But the entire affair had turned into a shameful debacle and she couldn't fault her parents for being angry with her for the additional shame she was bringing on the family.

"Highgate says the wedding will happen as soon as he can secure the license," the baron said.

"I can help with that," Derek replied.

"Father," Meg said, tears filling her eyes. "Will you be there? At the wedding?"

"We have no choice. To make this matter as respectable as possible, we must attend. We'll put off our move until after the wedding, but we still intend to go to the Continent."

Tears dripped down Meg's cheeks. "I may never see you again?"

"It's true," her father intoned.

"What about . . . your grandchildren? Will you ever visit them?" A sound that sounded suspiciously like a sob escaped her throat.

"That is up to you," Father replied. "I doubt we'll have the funds to visit."

Meg buried her face in the handkerchief Lucy had given her in the coach. Oh, what had she done?

"I suppose you'll offer to pay for the wedding gown," her mother sneered to the duchess.

"Of course. Meg will have whatever she needs," Lucy replied.

"It seems your gamble paid off, Your Grace." Mother eyed Meg up and down with disgust. "She'll be well able to repay you now with the money she'll have as Highgate's wife."

"Stop it," Meg murmured.

"Stop what?" Mother replied. "Isn't this what you wanted? What you planned for?"

It was so close to the truth and so awful that Meg jumped from her seat and ran for the door. There was no longer any doubt. She was going to retch.

CHAPTER THIRTY-ONE

The wedding was held precisely three days later in the drawing room of the Highgates' town house at nine o'clock in the morning. The wedding party consisted of the nervous bride, who was still convinced she would retch at any moment; the bridegroom, whose face remained an angry mask of stone; the bridegrooms' parents, who looked as if they were equally torn between anger and retching themselves; the bride's parents, who both looked completely outraged; the groom's sister and brother-in-law, who looked worried; the Duke of Claringdon, who looked stoic; and the Duchess of Claringdon, who looked ebullient.

As the archbishop intoned the words that would forever bind Meg to Hart, she fought tears. Not happy tears. It was entirely different from how she'd envisioned this moment in her dreams. This should have been a joyful time, a fantasy-come-true. Instead, as she'd walked the length of the drawing room to meet Hart in the front next to the archbishop, she felt as if she walked the gauntlet. She considered running away, hiding even, but those would be cowardly acts. She had to summon the courage to face this.

It was her fault. She'd been the one to ask for Lucy's help. She'd been the one to go out into the gardens and wait for Lucy to send Hart. Whether she'd known how it would happen or not, she was still the guilty party and she must face the consequences. She'd fretted over the possibility that Hart might run away or hide. Or might not arrive. In the end, however, she'd known Hart would never be so unchivalrous as to hide from this. He wouldn't run, and she owed it to him not to embarrass him or his family any further by running herself. It would shame him if she refused to appear at the wedding.

Hart didn't look at her. It was the first time they'd seen each other since that awful moment in Lucy's garden. Meg had hoped he'd pay a call, come and talk to her, give her a chance to explain, give her a chance to offer him a way out. She'd tell him she would be all right. Her parents had planned to take her to the Continent regardless. She could weather the scandal much better from there. Of course there would be visitors from England and the gossip would eventually spread. She wasn't naive enough to believe she could save her reputation, but she would be more than willing to live a life of shame if it meant saving Hart from a marriage he didn't want. She loved him desperately, but she didn't want a husband who had married her out of obligation.

Hart never paid her a call. The note she'd sent him

through Sarah, in which she'd asked him to come so they could decide how best to handle this debacle, had gone unanswered until early this morning when Sarah brought her a note with one scrawled line. Meg had been unable to breathe as she'd opened it and her heart had dropped into her slippers. "The wedding is set for nine o'clock." Not a word to indicate his emotions, but Meg knew. He was furious.

Sarah and Cassandra had attended Meg this morning. Jane had recused herself by saying she had nothing nice to say and didn't intend to aggravate the situation by being surly, a sentiment that Meg appreciated.

Lucy had been banished by both Meg and Sarah. The duchess showed no remorse for her actions and had merely offered her husband's experienced help in procuring a quick wedding license.

So it was that Sarah and Cassandra saw Meg outfitted in a pale peach gown, her hair arranged with white rosebuds. The entire time, Meg and Sarah had been on the verge of tears. Poor, dear, sweet Cassandra had looked as if she might cry, too, while trying to say encouraging things like "Won't it be lovely for the two of you to be sisters-in-law at long last?"

Sarah did her best to muster a smile. Meg couldn't summon any enthusiasm. Her stomach remained a mass of knots as she imagined facing Hart. What could she possibly say to him? What could she possibly do? She entertained a brief fantasy that involved grabbing his hand and running away with him. They could both run, couldn't they? She could save him and then leave and cause him no further trouble. But the moment she'd seen his stoic face and his ramrod-straight back as he stood in the drawing room, her courage fled and the rest of the wedding was a blur of recited words and worry.

When it was over and the vows were said and sealed, her husband turned on his heel and walked out of the drawing room without so much as looking at her.

CHAPTER THIRTY-TWO

If drinking too much champagne before noon was incorrect, Meg didn't want to be correct. The wedding breakfast was held immediately after the ceremony and Meg couldn't manage to choke down so much as a bite. Hart, who sat like a statue at her side, had no such compunction. He ate and drank as if he hadn't a care in the world and talked to the Duke of Claringdon and Lord Berkeley as if he *weren't* steadfastly ignoring his wife. Wife. The word made her gulp, made her belly tie into stricter knots. How in the span of three short days had the concept of being Lady Highgate gone from a fantasy to a nightmare?

Sarah sat on Meg's left and squeezed her hand reassuringly from time to time, but the two friends didn't speak. Meg downed glass after glass of champagne, nervously contemplating something she hadn't allowed herself to dwell upon until this moment: her wedding night. Regardless of how a wedding happened, joyful or solemn, wanted or unwanted, angry or pleasant, a wedding *night* was inevitable. It had to happen. If it didn't, their marriage wouldn't be consummated and that would render it unlawful. The thought of *how* it would happen was what kept her tipping back champagne glasses.

Hart wouldn't look at her. He wouldn't speak to her. His vows had been recited in a monotone voice while staring straight ahead. She couldn't think about a cold, unfeeling act in Hart's bed. Would it be painful? Surely Hart wouldn't punish her with his body. The only thing that made her feel more calm was the bubbly champagne. Champagne didn't judge her or ask her questions. Lovely, lovely champagne. When she reached for her fourth glass, Sarah's hand shot to her wrist to stop her.

"You may want to slow down," Sarah whispered.

"I'm frightened out of my wits," Meg whispered back, through a fake smile meant entirely for the archbishop, who eyed her over a heaping plate of salmon and eggs.

"I know, but Hart will have to speak with you eventually."

"He'll have to do more than *speak* with me eventually." Meg's voice shook.

"Is that what you're worried about?" Sarah whispered.

Meg managed a wooden nod. "I can hardly think of anything else."

"Come with me." Sarah pushed back her chair and grabbed Meg's hand. They both stood. "Excuse us for a moment, won't you?" Sarah announced to the table at large. The men stood as the ladies left the room, and even though he stood, too, Hart didn't make eye contact with Meg.

Sarah pulled Meg from the dining room, through the corridor, past the foyer, and into the front drawing room. She closed the door behind them and turned to face Meg.

"I hate to ask this, but I feel I must." Sarah smoothed her hands down her skirts. "How much has your mother told you . . . about your wedding night?"

Meg rubbed her hands up and down her freezing arms. "Absolutely nothing."

Sarah sighed. She pressed two fingers against her closed eyes. "That's what I was afraid you would say."

Meg made her way over the fireplace to warm herself. "It's going to hurt terribly, isn't it?"

"No." Sarah cleared her throat. "I mean, not necessarily."

Meg turned to face her. "That's hardly comforting."

"Forgive me. This is my brother we're speaking of. It's not a comfortable subject for me. If I don't mistake my guess, Hart's had, ahem, a great deal of experience, and I would venture to say he knows exactly what he's doing in bed."

"That's not comforting, either," Meg said, her stomach performing a somersault this time.

"Yes, it is." Sarah smiled. "An inexperienced husband can be a nightmare. Trust me. I've heard as much from other married friends."

Meg's eyes widened. "Surely not Lucy, Cassandra, and Jane?"

Sarah snorted. "No. Not them. *None* of them. We're the fortunate ones."

Meg continued to rub her arms. "I'm sorry if I cannot summon the enthusiasm to be happy about this."

Sarah floated over to her and patted her shoulder. "I

know, and I apologize if I'm not making it better. Just know that whatever happens, I've no doubt Hart will be gentle with you. I'm certain he'll make it pleasant for you. Do you want me to tell you the details so you'll be prepared?"

Meg swallowed hard. *Did* she want Sarah to tell her the details? "I'm not certain. If I know the details will I be apt to drink more or less?"

Sarah wrinkled her nose. "You have a point. Perhaps I should leave it to your imagination. I know if someone had told *me* the details before my first time I wouldn't have believed them."

Meg gasped. She pressed a palm to her cheek. "It's that outlandish?"

Sarah shrugged. "Rather."

Meg glanced about. "Oh heavens, where is my champagne glass?"

"It can be excessively pleasant, too," Sarah hastened to add.

"Can be?"

"When you're with the right partner. I, myself, look forward to it and I know Lucy, Cass, and Jane do, too."

Meg wrinkled her brow. "Are you certain about that?"

"Yes, why?"

"Because my mother hasn't mentioned much to me but from the few things she *has* said, I got the distinct impression it is something she has in no way ever looked forward to."

Sarah twisted her hands together. "Oh dear, that's unfortunate. It depends entirely upon your partner, I'm afraid."

Meg sighed and stared into the fireplace. "He hasn't looked at me. He won't talk to me."

"Which causes me concern. I think you need to speak with him, privately, before . . . you know. Try to explain what happened."

Meg rubbed her arms more quickly. "How can I explain it when I don't even know myself?"

"You must explain to him how you intended to tell him you loved him that night."

Meg rubbed the back of her hand against her forehead. "Oh yes. It's not possible that *that* won't sound entirely made up at this point. He'll never believe me."

Sarah placed a comforting hand on her shoulder. "You have to tell him, Meg."

Meg blinked back tears. "No. I don't. I can't. I never will."

CHAPTER THIRTY-THREE

It was his wedding night, but Hart took his time undressing. He dismissed his surprisingly sober valet so the man wouldn't have anything to gossip about and proceeded to remove every last shred of his clothing as slowly as possible. It was petty of him, but he wanted to make Meg wait.

She was worried. She was nervous. Good. She should be. He hadn't decided how this evening would go, but as each article of clothing came off he was more and more certain.

His father had gifted him a magnificent town house. One his father never used. One meant for Hart since birth, to live in with his *wife*. Raise a family. Hart had had his things brought from his apartments in St. James and put into the master suite. That's where they were now.

He and Meg had spent as long as they could at his parents' house today. The wedding this morning, then the insufferably long breakfast celebration, in which his new wife had become decidedly drunk. Then a long afternoon of talking in the study with his father and Berkeley while the ladies took naps. Finally, they'd had a late dinner, one during which his wife seemed particularly sober and nervous, and then they'd been carted off to Belgravia to spend their first night together in their new home.

Father had been ruthless this afternoon after the Timmonses had left. "Not only did you manage to get yourself forced into marriage, you couldn't have possibly picked a less deserving bit of baggage. Didn't I warn you about this? Hell, didn't you already have one such experience with that Cardiff chit? Yet somehow you managed to fall into the same trap with the last girl on earth I'd pick for you. She is a money-seeking whore."

Some of what his father said had been true, of course, but he refused to listen to the old man call Meg a whore. Hart slammed his fist onto the mahogany desk his father sat behind. "She's my *wife* now, Father, and I won't allow you to call her names."

Why he'd defended her, Hart didn't know. Perhaps it was because he enjoyed taking the opposite stance of his father. Partially it was because he'd been the one to traipse out to the gardens. He'd walked directly into the scandal that brought him down. That was his fault.

"So she *is* your wife," Father had replied. "I hope you're happy with her. Especially since she didn't bring a bloody red cent with her in marriage. Your mother said she doesn't even have a trousseau."

"There was no time for a trousseau," Hart ground out.

"Yes, because you couldn't bloody well keep your hands off that rubbish."

"Call her a name one more time and I'll call you out," Hart ground out, bracing both fists on the desktop and glaring straight into his father's eyes.

While the two men argued, Berkeley had merely raised his brows and taken a stiff drink of brandy—and if Berkeley was drinking, you knew it was serious.

Father leaned back in his chair and contemplated Hart over his steepled fingers. "I knew all along that Annabelle Cardiff wanted nothing more than your title and your money. I tried to tell you that. But did you listen? No."

"Are you serious? You pressured me to marry her."

His father ignored that. "I even tried to warn you about this Timmons chit recently when you brought her up, and you still didn't listen. What's wrong with you?"

Hart paced away from his father's desk. "I don't know. I suppose the apple doesn't fall far from the tree."

His father half rose from his seat. "You dare to compare yourself to *me*? At least I didn't marry a penniless nobody who brought shame upon my household."

Hart lunged toward his father. Berkeley intercepted him, backing him away until he'd calmed down enough to pace in front of the fireplace.

"Why would you defend her?" His father leaned back in his chair, his face still red with wrath.

"She's my *wife*," Hart said through clenched teeth.

"Don't remind me." Father nearly spit the words.

Hart growled but finally took a seat.

Berkeley made his way to the sideboard and poured more brandy into his glass. "Come, gentlemen, there is a bright side to this."

"What's the bright side?" Father glared at Berkeley.

"Your son is finally married. An heir is certain to follow," Berkeley replied.

Those words haunted Hart now. An heir? An heir is certain to follow? He wasn't less certain of anything at the moment. The last three days had been a blur. A blur of anger, confusion, and betrayal. Every dark emotion had roiled around in his brain while the words Delilah Montebank had called out were seared in his mind forever. "Your Grace. I found them. And it's a scandal just like *you said it would be*."

The events from the days prior to that moment had kaleidoscoped in Hart's mind. The dinner at Lucy's house, her asking him to fetch Meg from the silver closet. The dancing, even Sir Winford. It had been an elaborate ruse. A ruse that his own *sister* had been part of. Sarah had been the one to insist he go to dinner at Lucy's house so Lucy and Meg could spring their trap.

He'd never forget the moment he saw Lucy whispering to Meg in the dining room just before she got up and left. Left to go out in the gardens. Left to hide in wait for him. He'd walked straight into it, fool that he was. He'd trusted Meg, but she and Lucy and Sarah were nothing more than wretched schemers.

Meg had been clear about wanting to find a husband. She'd been nothing but honest about the fact that she needed a proposal to keep her father from taking her off to the Continent. After Sir Winford failed to come up to scratch, she'd sprung her trap on Hart.

Damn it, how had he made it all these years, escaped the scheming clutches of Annabelle and become more world-wise, only to be trapped into marriage by his sister's meek little friend? He pulled his shirt over his head. That was why, wasn't it? Meg didn't *seem* scheming, didn't *seem* evil. She *seemed* sweet, and pretty, and kind, and gentle. With Annabelle, he'd always been on edge. Something about her told him she wanted him enough to stop at nothing to get him. With Meg, he'd let down his guard. He'd *trusted* her. Idiot that he was.

He ripped off his breeches. Completely nude, he stomped over to his wardrobe and yanked his navy-blue velvet dressing gown from a peg inside the door. He shrugged it on and belted it tightly around the middle. Then he made his way to the door that separated his bedchamber from his wife's.

He knocked only once, one harsh rap before twisting the handle and pushing open the door. The room was dark save for a brace of candles burning on the mantelpiece and the fire in the hearth. As his eyes adjusted to the darkness, he scanned the room. Meg sat on the bed, wearing a gossamer white dressing gown. Despite himself he sucked in his breath. Blast it. Why did she have to be so bloody beautiful, his treacherous wife?

"Meg?" His voice sounded thunderous in the tomblike quiet of the bedchamber.

She was shaking and her eyes were wide. He fought against a surge of tenderness as he slowly made his way over to the bed and looked down at her. She hadn't been crying. No. Her eyes were quite dry. She'd got her way, after all. Why would she cry? The shaking and wide eyes were probably an act. He would call her bluff.

He traced his finger along the décolletage of her gown and tilted his head to the side. She shivered but didn't pull away. Gooseflesh popped along her skin where he'd touched. He moved his hand up to her cheek and cupped it. He owned her now. He could do whatever he wanted with her.

"So beautiful," he said.

She blinked at him.

"But *such* a liar."

She flinched and pulled her cheek from his hand.

"No maidenly tears to accompany your act?"

"What act?" Her voice shook.

"Don't pretend you didn't orchestrate that entire charade in the garden along with Lucy Hunt. Sarah admitted it."

"I—"

"What? You didn't go out there hoping I'd follow you? Is that what you're going to tell me?"

She hung her head.

"Lucy didn't send me out there knowing what would happen?" he continued.

"It wasn't—"

"Wasn't what?" Surely she would manage to muster a tear or two now. Instead, she lifted her chin and stared him straight in the eye.

"I never lied to you." She sat up straighter and jerked her body away from him.

"Didn't you?"

"No." She lifted her chin and glared at him.

"So you *did* want to marry Sir Winford? I was never your target?"

Her gaze swung away from his. He hadn't mistaken the guilt in them before she turned away. Her silence said it all. At least she was willing to admit to *that* lie. He pushed the strap of her gown off her shoulder. It would be so easy to take her. Not to make love to her, never that, but to shove her back on the bed and rut with her. Get about the business of making an heir. No doubt she'd be thrilled with it. That's what she wanted, after all. She wanted children. It would be worse for her if he didn't consummate their union. She'd remain in a state of doubt, insecurity. Of course there would be no children. At least none that he would claim. That was it. His mind was made up.

Her voice shook again. "You won't . . . hurt me, will you, Hart?"

His laughter was cruel. "Not unless what I've already done has hurt you."

"What do you mean?" She shivered. Such a good actress.

"I mean I intend to turn around and leave this room now. And I won't be back."

"You . . . you don't intend to bed me?" Her voice was quiet but filled with surprise.

"I have no intention whatsoever of bedding you."

Her brows drew together. "I don't understand."

The look of relief mixed with the confusion on her face served to steel his resolve.

He crossed his arms over his chest and regarded her down the length of his nose. "My dear, you have what you *think* you wanted. A husband. A name. Money. A reason to stay in London and not have to go to the Continent. But I refuse to give you what you *really* want."

Confusion flitted across her features. "What I really want?"

"Children. A family. You told me once that you wanted those things."

She nodded. "I do."

"I have no intention of giving them to you." He forced a humorless smile to his lips.

She expelled her breath in a heated rush. "What are you talking about? You need an heir."

"The only thing that will make forgoing an heir palatable to me is knowing that *you're* not going to get what you want. I can leave the estate and the title to Sarah and Berkeley's children."

A hint of anger flashed across her face. "You cannot be serious."

He turned on his heel to walk away. "I've never been more serious."

CHAPTER THIRTY-FOUR

The next morning at precisely half past ten, the Duchess of Claringdon's coach pulled to a stop in front of Meg's new home. Meg had spent the better part of the morning hiding in her room. Wedding gifts and congratulatory notes poured through the front door. Apparently everyone in the *ton* was eager to wish the new Lord and Lady Highgate well.

Knowing Hart was locked in his study, Meg had ventured downstairs to walk past the tables full of gifts when she'd spotted a lovely bouquet of white azaleas. The accompanying note was from Sir Winford. The knight wished her well on her marriage and congratulated her lucky groom, wishing them both a lifetime of health and happiness. *That* had sent her straight to her room in tears.

She'd been hiding in her bedchamber contemplating the rubbish heap she'd made of her life when one of the maids tentatively knocked and informed her that Hart had gone out to the club. Meg wiped away her tears and decided to venture forth to explore her new home. The housekeeper, Mrs. Grintley, was still proudly showing her around when the duchess arrived along with Sarah, Cass, and Jane. Lucy was crafty, Meg had to admit. If she'd come alone, Meg would have refused her, but bringing the other ladies guaranteed her admittance. Why had Sarah agreed to come with her, though?

Meg received them in the light blue drawing room. It was the first time she'd been in the room. It was lovely in its subtle blues and white. The entire house was lovely. Much grander than anything she'd ever imagined living in. A far cry from the shabbiness her father's town house had become. She didn't deserve to live here.

As soon as the butler left the ladies alone together, Meg turned to Lucy. "You have a great deal of nerve showing your face here, Your Grace."

Sarah interjected. "Please, Meggie, hear her out."

"What can she possibly say that will make this better?" Meg glared at Sarah.

"That was my point, but no one listened to me, did they?" Jane pushed up her spectacles and glanced around at the others accusingly. "However, I was told there would be teacake." She looked anxiously toward Meg.

Remembering her manners, Meg rang for tea (and cake) before settling back to glare at Lucy. To her credit, Lucy did look sufficiently chagrined.

"Where is Hart?" Sarah asked.

"He went to the club," Meg replied.

"And did you . . . have a pleasant evening?" Sarah asked, her voice tentative.

"My husband hates me, what do you think?" Meg kept her arms crossed over her chest.

"May I speak now, pleeeease?" Lucy clasped her hands together in front of her and stared at Sarah.

"Very well." Sarah nodded stiffly. "Go ahead."

"You managed to keep her from speaking?" Meg asked, blinking.

"It was a condition of my coming with her," Sarah replied.

"Really?" Meg asked. "What were the other conditions?"

"One was that she didn't make anything worse," Jane pointed out.

"Oh, Meg, dear," Cass finally said. "Do hear Lucy out. She wants to make things better for you."

Meg crossed her arms over her chest and glared at Lucy. "How do you intend to do that? I'm quite through with your scheming. I believe I was entirely clear on the multiple occasions I told you that I never wanted Hart forced into marriage."

Lucy cleared her throat and sat up straight. She glanced at Sarah as if to confirm her permission. Sarah nodded. "First, I would like to point out that you are married to the man of your dreams as a result of my scheming."

Meg opened her mouth to retort.

"Lucy . . . you promised!" Sarah nearly shouted.

"I know. I know. But I think it's a relevant fact that should not be *entirely* overlooked," Lucy said.

"And?" Sarah prompted, eyeing Lucy warily.

Lucy turned back to face Meg. "Delilah has a great deal of potential as a plotter, but I'm afraid she's still a bit rough around the edges. I would like to apologize for the method in which I carried out my plot. It was poorly done of me." Lucy finished by folding her hands in her lap.

"An apology?" Jane asked, scratching the tip of her nose with a finger. "I honestly didn't think Lucy had it in her."

"Of course I do." Lucy sniffed and lifted her nose in the air. "I know when I've made a mistake and I can admit it."

"Really?" Jane looked skeptical. "When was the last time you were wrong?"

Lucy's brow wrinkled into a frown. "Well, I . . ." She tapped her finger against her cheek. "I . . ."

"I'll wait," Jane replied sweetly, batting her eyelashes at Lucy.

Lucy tilted her head to the side. "I'm certain there have been other times. I simply cannot remember any at the moment."

"Please ladies, can we return to the matter at hand?" Cass asked. "Lucy was apologizing to Meg."

"Yes," Sarah added, nodding to Lucy again. "Go ahead, Lucy."

Lucy straightened her shoulders. "As I said, I'm ever so sorry for the way in which I bungled things and I would like to offer my assistance in making everything right."

Meg smoothed her hands over her skirts. "Thank you for the apology, Lucy, but I'm afraid there's nothing you can do to make it right. I will, however, repay you for the expenses you incurred on my behalf for the gowns and—"

Lucy clenched her fists. "I don't give a damn about the money for the gowns," she nearly shouted.

All four ladies gasped. Lucy traced one brow with a fingertip and took a deep breath. "What I mean to say is, there must be *something* I can do. Tell me what Hart said to you last night and I'll think of something to help."

"He called me a liar," Meg replied sweetly. She'd love to see Lucy Hunt talk her way out of *this* circumstance.

"No!" Sarah gasped.

Lucy winced. "And?"

Meg took a deep breath. "And he accused me of orchestrating the entire charade in the garden along with you, Lucy."

"No!" Cass said this time.

"But you must have . . . made up before you . . . you know?" Sarah's face turned pink.

Meg's cheeks burned, too.

"What? What is it, Meggie?" Sarah leaned forward and patted Meg's knee.

"I can't. I just can't say." Meg's face was on fire.

"You can tell us, dear," Cass said encouragingly. "We're all married ladies here. You needn't be embarrassed."

Meg took three deep breaths. All morning she'd been contemplating the awfulness of what had—or, more correctly what *hadn't*—happened last night. Nothing she could think of could make it less horrible. Would telling these ladies make it more shameful or would she feel better if she admitted it to someone?

"Go ahead, Meg," Sarah prompted.

"Very well, but you all must solemnly swear not to tell another soul."

Each lady in turn crossed their fingers over their heart.

Meg closed her eyes and counted three before blurting, "Hart didn't touch me last night."

Sarah gasped. "What?"

Cass gasped. "What?"

Jane cupped a hand behind her ear. "Pardon?"

"It's true." Meg felt more ashamed with each passing moment. "He didn't touch me and he vowed he never would."

"Oh my God. He's an idiot!" Sarah declared, tossing her hands in the air.

"It's certainly surprising," Cass offered, her pretty face scrunching into a decided frown.

"I wonder what's keeping the teacakes," Jane murmured, looking about.

"Jane!" Cass scolded. "This is hardly the time to discuss teacakes."

"Very well, I agree. It is *quite* surprising," Jane added.

"It's humiliating," Meg replied, covering her face with her hands. "My own husband won't touch me. Our marriage is not legal."

Finally Lucy spoke. "Is that all?" She pushed a dark curl behind her ear.

"Perhaps you didn't hear me correctly," Meg replied, pulling her hands away from her face and narrowing her eyes on the duchess. "My husband refuses to touch me."

"Yes," Lucy said. "I heard you and I asked if that was the worst that happened."

Meg wanted to shake Lucy. "Yes, as a matter of fact it is." She planted both fists on her hips.

"Good, then, because I hardly see that as an issue at all. The easiest thing in the world is to convince a young, healthy man to take a young, beautiful woman to bed," Lucy said.

"What are you talking about?" Sarah asked.

"Yes, Lucy, what are you talking about?" Meg added.

"It's quite simple," Lucy replied with a sigh. "All you have to do is seduce your husband."

CHAPTER THIRTY-FIVE

Seduce your husband. Seduce your husband. The words chased themselves in Meg's mind that night as she waited in her bedchamber. Would Hart come to her? He'd had all day to think. Perhaps he'd changed his mind. Perhaps he'd realized that not consummating their marriage was madness. Perhaps he still hated her and blamed her for his being forced into an unwanted marriage.

He'd told her how much he detested scheming women. Annabelle had tried to snare him into marriage in the exact same way. No wonder he was angry with her. Meg hadn't even been able to deny it when he'd asked her outright.

In her own way, however, she'd tried to tell him the truth, to explain how she'd come to be in the garden waiting for him. The man was stubborn as a mule. Not just any mule. An elderly, recalcitrant mule. He wouldn't listen and he certainly wouldn't believe her. She wasn't about to beg him to hear her out. She wasn't about to try to convince him she'd planned to tell him she loved him that night. There was no possible way he'd believe that now. She had to think of another way to get through to him.

This morning the other ladies had all seemed to agree. Seduction was a fine idea. They all also seemed to think it would be a simple task.

"Let him know you're willing. Show a bit of décolletage and *voilà*," Lucy had said.

"But he hates me," Meg had countered.

"Décolletage works wonders." Lucy had winked at her.

The other ladies nodded and agreed with Lucy. "Men really are quite simple when it comes down to it," Jane said, finally taking a bite of her coveted teacake.

"I must admit, there's some truth to that," Sarah said, biting her lip.

"Décolletage has worked for me in the past," Cass added, shrugging.

It was unanimous, but now that Meg was sitting alone in her bedchamber with plenty of décolletage visible, she realized she'd failed to ask the ladies what to do if he didn't even speak to her. Should she knock on his bedchamber door and show him her décolletage? *That* seemed exceedingly awkward. As the minutes ticked by and there was no sign of him, she began to wonder if she would have to march into his bedchamber after all.

Hart hadn't come home for dinner. She'd eaten alone at the huge dining table with the servants giving her varying degrees of pitying looks. She heard two of the maids whispering about Hart, and the word *rogue* had definitely been discernible. The consensus among the staff was that they'd always expected their master to take a wife and ignore her. His reputation preceded him. This was why Sarah hadn't encouraged their match. Oh, why hadn't Meg listened to Sarah?

Meg looked down at herself. Was she enticing? Was she desirable? According to her mother she never would be, but Lucy proclaimed there was no way her husband could ignore her if she wore the right garment. Of course Lucy had ensured she *had* the right garment. Meg contemplated the lovely lacy shift Lucy had had made for her as a (albeit inappropriate) wedding gift.

Meg had picked out a soft light-blue gown and matching robe, and ensured her décolletage was on full display, before she sat on the bed, attempting to read, and waiting to hear her husband come home.

As minutes turned into an hour, she had doubts he'd ever return, but before midnight she heard noises in his bedchamber and the unmistakable sound of him dismissing his valet. Confound it, the timbre of his voice still gave her gooseflesh. The man was being a complete ass but she loved him madly. Did it even matter anymore, why? Her heart belonged to a man who hated her, and she was about to stoop to trying to seduce her own husband.

After another quarter hour passed, she suspected he wasn't going to come into her room. Very well, she'd go to him. Courage, Lucy had said. Be bold. This would take every drop of boldness she had.

She stood, set her book on the nightstand, smoothed her hands down the front of her diaphanous gown, and took a deep breath. She considered wearing her dressing gown over the skimpy concoction, but decided against it. If seduction was her goal, she might as well get right to it.

She made her way across the wide expanse between her bed and the door that led to Hart's bedchamber. Blood pounded in her ears with each step.

When she came to the door, she took another deep breath before rapping twice and pushing open the handle with her sweating hand.

She took a tentative step inside her husband's bed-chamber. He stood next to the bed, his shirt and boots off, wearing only his breeches. The firelight glanced off his muscled abdomen and Meg swallowed. Oh, this was going to be more difficult than she'd thought. What if he refused her?

He turned to face her. "What are you doing here?" His voice was harsh, accusing.

"I came to . . . I wanted to . . ." She couldn't force the words past her dry lips. All she could do was stare, fascinated, at his naked torso and the six muscles that stood out in sharp relief on his abdomen.

His eyes flared, possibly because of what was visible under her flimsy gown. She could only hope.

"Wanted to what?" His voice was still harsh.

"I thought perhaps . . ." No. She still couldn't say it and she was turning red under her blue gown. That couldn't possibly be an attractive combination. She needed to retreat.

"Perhaps *what*?" His voice bit through the silence.

She clung to the last bit of courage she possessed. "Perhaps we might . . ."

His eyes narrowed to slits. "Do you think I've changed my mind?"

She met his gaze. "Have you?"

He made his way toward her and stopped a pace in front of her. His eyes moved up and down her body.

"Where did you get that gown?" he asked, the edge lingering in his voice.

"Lucy gave it—"

The flare in his eyes burned out. "Ah, Lucy. Of course, Lucy. Your partner in scheming. Still trying to help you, I see."

She shouldn't have mentioned Lucy. "You don't like it?" Meg countered, lifting her chin even higher.

"On the contrary, what husband wouldn't?"

She swallowed. "A husband who wants to punish his wife for something she didn't do." Meg had no idea where this defiance was coming from, but she would not allow him to control the situation. If he refused her, so be it.

"Unfortunately, I know of no such husband."

"You cannot ignore me forever, Hart." She knew it was the wrong thing to say even before the words came out, but anger burned in her chest and she couldn't stop herself.

"Really?" he drawled. "Try me." He lifted one brow, taunting her.

Courage. Courage. Boldness. Courage. The words rang inside her head. She'd already used nearly every drop of both, but the words *try me* presented a challenge she couldn't refuse.

She forced herself to move even closer to him, coming to a stop directly in front of him, her bare toes only a pace from his. They faced each other, the heat from his body palpable. Shaking, she made herself rise on her tiptoes. She pressed her lips against his.

It was like kissing a statue. His lips didn't move. His body didn't, either. He stood stock-still while she felt like an idiot. Finally, his mouth opened and his lips slanted across hers. His tongue plunged inside and she gasped against his mouth. His arms enveloped her and he began walking her backward toward the door. Oh God, she'd won. He was taking her to her bedchamber. He was going to make love to her.

She wound her arms around his neck as the kiss intensified. He leaned down to keep the contact between their mouths as they continued to make their way to the door. He slammed her back against the door and kissed her, long and hard. The heat of his hardness pressed against her belly. She was panting and mindless when he pulled her to him, broke the contact of their lips, and yanked open the door to her bedchamber. His smile was tight as he shook his head, pushed her firmly into the room, and pulled the door shut in her face.

Meg stood on the other side of the closed door, shaking with lust and anger. She clenched her hands into fists and squeezed them as hard as she could. He was an ass and she wanted to slap him, but the kiss had told her something valuable. She'd felt passion in his response. Hart wasn't entirely immune to her. She had a chance to win him back.

CHAPTER THIRTY-SIX

The next morning, Hart sat in his coach outside of Meg's parents' house and stared at the black front door. The bloody thing could use a coat of paint. Hell, for that matter, the stairs needed to be scrubbed and the entire facade looked sorely in need of repairs. He shook his head and pushed open the coach door. Might as well get this unpleasant business over with.

His knock on the front door was answered after several minutes by the same disheveled-looking butler he'd seen the night he'd come to inform Meg's parents he intended to marry her. Just as he had that night, the butler immediately became alarmed at the presence of a viscount on the front step. Apparently, the Timmons residence wasn't accustomed to visitors.

After Hart asked to speak with the baron, the butler ushered him into the same sadly worn drawing room he'd been ushered to the last time. He sat staring at a crack in the stained ceiling for several minutes before his father-in-law came hurrying in. The man's face was red and he looked as if he'd come running. Probably not the best idea, given the man's health concerns.

"My lord," Tifton said, bowing to Hart. "To what do I owe the pleasure?" Despite the nicety of the words, Hart heard the unmistakable snideness in the man's tone.

Hart stood to shake Tifton's hand. It was a rough shake, over quickly, and the two men took seats opposite each other.

"I'm here to make you an offer," Hart said. He might as well get right to this odious business.

The baron's green-and-gold eyes, which reminded Hart of Meg's, narrowed on him. "What sort of an offer?"

Hart opened his coat and pulled a bank draft from his inner pocket. "I've been doing some investigating into your affairs."

The baron opened his mouth to protest but Hart shot up a hand to stop him. "Allow me to finish."

The baron pressed his lips together and nodded curtly. "Fine. Proceed."

"My solicitor has paid off all of your debts. Every last one of them. I personally owe every single debt you're responsible for at the cost of a small bloody fortune."

The baron tugged at the lapels to his coat. He cleared his throat. "I highly doubt—"

"To the tune of nearly fifty thousand pounds. Does that sound about right to you?"

The baron snapped his mouth shut and hung his head. "What do you want in return?" His voice was low.

"This." Hart waved the bank draft in the air. "Is more

money than you've probably seen in your lifetime. I'm prepared to give it to you on three conditions."

Tifton lifted his head again to look at the draft. He pressed his tongue against his cheek. "What conditions?"

"The first is that you use this money to restore your household and live in a manner more befitting your station." Hart glanced around at the worn room.

The baron nodded slowly. "And the second?"

"If I ever hear of you gambling or ringing up debts again, you will *not* like the consequences."

The man opened his mouth to speak, but Hart wouldn't let him. "You are no longer welcome in any of the gentlemen's gaming hells in the city and I promise you I will hear about it if you attempt to go to less desirable places to game. I have friends *everywhere*. Do I make myself clear?"

The baron gave Hart a tight nod. "Perfectly. And the third condition?"

Hart settled back in his seat and regarded the man down the length of his nose. "If I ever hear you or that wasp you call a wife say an unkind thing to Meg *ever again*, I will have you and all your belongings packed up and carted off to the outer reaches of India."

The baron had the grace to look guilty. He threaded his fingers together and hung his head. "I understand."

"Good. I'm glad we see eye-to-eye. I know why you and my father hate each other, but Meg doesn't and I'd like to keep it that way."

The baron cleared his throat again and faced Hart. "Why are you doing this?"

Hart considered the question. He might want to punish

Meg for her treachery, but he wasn't about to allow her father to be murdered or sent to debtors' prison. Like it or not, they were family now.

And there was another reason.

"For some unfathomable reason, Meg loves you and her mother and she would be sad if you moved to Spain. Now, do you agree to my terms?"

"Yes."

"I thought so. Let me be clear . . . if you make a mistake, I'll send you to Newgate myself."

Minutes later, Hart was gathering his hat from the butler in the foyer when Meg's mother sashayed up to him. The butler quickly disappeared. "Lady Tifton," Hart intoned, inclining his head to the woman.

"My lord," she answered. Her eyes were narrowed, but she had what probably passed as a smile on her face. "I heard what you said to my husband."

"Which part?" Hart asked, wanting nothing so much as to leave the odious house as soon as possible. How the hell had Meg lived here so long with the two of them? "The part about paying off the debts or the part about sending him to Newgate if he makes any more mistakes?"

"Both," Lady Tifton replied. She crossed her arms over her chest.

"Listening at doors, are you?"

"My husband rarely tells me anything."

"I cannot imagine why."

She ignored that. "I also heard what you said about us saying anything bad to Margaret."

"I meant that, too," Hart replied. "Will it be a problem?"

She paced away from him. "You have no idea how difficult the girl is."

"She's not difficult. I've known her for years." The fact that he had to defend Meg to her own *mother* sickened him.

"She's meek and mild and weak, just like her father."

"No, she's nurturing and kind and sees the best in people, unlike either of her parents."

Lady Tifton scoffed. "She's just not—"

"A son?"

The baroness gasped. "What?"

"Don't pretend. That's the reason you dislike her so much, isn't it? You only had one chance to produce a son and you had Meg instead. My father tells me many things when he's deep in his cups."

The woman's silence spoke volumes.

"Your husband stopped touching you years ago. His affairs are as legendary as his gambling debts."

"I wouldn't allow him to touch me," the baroness spat.

"Yes, well, it's not Meg's fault she wasn't born a son and it certainly wasn't her fault that you two had no more children."

"But she—"

"I've personally heard you say horrible things to Meg. If I hear anything like it again, I'll take back every pound."

"You can't do that."

"I'll call in all the debts he owes me."

"You wouldn't!"

"Try me."

The baroness scrunched up her nose in a sneer. "You

people with money make me ill. You think you can buy anything."

Hart pulled his hat from a nearby table. "If my money buys your decency to my wife, then I don't give a bloody damn if it makes you ill in the process." He placed his hat on his head and walked out the door.

CHAPTER THIRTY-SEVEN

Hart spent the next two days drinking at the club, boxing at the club, playing cards at the club, and doing whatever the hell else he could to keep his mind off his new wife.

When Meg came to his room three nights ago, it had been a bloody act of heroism to send her away. She'd been wearing a wisp of a gown, the lines of her seductive body clearly visible underneath . . . and her décolletage. By God, her décolletage. The sight of it had nearly sent him to his knees.

He'd had to shake his head instead of saying anything to her when he pulled that blasted door closed between them because he hadn't been convinced his voice wouldn't shake if he'd actually spoken. It had been one of the hardest things he'd ever done, to pull the door shut, but he was a grown man, not an untried lad, and he wasn't about to forgive the woman her treachery over some décolletage and a misguided attempt to seduce him.

Hadn't he just told her the night before that he wasn't going to touch her? She clearly thought she could control him with her body. He refused to allow that to happen. If he gave in to her, he'd never have the upper hand again, and he did not intend to relinquish it. No, even if he had to stay away from his house and hide from the confounded woman, he would not touch her.

Tonight he'd gone out and boxed until his knuckles were bloody and worn. Anything to tire himself out, to make it so that he could fall into sweet oblivion in bed, not thinking about his wife in the next room the way he had been tortured each night since their wedding.

He almost didn't hear the tentative knock when it came. Bloody hell. She was going to try again. By God, did the woman have no shame? He closed his eyes briefly, trying to steel himself against the sight of her. She clearly wasn't going to make refusing her easy for him. She hadn't made any of this easy for him. Why should she begin now?

"Come in," he said in as domineering and cold a voice as he could muster.

The door swung open slowly and in walked Meg wearing a cream-colored dressing gown tied tightly around her slim waist. At least she was more clothed tonight. Perhaps she merely wanted to talk. He had to admit he was curious as to what she might say.

"Yes," he intoned, not looking at her as he went about his evening ablutions.

"Did you . . . have a good evening?" Her voice was slight, hesitant.

So, she wanted to begin with small talk. He could do small talk. "As good as can be expected."

"Were you . . . at the club?"

"Among other places." He'd let her think about that. The truth was he'd gone to a gaming hell after the club and gambled away a small fortune because he couldn't keep his mind on the play. He'd been tortured by images of Meg in her diaphanous dressing gown.

He'd bloody well been offered woman after woman at the hell. It was the sort of place one could find a willing partner ready to go upstairs and have a tumble. He'd considered it, of course he had, but in the end he found he couldn't do it. He'd be thinking of Meg the entire time and that was distasteful to him. He'd never had a problem like this before. Being-married was a damned nuisance.

"My parents came for a visit today," Meg said. "They have decided not to leave London after all."

"And that is of interest to me because . . ." He let his voice trail off, keeping his face blank.

"I suppose it's of no interest to you," she replied. He could tell she was angry. Fine. They both knew who had the right to be angry here, but if she wanted to play that little game, she was free to.

"Are you finished?" he asked. "I'm exhausted. I've had a long night." He'd let her think about that, too.

"I suppose being a rogue is exhausting," she replied in a sharp tone, one slender hand resting on her hip.

"No doubt every bit as exhausting as being a schemer is," he countered.

"One can only imagine how much energy it takes to be such an ass to one's wife." She gave him a tight smile.

"Oh, *I'm* an ass?"

"If the shoe fits."

"What about the other shoe? The one you were wearing the night you trapped me into marriage?"

"My compliments. You do play the victim so well. Perhaps it's time for the truth. I know you don't want to hear it, but the fact is that I had absolutely no intention of trapping you into marriage."

"You're right. I don't want to hear it and I certainly don't believe it."

"Fine, be stubborn. Be an ass. I've said all I can say on the matter."

That was it. He was through trading barbs with her. This couldn't end well. To make matters worse, he was actually taking pleasure in trading barbs with her. *That* was an unwelcome thought. He needed to get away from her. If he continued to enjoy his time in her company, he might weaken and take her to bed. He grabbed his dressing gown and brushed past her, stalking out the door. "I'll sleep in my study tonight."

CHAPTER THIRTY-EIGHT

"I need you to be much more specific," Meg said to Lucy the next morning over tea at the duchess's town house.

Lucy stirred an obscene amount of sugar into her tea. Obviously, at the duchess's town house, the cost of sugar was no object. "Specific? About what, dear?"

"About the whole . . . seduction business."

"Oh dear. Didn't it work?" Lucy searched Meg's face.

"No. I failed miserably. The first night he essentially ordered me to get out of his bedchamber, and last night he left his own room to sleep in the study." She decided to leave out the part about the kiss. She'd shared enough with Lucy. She was merely here for some good, solid advice from a married lady.

Lucy *tsk*ed under her breath. "Are you telling me your husband still hasn't consummated your marriage?"

Meg pressed a knuckle to her forehead. "That's precisely what I'm telling you."

Lucy continued to stir the tea. "Egads. Who knew

that once Romeo and Juliet actually married, it turned into a farce? What were you wearing?"

Meg's jaw was tight when she said, "Does it matter? By the time it was over, I wanted to slap him, not seduce him."

Lucy lifted her green skirts with her free hand and made her way over to a tufted chair. "Very well. You're going to have to be much more obvious next time."

Meg followed Lucy and sat in a similarly tufted chair next to hers. "Obvious? What does that mean?"

"I mean go to him wearing *only* your dressing gown."

"I had that on last night." Meg took a sip of her own, far less sugared tea.

"You didn't let me finish." A catlike smile perched on Lucy's lips. "Go to him wearing only your gown and nothing beneath, then . . . drop it."

Meg choked on her tea. She set the cup on the table beside her and pounded her chest. "Pardon?"

"You heard me." The catlike smile remained.

"Are you suggesting I go to my husband . . . *nude*?"

"No. I'm suggesting you go there in your dressing gown. Then become nude." Lucy continued to stir her tea.

"What if he refuses me? What if he brushes past me and sleeps in the study again? I'd be standing there like a naked fool."

"I cannot promise those things won't happen." Lucy finally took a sip of tea. "I can only assure you that you have a much better chance to convince him to stay if he's confronted with your naked body."

"I cannot believe you're saying this to me. I truly cannot." Meg covered her rapidly heating cheeks with her hands.

Lucy took another quick sip of tea and set her cup on the same table where Meg's rested. "Prepare yourself then, because I'm about to tell you how to do something that is certain to scandalize you—but I guarantee, if you're given the chance to try it, it will work wonders."

Bleary-eyed, with a smashing headache, Hart slid into a large leather chair at Brooks's the next morning. His friends Harlborough, Norcross, and Wenterley sat across from him.

"You look like hell," Norcross said. The blond earl was a crack with a pistol and had been Hart's friend since they were lads growing up on neighboring estates.

"I feel like hell," Hart admitted.

"Marriage not agreeing with you?" Harlborough drawled. The duke was dark-haired, had a wicked sense of humor, and was the only man of Hart's acquaintance who had a finer set of horseflesh than he did. A damn fine rider was Harlborough. He'd known the duke since their days at Eton.

"An understatement," Hart replied.

"I don't understand. We met your wife. We danced with her. She seemed a lovely, accommodating sort," Harlborough replied.

"She is if you count scheming seductresses as lovely and accommodating," Hart sneered, just before he ordered a brandy from a footman.

"Scheming? How so?" Wenterley asked. The brown-haired, brown-eyed viscount was by far the most studious of Hart's group of friends. He'd met Wenterley at Oxford while trying to cheat off his paper. The viscount had promptly called him out, Hart had promptly bested him with his fists, and they'd ended up drinking together in a pub and deciding they could help each other.

"You didn't hear the story about how my marriage came to pass so quickly?" Hart asked.

"Of course we did," Harlborough said. "Got caught in a scandal and all that. What does that have to do with anything? Could've happened to the best of us. I, for one, can't blame you for not being able to keep your hands off her till your wedding day. She's a fine-looking lady, that one. If you don't mind me saying." Harlborough held up a finger to order a brandy for himself.

"That's just it," Hart replied. "She wasn't *supposed* to be my wife."

"Could've fooled me," Norcross replied. "You spent a great deal of time with her this Season."

"I was doing her a favor and—"

"And you merely happened to be compromising her in the Duchess of Claringdon's garden? Was that a favor as well?" Wenterley snorted. The other two laughed.

Hart snapped his mouth shut. When his friends put it like that . . . he seemed less . . . right about the whole thing. "My sister and the duchess were in on it, too. They sent me out there knowing she would be there and knowing—"

"Knowing you'd compromise her?" Wenterley blinked at him innocently.

Hart wanted to punch bloody Wenterley. Why did the viscount always have to be right? Damned annoying trait.

"What does it matter?" Norcross asked. "You needed to get married, didn't you? You told us you liked her. Why not marry her?"

"She planned it," Hart said.

"Marriages are often planned," Norcross replied.

Hart slapped his hand on the table, making the glasses bounce. "It was a scheme. She doesn't have a dowry."

"What do you care if she doesn't have a dowry?" Harlborough replied. "You and your father have more money than the pope. Besides, I've never known you to shy away from doing something that would give your father a fit."

Hart didn't have time to respond before Wenterley said, "I'm more interested in the seductress part. What did you mean when you called her a 'scheming seductress'?"

"She's been trying to lure me into bed," Hart ground out, feeling like an utter fool.

"What in the devil's name are you talking about, Highgate?" Norcross's face had turned a reddish-purple color. The earl looked nearly apoplectic.

"I mean I vowed not to touch her after our wedding," Hart mumbled, feeling like a damn fool.

"Have you lost the bit of your bloody mind you had left after all the drinking you've done, Highgate?" Harlborough wore a horrified expression.

Hart slammed his fist on the table again. "Damn it. You don't understand—"

"Do I understand that your gorgeous wife is trying to seduce you and you're not taking her up on the offer?" Harlborough shook his head in disbelief.

"Yes," Hart ground out, crossing his arms across his chest and giving all three of his friends a condemning glare.

"Then I also understand you're a bloody fool," Harlborough added.

Hart tossed back his drink in one gulp. Blast.

CHAPTER THIRTY-NINE

That night, Hart came home at a decent hour. He'd imbibed several more drinks at the club but had quite appallingly sobered up by the end of the evening. He'd told his friends in no uncertain terms that he no longer wanted to speak about his new wife or his new marriage, but that hadn't stopped the chaps from giving him digs throughout the evening.

They'd finally told him he needed to go home and make love to his beautiful new wife. While he hadn't agreed to any such thing, he *had* ordered his coach to go straight home.

As soon as he entered his bedchamber, he dismissed his valet and ripped off his clothing. Was he in the wrong? No, by God, he wasn't. Meg *had* schemed. She *had* plotted with her friends. Sarah admitted it. Meg was no better than Annabelle. Bloody hell. He may have *given* Meg the damn idea.

On the other hand, she insisted she hadn't been trying to trap him and he'd refused to listen. He'd known he was being an ass, but she deserved his anger. Didn't she? Damn. None of it made sense any longer. Meg probably wouldn't be coming back in here, not after he'd refused her so many times.

Would he refuse her again? Should he refuse her again? He didn't know anymore. If she didn't come, would he go to her, demand his husbandly rights? No. He'd feel like an even bigger arse. Bloody hell! What if his blasted friends were right?

On the other hand, what if his father was right? His father had told him how his own mother had schemed to wring an offer of marriage from the earl. His father had fallen helplessly, hopelessly in love with her, but she'd been unfaithful to him throughout their marriage. Hart had heard about it often enough.

"Never give a woman your heart," the earl had repeated to his son on countless occasions. "She'll crush it in her palm."

Hadn't Hart watched his father give his mother jewels, gowns, expensive coaches, all to be rebuffed and ignored? His father had stayed home night after night while his mother went out to pursue her friends and her amusements. The details were kept hidden from Sarah, but Hart knew.

Hart had sat in his father's study with him many a night, knowing his mother had never come home from the ball she'd attended. For years, he'd listened as his father poured out his heart and tried to find solace at the bottom of a brandy glass. Finally, his father had stopped trying and had gone out to find his own amusements.

His parents treated each other like strangers. Hart refused to have a marriage like that. If he kept the upper hand with Meg, he wouldn't suffer like his father. He would never have his heart crushed.

Hart almost didn't hear the tentative knock. He sat in silence. She didn't open the door. She was waiting for his approval. "Come in," he intoned.

When she entered the room he was standing near the bed wearing only his breeches, just as he had been the other night.

She wore her diaphanous blue dressing gown again. If he didn't mistake his guess, this time she was . . . completely nude underneath. He couldn't swallow. His mouth was so dry it hurt.

"Not such a late night tonight?" she asked in a voice as smooth as glass.

"No," he mumbled like an idiot.

"Dare I hope it's because you wanted to come home to me?"

He wanted to say no, prompted himself to, but he couldn't make the word move past the lump in his throat, and he couldn't take his eyes off her glorious body outlined by the firelight.

She untied her dressing gown quickly, pushed the material off her shoulders, and let it drop. She stood naked in front of him. Hart's eyes flared and he sucked in his breath. Of all things, he hadn't expected this. His body instantly reacted, hardening.

"Damn it, Meg. What do you think you're doing?" He tried to look away but couldn't force himself to.

"Isn't it obvious? I'm trying to seduce you."

"Why?" His breathing was ragged.

Meg took a deep breath. "This is it, Hart. This is the last chance. I offer myself to you willingly tonight. If you refuse me again, I'll leave and not return. I refuse to beg you."

Hart fought an internal war. Fought it and lost it. When he raised his eyes to hers, he knew that he'd been bested. "You don't have to beg."

He took two long strides and she was in his arms. His bare arms swept around her body, pulling her close, crushing her naked breasts against his bare chest. She moved up on tiptoes and wrapped her arms around his shoulders. His mouth ravaged hers, his tongue pushing against her lips until she opened for him. He kissed her mouth, her cheek, her neck. His lips began to move down the slim column of her throat. He nipped at her collarbone. "God, Meg, I—"

"No," she whispered. "No more talking. Only this."

He scooped her up into his arms and carried her through the doorway to her bed, where he laid her down gently. "You *are* beautiful." He stood up and drank in her body with his eyes while he divested himself of his breeches.

He would make love to her and not give her his heart. He did need an heir. He'd been foolish denying himself one. She could busy herself taking care of the houses and the children and he could avail himself of her gorgeous body once in a while. That didn't mean he'd give her his heart. That didn't mean he loved her. Yes, he could do this. He was a master, a rogue. This was only sex.

Once Hart was completely naked also, he slowly lowered himself down to the bed. Meg's eyes scoured over him.

"You're . . . perfect," she whispered, watching him intently. His body looked as if a sculptor had carved it out of stone. His sinewy neck, wide shoulders, taut chest, and flat abdomen tapered into narrow hips and long legs. He was ready for her. Sarah had explained enough about it that Meg knew that much. Lucy had explained something else Meg couldn't contemplate lest she blush from head to toe. There would be time for that later. For now she had the distinct impression that Sarah had been right. Her husband knew precisely what he was doing in bed and he was about to show her.

He moved atop her and there was the strange sensation of a male body pressed against hers, all sinewy and hairy and hard and hot and heavy. He kissed her neck again and she thought she might go half mad with longing. He moved down her body and cupped one of her breasts in his palm. His mouth came down to meet his hand and he sucked her nipple into his mouth. Meg gasped. She arched her back to meet his lips, her nipple an aching tight point as he laved it. She clasped the back of his head, letting his soft dark hair filter through her fingers.

"Hart," she whispered, her head tossing fitfully against the pillow. He tugged at her nipple with his teeth and sucked it hard. She closed her eyes, awash in a tide of sensations she'd never experienced before. His hand moved down between her legs and lightly traced the outline of her most intimate spot. One of his long fingers slid between her cleft and stroked the soft, wet skin there. The sensation overwhelmed her. She twisted her hips away.

"No," he said. "Let me touch you, Sweet. Relax."

Relax? How was she supposed to relax when he was

doing things to her body that made her tighter than a bow? She closed her eyes and his finger slid inside her. She cried out and arched up.

"Hart," she called. He kissed her to absorb the sound. His finger began to move inside of her and she forgot everything else. She forgot her shyness and her embarrassment and her uncertainty as a wave of pleasure rode through her. He eased his finger out and with the tip he circled a spot so perfect she cried out again. Her feet tensed and her back arched. She tried to sit up. "Hart, I can't—"

"Shh," he whispered in her ear, sending goose bumps skittering along her skin. "Yes, you can. Let me touch you. I promise, it'll be worth it."

Worth it? Was he mad? It was already worth it. She never wanted him to stop touching her, but could she handle any more? She was on fire. He kept circling the spot with his finger until she dug her fingernails into his back, until her feet pushed against the mattress, until her knees squeezed his hips, until she called his name and exploded in a shower of light and feeling unlike anything she'd ever experienced.

When Meg floated down from of the haze he'd shot her into, she opened her eyes and blinked. Suddenly shy, she gave him a tentative smile and pulled up the sheets to cover her breasts. "I had no idea you could do that. If I'd known, I would have demanded my marital rights on our wedding night."

He gave her a boyishly handsome grin. "I'm glad you enjoyed it." He nudged his forehead against hers and kissed the tip of her nose.

"*Enjoy* is not the correct term. I've been told how to do some awfully scandalous things but I had no idea that—"

He shot up onto an elbow. "What sorts of things?"

Meg darted her nose under the sheet and blinked at him. "Nothing."

"No, you said you've been told how to do some scandalous things. Like what?" His grin was roguish.

Meg pulled the sheet back down to her chest and bit her lip. "My friends and I were discussing seduction."

Hart traced the outline of her ear with his finger. He bent to trace his tongue along the same path. Meg shuddered. "I gather. What did they tell you?"

"I can't say it." She turned her head and buried her face in the pillow. "I'd die of embarrassment."

"Very well, what if I lie here and you *do* it then?" He waggled his eyebrows at her.

Meg turned her head to allow one eye to peek out from beneath the sheet. She nodded.

Hart flipped onto his back and crossed his arms beneath his head, his naked body open to her. Meg regarded him. The man was a work of art. Even his knees and calves were manly. She traced her finger along the inside of his thigh and he flinched. Drunk with the knowledge that he reacted to her touch that way, she moved her hand to the juncture between his thighs and wrapped her fingers around his length.

The moment Meg's hand touched him, Hart groaned. She'd surprised him, his innocent wife. He was eager to see what she'd learned from her married friends. He wanted her so badly he thought he might explode. Her eyes explored his body, and he reveled in it. He was young and fit and had never been more pleased to display his assets.

She'd come apart in his arms and it was the most

erotic thing he'd ever seen, giving her an orgasm while she was still innocent. He hadn't done that with a woman in ages, but with Meg he felt like a lad again. It was almost as if it was the first time he'd been touched or touched a woman. Such a different experience than he was accustomed to.

How did Meg manage to make everything feel fresh and new? When his beautiful innocent wife wrapped her delicate fingers around his cock, he nearly exploded with desire. When his beautiful innocent wife lowered her sweet, pink lips to his cock, he was certain he would go up in flames. She kissed the tip and stopped. For a moment he thought she would stop there, and he nearly sobbed. But then the slightest hint of wetness flickered across the tip. She'd licked him. She was using her tongue. Sweet Jesus. Her lips opened over him and she sucked the tip, hard. Hart dug his fingers into the sheets, nearly ripping them. "Jesus Christ." His voice was a harsh whisper.

"Is this too much?" came Meg's sweet tone. Her breath was a hot puff against his cock. "Do you want me to stop?"

"On the contrary," he managed to pant. "Please don't stop." His voice was a husky rush of air.

Her mouth descended once more and this time she slid him into her throat. Hart pushed himself up on his elbows to get a better look. He'd had whores who hadn't been this damn good.

Her mouth worked over him and her soft pink tongue rubbed him as she moved up and down his throbbing length. He tried to regulate his breathing, to keep from spilling his seed inside her mouth. If they were going to consummate their marriage tonight, by God he wanted to do it right. He wouldn't be able to if he allowed this to continue for much longer.

Wives did this sort of thing? "Meg, where did you . . . How did you . . . ?" Did it even bloody matter where she'd learned how to do this? He didn't care. Definitely didn't care.

Meg's mouth came off him with a sucking sound. Her cheeks were pink.

Hart panted. "Never mind. I don't want to know." He groaned again as his wife's mouth covered him once more. As much as he was loath to, he had to put a stop to this. He wanted to make love to her. This was not helping.

He cupped her shoulders and gently pulled her up on top of him. He kissed her again. His mouth ravaged hers. She kissed him back with fiery passion. He rolled her over so he was on top of her. "Meg," he said. "I'll try my best not to hurt you, but I'm told it . . . I understand it can be . . ."

"Sarah told me." Meg looked at him with those unfathomable pools of green she had for eyes.

Hart gathered every bit of patience he'd ever had and every ounce of finesse he possessed. He wouldn't allow her first time to be uncomfortable.

He leaned down and kissed Meg. He played with her nipples, sucked them, stroked them. He slipped a finger inside her again and circled that same spot she responded to. He didn't stop until her legs thrashed and her head moved fitfully on the pillow. Then he pressed her thighs wide with his and slowly, more slowly than he'd ever moved in his life, slid inside of her. He pressed himself in bit by bit, higher and higher until finally he was in to the hilt. He stared down at his wife, whose eyes were squeezed tightly shut. He didn't want to laugh at a time like this, but she was adorable. Doing his best not to move while her body adjusted to his, he memorized the freckles along the bridge of her nose.

"Meg," he whispered. "It's all right."

She gasped for air but kept her eyes screwed shut. "Yes, I'll be all right. Please tell me when to expect the pain."

He buried his face in her neck to keep from laughing. "The, ahem, painful part is over."

"What?" Her face exploded in ecstasy as Hart moved inside her for the first time. He pulled out a small bit and slid back in.

Meg moaned. "Oh."

He pulled out again, farther this time, and slid back in. "My," Meg groaned.

The third time he pulled out nearly all the way and slid back in ever so slowly.

"God," Meg cried.

Hart bit his lip, sweating with the effort of control. He wanted this to be the most unforgettable night of her life, and he would make it good for her if it was the last thing he did. How he'd kept from coming already was a bloody miracle. She was so tight and wet and felt so good and was so responsive. When he remembered how she'd sucked his cock . . . that wasn't helping.

He buried his face in her neck. Passionflower. God how he loved the scent of passionflower. It drove him mad. He pumped into her again and again, trying to ignore the soft cries that came from her lips every time he moved. He reached down between them and touched the spot he knew she needed. Forcing himself to stop moving inside her, he circled her again and again as Meg's body thrashed beneath his.

She moved up and down beneath him, forcing him to pump into her. He groaned and steeled himself against the thrumming in his balls that told him he was about to come. She had to come first. Had to. He flicked his finger back and forth on the nub of soft flesh. Sweat beaded on his brow and he bit the inside of his cheek, hard. She tensed against him, her nails carving into his shoulder blades. She cried his name against his cheek as Hart pushed one last time, allowing his seed to spill inside her.

CHAPTER FORTY

Meg woke the next morning in her bed. She sighed and stretched. Had she and Hart actually done what she remembered doing last night? Had she actually performed the scandalous act Lucy had explained to her? She'd pinched herself to ensure she wasn't dreaming. It had happened. The night flashed through her mind in a series of highly tempting images. A smile spread across her face. They'd consummated their marriage in her bed. There was no doubt about it.

She reached out, wanting to trace the outline of Hart's muscled shoulder with a fingertip. Goose bumps popped along her skin as she remembered in explicit detail everything they'd done last night. Her dreams had come true. She was married to Hart, was desperately in love with him, and he'd made unforgettable love to her. It was so much better than she'd imagined. She would tell him she loved him now. He had to believe her after last night.

Her searching hand met only with the sheets. She turned over and sat up. The space next to her was empty.

She frowned. Perhaps he'd had an appointment today, some reason to wake early and leave. Perhaps he hadn't wanted to bother her. She slid from the bed and padded over to her wardrobe to get another dressing gown, which she pulled on and fastened around her waist. Then she made her way over to the door between their rooms. She knocked once, tentatively, and was greeted with, "Come in."

She pushed open the door. Hart sat on the edge of his bed, pulling on his boots. His valet was nowhere to be seen. She couldn't help but smile at him. "Good morning, husband."

"Good morning," Hart replied. He didn't look at up at her.

Something was wrong. "I thought we might have breakfast together."

"I have some business to attend to."

"Very well." She forced herself to nod. "Will you be home for dinner?"

He finished with his boots and stood. "No."

"But I thought—"

His face turned to stone. "Look, Meg, last night didn't change anything."

The smile vanished from her face. Those five words sent ice water slicing through her veins. Those five incomprehensible words, uttered from her husband's handsome yet treacherous lips.

Last night didn't change anything? It didn't make sense. They'd made love. They'd consummated their marriage. Was the man mad? What they'd done last night had changed *everything*. For Meg at least.

She didn't utter a word. She stood, blinking like a fool, trying to make sense of how her world had gone from perfection to confusion in the span of five words.

Hart strode to his wardrobe and choose a coat. "Things can be . . . pleasant between us but there's no need to lose our heads."

"Pleasant between us?" she echoed, confused. She knotted the dressing gown tighter around her middle, pulling the collar together to cover her throat.

"Yes, like last night." He turned to look at her, shrugging on his coat.

She swallowed hard and forced herself to look away. "Pleasant is the word you use for what happened last night? *Pleasant?*"

He made his way across the room, stopping to scoop up the dressing gown she'd dropped last night from the floor next to the bed. He handed it to her. "You know how these things go, Meg. You're not a child."

Her head snapped to the side as if he'd slapped her. "What 'things'?"

"*Ton* marriages. We can be cordial to each other. Have fun every now and then and go about our days normally. No need to be in each other's pockets, is there?" He looked as if he was trying to manage a smile for her. "What happened last night doesn't change anything," he repeated.

The words ripped like a knife through her heart. What was wrong with him? She didn't understand.

Then it struck her. It hit her over the head with the force of a club. What they'd done last night hadn't been special to *him*. He'd done it before, probably with dozens of women.

It had been special to her. Too special. His words

devastated and angered her, but she couldn't let him know it. She must feign nonchalance. He meant to keep his distance and she must, too.

"Of course not," she murmured in a monotone voice.

Numbly, she turned away from him. She moved toward the adjoining door, entered her own room, and silently shut the door behind her. She leaned back against it, closing her eyes and forcing herself to take a long, deep breath. Tears rushed to her eyes but she refused to allow them to fall. She was through crying over her husband. If he wanted to keep her at arm's length, she wouldn't fight him.

She shook out her hair and lifted her chin. She would simply go about the business of being a good wife. Even if her husband was absent. She was used to being alone. She was accustomed to living in a household full of unspoken words and anger.

She rang for her maid and asked Emily to draw a bath. While she waited in the antechamber for the footmen to bring up the steaming-hot buckets of water to fill the tub, Meg fought more tears as well as the urge to stomp into Hart's room and demand an explanation. Once the bath was ready, she dismissed the servants, shed her gown, and slid deep into the water, letting it cover her head. She bobbed to the surface and grabbed the bar of French soap Emily had left on the stool next to the tub.

Last night in Hart's arms, in Hart's bed, she'd known he felt something for her. Perhaps not love, perhaps not yet, but something deeper than lust. He'd been so caring, so gentle, so attuned to her. He'd so obviously wanted to make it good for her, and he had. He *had*. She refused to believe it meant nothing to him. That it didn't change anything as he'd said. Why did her husband have to be so confoundedly stubborn?

She finished her bath and rang for Emily again. The maid hurried to help her dry off and dress.

"Has His Lordship left?" Meg asked while Emily arranged Meg's hair.

"Yes, my lady, I believe so."

He'd said he had business to attend to but no doubt he'd gone to his club again. He wasn't coming back tonight. She could *feel* it. He'd told her as much when he said their night together didn't change anything. He intended to go right on behaving as if he weren't even married. Just as Sarah had predicted.

Meg had had enough. He was out at his club doing as he liked. By God, she would do the same. Once Emily finished her ministrations and left the room, Meg sat down at the small white writing desk in the corner of her bedchamber and scribbled off a note to Sarah asking her to come and get her tonight on her way to the latest ball.

"Hart's going to be there tonight," Sarah said hours later as their coach rattled along toward the Hartleys' soiree.

Meg was busily plucking at the strings of her reticule. Her head snapped up at Sarah's words. "How do you know?"

Sarah bit her lip, a guilty look on her face. "He told me."

Meg had shared enough of the details with her friend for Sarah to know they'd finally spent the night together and that Hart had told her it didn't mean anything. Sarah had promptly declared her brother a fool and apologized to Meg. Meg had told Sarah she didn't want to discuss her maddening husband any more this evening. She'd hoped to forget all about him until Sarah informed her he'd be at the party.

"You saw Hart today?" Meg smoothed a hand over her skirts, feigning nonchalance.

Sarah winced. "He came over to speak to Christian this morning. On his way out Hart asked where I'd be going tonight and when I told him the Hartleys', he said he planned to go, too."

Meg's brow remained furrowed. "Why would he go there? He prefers his club and his gaming hells."

"It is curious," Sarah agreed. "You didn't tell him you'd be there, did you?"

Meg shook her head. "I didn't even know I would be there until after he left."

The rest of the way to the party, Meg stared out the coach window into the darkness. Try as she might, she couldn't stop thinking about him. Why would he want to attend the Hartleys' party? Would he be angry with her? Would he ignore her? Would he even notice her? God, she'd rather he was angry with her than distant.

The coach pulled to a stop in front of the Hartleys' town house. Sarah and Meg alighted and Lord Berkeley escorted them inside. Meg stayed by Sarah's side and did her best to make a show of talking and laughing with Sarah and Christian's friends. Anyone watching her would have thought she was having a lovely time.

But her eyes darted around the ballroom, looking for her husband. She'd been there the better part of an hour with no sign of him. Perhaps Sarah had been mistaken. Perhaps Hart had changed his mind. Perhaps he'd come and gone already.

Yet another hour passed before Lady Cranberry

stopped Meg near the refreshment table. "Ah, Lady Highgate. I saw your husband out on the veranda. I congratulated him but I've yet to offer you my best wishes on your marriage."

"Th . . . thank . . . you," Meg managed. She wasn't used to people calling her Lady Highgate, let alone speaking to her.

Lady Cranberry moved off into the crowd and Meg took a deep breath. The veranda? That's where he'd been all this time. Why did she have a sinking, awful feeling he wasn't alone?

Meg took her time sauntering toward the veranda. She didn't want Lady Cranberry, one of the *ton*'s biggest gossips, to see her fly off in search of her husband like a jealous fishwife. Instead, Meg meandered in that general direction, greeting people and stopping for strategic conversations with friends of Lucy's or Sarah's, all the while trying to tamp down her panic as she speculated about who Hart was with on the veranda.

When she finally reached the French doors that led outside, Meg took a deep breath and peeked out. The veranda appeared to be empty, but she couldn't see the entire space. She pushed open the double doors and walked out into the soft night air. Taking another deep breath, she turned the corner to see the rest of the space and sucked in her breath. Hart was there, tall and handsome, dressed in fine black trousers with a black coat and expertly tied white cravat. As Meg suspected, he wasn't alone. He towered over a gorgeous brunette who wore a sparkling silver gown. The lady laughed at something Hart said. She turned her head and Meg caught a glimpse of her.

Lady Maria Tempest.

As Meg watched wide-eyed, Lady Maria lifted her hand and brushed the hair away from Hart's forehead. It was a tender gesture . . . an intimate one.

Meg hadn't even realized she gasped until Hart and Lady Maria turned to look at her.

"Meg," Hart said. He didn't even have the grace to look guilty. He looked more bothered at the interruption than guilty. "What are you doing here?"

"Looking for my *husband*," Meg ground out. She crossed her arms over her chest, her gloved fingers digging into the opposite elbows.

"Is this your wife, darling?" Lady Maria said in a sultry voice. "She's absolutely adorable."

Meg had had enough. She'd tried to tell him the truth. Given him her body. Nearly admitted she loved him. He was a fool. Worse than a fool. He was an arse, a scoundrel, a *rogue*. He could have his lover. Meg was through with him.

She eyed them both up and down. "My apologies for interrupting." She picked up her skirts, turned on her heel, and stalked away.

CHAPTER FORTY-ONE

The next day Lord Berkeley's coach set out from London, jostling its way north toward Christian's estate in Northumbria. Sarah and Meg were ensconced inside.

"You think I shouldn't leave, don't you?" Meg asked. "You think I'm being a coward."

Sarah tugged at her glove and pressed her lips together. "On the contrary, I only wonder why it took you so long. My brother is being a world-class ass and doesn't deserve you. I hate to say it, but this is what I was afraid of, Meggie."

Meg pressed her gloved hand to her forehead and leaned against the velvet-tufted seat. "I have only myself to blame. It is what I wanted. Or at least what I thought I wanted. Now I must live with it."

Sarah leaned over and patted Meg's knee. "We shall stay at Berkeley Hall as long as we choose. Don't worry about a thing. Mrs. Hamilton will take excellent care of us," Sarah finished with a nod.

"Do you think he spent the night with her last night?" Meg asked with a groan. "No. I don't want to know."

Sarah's eyes widened. "Who? Lady Maria?"

"Yes," Meg murmured. "I hate myself for caring."

Sarah shook her head. "He slept on our settee last night. Couldn't even make it up to the guest bedchamber, he was so deep in his cups."

Meg's head popped up. "Your settee? Truly?"

"Of course I didn't tell him where I was off to this morning. Or with whom. He doesn't deserve to know as far as I'm concerned."

Meg pulled her reticule off her wrist and set it on the seat next to her. "Thank you, Sarah. You're a dear friend. What does Christian think of this debacle?"

"You know Christian. He adores Lucy and always has. He's an admirer of her schemes. He's convinced it will all work out. I even reminded him of how angry he was with her last year when she inserted herself into *our* affairs."

Meg sighed. "Christian is a kind soul. I wish your brother was more like him."

"My brother is a stubborn ass, much as I am. I nearly ruined my future with Christian because I wouldn't admit I was wrong. I only hope Hart comes to the same realization before it's too late."

Meg pressed a hand to her cheek. "It may already be too late."

"Please don't say that. I didn't ask you before because I didn't want to pry, but now I feel I must. Did you ever tell him what you were going to say to him that night in Lucy's garden? Did you ever tell him you've loved him for years?"

Meg leaned her head back against the seat again and

groaned. "No, and he wouldn't believe me if I tried. I've attempted to tell him several times that he was wrong about what happened in Lucy's garden. He doesn't care. He doesn't want to hear the truth."

"I'm sorry, Meggie." Sarah took a deep breath. You may not want to hear it, but the truth is I think you both carry some of the blame. Hart was horribly hurt by Annabelle Cardiff's treachery and he's never been one to trust easily. He knows wc planned the events in the garden and I cannot entirely fault him for being angry. However, he's had plenty of time to calm down and hear you out, yet he stubbornly refuses to do so. But you're being stubborn, too. I think you should tell him you've loved him. It has to make a difference."

Meg stared out the window. Sarah made a good point. Hart wasn't a complete victim, but neither was she. However, telling him she loved him, especially after he'd been so cavalier about their night together and had run off to meet with his mistress, was too painful to contemplate. What if she told him the truth and he rejected her? She couldn't bear it.

The only thing she knew for certain was that leaving for Northumbria was the right thing to do. She had to go. For her own sanity. She couldn't stay with him, give him her body at night, and pretend they barely knew each other during the day. She didn't know why she thought things would be different once they made love, but they hadn't been and it broke her heart.

It also made her angrier than she'd ever been. Especially after she saw him with his lover the very next night. The image of Lady Maria brushing the hair away from Hart's forehead was burned in Meg's brain.

Meg wouldn't be like her mother, a wife whose

husband spent more nights in someone else's bed than her own. On the other hand, she couldn't give him both her body and her love with nothing in return. She refused to be the laughingstock of the *ton*, everyone knowing her husband spent time with other women.

She needed time to be alone or at least away from Hart. It was lovely of Sarah to not only give her a place to stay, but also come with her and keep her company.

Meg refused to spend any more of her life unwanted and unloved, on the sidelines of every dance, on the sidelines of life.

Where the bloody hell was his wife? Hart stomped out of her bedchamber, a note she'd left him crumpled in his hand. He'd come home from Sarah's house this morning prepared to speak to Meg. He'd known she was angry with him when she'd seen him with Maria last night. How the hell did she know what Maria had been to him in the past? He'd gone in search of Meg soon after she'd left the veranda, only to find she had left the party.

Their night together had been . . . unforgettable, but he couldn't allow himself to fall in love. She would destroy him the way his mother had destroyed his father, making him bitter and angry. To that end, he'd refused to chase her around last night. Instead he'd drunk far too much and ended up passed out on his sister's settee. This morning he was sober and planned to ask Meg why she'd left. He wanted to talk to her, perhaps even explain the scene she'd witnessed. A completely innocent scene, but he could imagine how it must have looked.

But Meg was gone. Her valise was missing and the note she'd left on her bedside table said that she needed some time to herself to . . . think. What the bloody hell did that mean? She hadn't even mentioned where she'd gone and he couldn't guess. Her father didn't own an estate. Hart's parents were hardly apt to have allowed her to go to their estate.

Was she staying with friends in town? She wasn't at Sarah's. He'd just come from there. The Duchess of Claringdon's perhaps? Damn it. He'd have to clean himself up and go over to the duchess's house and fetch his wife. Blast. Blast. Blast. He didn't know how to be a husband. He was making a bloody muddle of it.

Less than an hour later, Hart was sitting in a far-too-delicate chair in the Duchess of Claringdon's drawing room, staring at a cup of tea he didn't want, trying to allow enough time to pass before he could politely ask after his wife's whereabouts. They'd discussed the weather and politics. He had no more patience.

"Where is she?" Hart blurted.

"Who?" Lucy pushed at a dark curl along her forehead.

Hart expelled his breath. The duchess knew damn well who. He didn't have time for games. "My wife," he nearly growled.

Lucy took a sip of tea that he'd watched her drop an ungodly amount of sugar into. "Has she gone missing?"

Hart tilted his head to the side and sighed. "I take it she's not here, then?"

The duchess arched a brow. "Not unless she's stuck in the silver closet again. I'll give you the key and you can go look if you like."

Hart arched his brow. "That's not funny."

"I thought it was." Lucy took another sip of tea.

Hart leaned forward in his seat, hoping the chair

wouldn't crack from his weight. "You have no idea where she is?" His voice dripped skepticism.

Lucy lifted her teacup to her lips again, her pinkie finger pointed skyward. "If she's not at your house, I'd guess she's with Sarah."

Hart growled under his breath. "She's not at Sarah's. I came from there earlier."

Lucy regarded him seriously for a moment. "Did Sarah tell you she doesn't know where she is?"

Hart frowned. "No."

Another sip of tea. "Where's Sarah then?"

Hart was quickly coming to understand that Lucy didn't have any idea where Meg was. He'd made a mistake coming here. This was a waste of time. "I don't know. I didn't see her this morning before I left. The servants said she'd gone out."

"So Meg is missing and Sarah's not home?" Lucy asked.

"Yes." He clenched his jaw.

"Hmm." Lucy smoothed a finger over a dark brow. "I'd say find Sarah and you'll find Meg."

CHAPTER FORTY-TWO

Meg had been in Northumbria for three weeks. Three long weeks in which she'd had no communication with her husband. No communication with anyone except Sarah and Mrs. Hamilton, and the dear staff at Berkeley Hall, which was a perfectly lovely place. She'd spent her days riding horses, going for walks, and picking flowers in the meadows. Her journal was full of the details of the past several weeks, but she was no closer to understanding her husband or having a plan about dealing with him than she had been when she came.

She'd spent her nights tossing and turning, tortured by the thought of Hart and Lady Maria tangled in each other's arms in London. Had he invited the woman to their house? Were they spending their nights in naked ecstasy in the same bed he'd refused to take her to? It made Meg's stomach roil. Hart had slept on Sarah's settee that night Meg had found him with Lady Maria, but that didn't mean he'd remained celibate since. Perhaps

Meg had made a horrible mistake coming here. Still, she refused to crawl back to London and watch him and his lover together. That would be worse than being here and not knowing.

"I expect we'll have a visitor today, Meg," Sarah said over breakfast on the twenty-second day they'd been in Northumbria.

"A visitor?" Meg blinked. Her heart lurched. Surely Sarah hadn't invited Hart here.

"It's Christian," Sarah said, reaching for the pot of honey.

Meg breathed a sigh of relief. Of course Sarah wouldn't have invited Hart. Not without warning her first.

"Christian?" Meg took a sip of juice. She didn't want to admit she'd been disappointed when she realized their visitor wasn't Hart.

"Yes," Sarah continued. "I've written to Christian and told him that you refuse to return to London. He's been closely monitoring Hart's behavior, by the by."

Meg briefly closed her eyes. "Don't tell me. I don't want to know."

Sarah slathered honey on a piece of toast with a knife. "I know you don't, but you must. You cannot hide up here forever. Besides, we're missing all the best gossip. Christian told me Lady Eugenia and Sir Winford have become betrothed."

"No!" Meg breathed, a small smile popping to her lips. She was happy for Sir Winford. He deserved to find love.

"Yes," Sarah continued. "I was in agreement with you that you needed time, but it's been nearly a month and neither you nor Hart appears willing to be the first to attempt to reconcile. You must be in the same room with each other if you're to work this out."

Meg took a bite of eggs. "Who says we need to work this out?"

"Intend to live here forever, do you?" Sarah smiled at her and took a bite of honey-covered toast.

Meg pressed her lips together. She had to concede. Her friend did have a point. "Very well, what has my husband been doing in London without me? Drinking to excess and visiting Maria Tempest's bed, I expect."

Sarah smiled, clearly pleased with herself. "I'll let Christian tell you when he arrives, which should be any moment now."

The butler announced Lord Berkeley's arrival precisely a quarter hour later. Meg held her breath while the viscount made his way into the breakfast room. The servants hurried to place a plate full of food in front of him. He'd been traveling all night. No doubt he was exhausted.

After the greetings and niceties were exchanged and Sarah gave her husband an indecently long kiss, Sarah turned to Meg. "Very well, Christian, tell Meg what you told me."

Meg tried to keep her hand from shaking on her teacup. "My husband's exploits?"

Christian cleared his throat. "If you can call them that. He's been a complete mess since you left."

"A mess?" Meg blinked. Had she heard Christian correctly?

"He's spent more nights than not on our settee and they say he's gambled away a fortune at the clubs. He's completely distracted."

Meg took a breath. *That* was surprising. "Did Lady Maria reject him?"

"On the contrary. She's made it clear she'd welcome him back. Hart hasn't taken her up on the offer."

Meg closed her eyes briefly. Relief flooded through her. "Are you certain?"

"Told me himself not three nights ago when he was deep in his cups and being quite honest."

"No," Meg breathed.

"Yes," Christian replied. "He loves you, Meg. I'm convinced of it."

"Loves me?" Meg shook her head. If Christian had told her Hart was half wolf she could not have been more astonished.

Christian picked up his fork and stabbed it into a sausage. "Yes. It just takes some of us poor fools a bit longer than others to realize we're in love." He winked at his wife.

Sarah laughed and squeezed her husband's wrist. "So true, darling."

"What if you're wrong?" Meg asked. "What if he doesn't love me?"

"Meg, I owe you," Christian began. "If it weren't for you helping us last year, I'm not certain Sarah and I would be together now. Normally, I wouldn't involve myself in such affairs. I leave the meddling to Lucy, but there's only one way to find out if I'm right. Go back to London and talk to Hart."

That same afternoon, Lucy Hunt arrived at Hart's town house in London with Delilah Montebank in tow. Hart grudgingly allowed the two females into his study only because he was mildly interested in what the duo had to say. He was still feeling the effects of his excessive drinking the night before, however, and was hardly in the mood for company.

Lucy marched in, removed her kid gloves, motioned for Delilah to sit, and paced in front of the fireplace. Lady Delilah, dressed all in pink, took a seat, blinked at him with her big, dark eyes, and proceeded to look around his study as if memorizing everything inside. The girl had a nasty scrape on her arm. "What happened?" he asked, motioning to the scab visible above the line of her glove.

"I learned the difficult way never to tease a parrot about his lineage," Delilah replied with a sniff.

Hart pressed his lips together to keep from laughing. Lucy was right. The girl was unique. Instead, he turned his attention to the duchess. "To what do I owe the pleasure of your company, Your Grace?" Lucy's progress back and forth across the carpet was bringing his headache back.

Lucy clasped her hands behind her and regarded Hart down the length of her nose like a general preparing for battle. He was tempted to stand at attention.

"I've come to ask you a question, Highgate," the duchess said.

"And that is?" he replied.

Lucy stopped and rocked back and forth on her heels. "When are you going to stop being *such* an idiot?"

"I beg your pardon," Hart replied, frowning.

"She said, 'When are you going to stop being such an idiot?' " Lady Delilah repeated in a loud voice as if Hart were hard of hearing.

Hart gave the child a warning glare before turning his attention back to Lucy. The duchess had some nerve.

She'd executed a scheming plot against him and now she was in his home calling him an idiot? "I didn't realize I was being an idiot," he drawled.

"I find that difficult to believe," Lucy replied. "I must say, I've encountered some stubborn people in my time, my husband being one of them, but you and your sister are by far the most stubborn individuals I've ever attempted to help."

"Help," Hart scoffed. "You attempted to *help* me? That's rich."

"I not only attempted, I succeeded. You have me to thank for your lovely, perfect wife." Lucy continued her pacing in front of the fireplace.

"You to *thank*?" He couldn't believe what he was hearing. Was the Duchess of Claringdon truly marching around his study asking for thanks for the mess she'd created in his life?

"Yes, you dolt." Lucy paused to glare at him. "Are you honestly going to tell me you'd rather be married to Lady Eugenia Eubanks right now? You might have her dowry to spend in the clubs, but I hardly think she'd have made you happy. You looked bored as toast whenever you were with her."

"My wife hasn't exactly made me happy, either," Hart drawled.

"Well, not yet," Lucy replied. "That's because you're being such an idiot. If you would hear her out and allow her to explain, you could both get over this ridiculousness and be wildly happy together as you are so obviously meant to be."

Hart opened his mouth to tell the woman to get out of his house, but Lucy kept going. "It's high time you stopped acting like a spoiled child and began acting like a man who's thankful for the gift he's been given."

Hart narrowed his eyes on the duchess. Spoiled child? The duchess was clearly insane. He'd let her say her piece and usher her out the door as quickly as possible. "I suppose there's a reason you brought Lady Delilah with you today," he said in an effort to hurry along their visit.

Delilah hopped up to sit on the edge of her chair. "Yes. I was hoping to apologize to your wife, but Lucy told me when we were nearly here that Lady Highgate isn't home. Is that true?"

"Yes," Hart replied through clenched teeth. "That's true." Perfect. Now he was going to be made to feel guilty by a precocious girl. Could the day get any worse?

"A pity. I did so want to apologize to her," Delilah said, a crestfallen look on her face.

"For what, may I ask?" Hart replied, hating himself for asking, as it would no doubt prolong their visit.

"Go ahead, Delilah, tell Lord Highgate the truth," Lucy prompted.

Delilah took a deep breath and folded her hands in her lap. "That night in the duchess's gardens, Lucy and I were watching. The moment we saw you kiss Meg, I ran around the corner and Lucy went back to get the others."

"Yes, I remember," Hart ground out. "Thank you for admitting you planned the entire thing." He pinched the bridge of his nose. His headache was worse, throbbing behind his eyes.

"But what you don't know is that Meg never knew anything about it," Delilah continued.

"I find that difficult to believe, since I saw the duchess talking to Meg just before she went out to the gardens.

Do you deny that, Lucy?" He gave the duchess a challenging stare.

"Of course I don't deny it," Lucy said. "I sent Meg out there."

"I rest my case." Hart allowed a smug smile to settle on his face.

Lucy stamped her boot-clad foot. "You rest nothing, you fool. The reason Meg went out there, the reason I was able to *convince* her to go out there, was because she had something she wanted to say to you. I merely made a mess of the timing and assumed she'd said it *before* you began kissing. Which you'd understand was quite an honest mistake if you'd known what she planned to say."

"What she planned to—" A niggle of doubt swirled through Hart's brain. Meg's words from that night skittered through in his mind: "There's something I must tell you. Something important." He'd forgotten that until now. His next words came from a suddenly dry throat. "She *was* going to tell me something . . . before . . ."

"You nearly ravished her?" Lucy said. "Was that her fault, by the by? It looked quite mutual to me. She still has something to tell you, something quite important, but it's not for me to say. I suggest you find your wife and ask her."

CHAPTER FORTY-THREE

"Lucy says I should talk to Meg." Hart lay on the settee at his brother-in-law's town house, a half-drunk bottle of brandy sitting on the floor next to him, within arm's reach. Christian sat behind his desk not ten paces away, seeing to his paperwork and humoring Hart. Berkeley had just returned from a trip up north.

"Do you agree with her?" Christian did not glance up from his ledger.

"I don't know. Should I?"

"That's not for me to answer, old boy," Berkeley replied.

"Damn it, Berkeley. I don't know how to be a husband. You've seen my parents. They have no love for each other."

"Yes, Sarah's mentioned that. I suspect it's why they were hell-bent on securing miserable marriages for their children . . . because they're miserable themselves."

Hart rubbed his eyes with the heels of his hands. "I never thought about it like that."

"Yes, well, you should. Whenever anyone is hell-bent on you doing something, always ask yourself why."

"Why does Lucy Hunt want me to talk to Meg then?" Hart mumbled.

Berkeley tapped his quill against his ledger. "Perhaps because it's the right thing to do?"

Hart emitted a groan. "You agree with her?"

Berkeley sighed and shook his head. "How did your parents choose each other, by the by? I've often wondered. I assume it was arranged."

Hart snorted and lifted the bottle to his lips for another swig. "Yes. Arranged by my mother."

Berkeley leaned back in his chair. "How?"

"The year my mother made her debut, she set her sights on my father. My grandfather had died not eighteen months earlier, and my father was the earl by then."

Berkeley crossed his arms over his chest. "Ah, couldn't resist the title?"

Hart took another swig. "She tossed over a baron she'd been close to marrying when my father arrived at a ball she attended."

Berkeley tapped his quill against his ledger. "She must have captured his interest."

"She flirted with him outrageously. Told him she liked everything he liked. Pretended to be madly in love with him."

Berkeley nodded. "And your father believed her?"

"Yes. He offered for her within a fortnight. I think he was still grieving for my grandfather. My grandmother apparently tried to talk him out of his choice."

Berkeley smothered a laugh. "That must have made for awkward dinner parties in the future."

Hart rested the back of his wrist atop his forehead. "Grandmother never accepted Mother, and my father soon came to regret his choice. Mother racked up huge amounts of debt and took off with her lovers soon after Sarah was born."

"Really?" Berkeley raised a brow.

"That's why he abhors scandal so much. He had to chase his wife out of bed after bed. Is it any wonder marriage makes me queasy?" Hart groaned again.

"I never knew. I don't think Sarah knows."

"She doesn't and I hope you'll keep it to yourself."

"You have my word. My parents barely spoke to each other. That didn't keep me from loving your sister more than my own life."

Hart sat up and blinked at his brother-in-law. "Really?"

"Yes, really. It's a fallacy that one must have a good example to set a good example. Some of us invent our own image of the way we want things to be, regardless of the messes around us."

"That's heartening, I suppose. My father's been trying to get in touch with me for days. I haven't replied to his notes."

Berkeley laughed. "Wonder what he wants."

"To control me, no doubt."

"That sounds likely."

Hart folded his hands over his chest and lay quietly for a moment. "Berkeley, may I ask you a question?"

"Haven't you been doing that for the past quarter hour?"

"Another one?"

"Go ahead."

Hart took a deep breath. This was not easy to ask. "What does . . . jealousy feel like?"

Berkeley laughed. "Think I would know, do you?"

"You must have felt it when you saw Sarah about to marry Branford last summer."

Berkeley's voice was tight. "You're damn right I did."

"What does it feel like?" Hart continued.

"You've never felt it?"

"Father told me it was the worst feeling in the world. I've always ensured it didn't happen to me. I'm not certain I'm capable of it."

"Allow me to reassure you then. If you felt it, you'd know," Berkeley replied.

"Then I suppose I haven't." Hart took another swig from the bottle. "Describe it to me."

Berkeley was silent for a few moments. "It feels like a mix between wanting to vomit and wanting to rip another man apart limb from limb."

"Is that all?" Hart said with a laugh. "Another man?"

"Whomever you're jealous of."

Hart put the bottle back on the floor. "I've been angry, of course. But not over a woman."

"Never had a thought or two about planting a facer on Sir Winford?"

Hart nearly growled aloud. Sir Winford? By God, he *had* had a thought or two about planting a facer on Sir Winford. Was *that* what jealousy felt like?

"I need to talk to her, Berkeley. What should I do?"

"Finally," Berkeley replied. "It's a surprising thing when you realize that a happy marriage is within your reach. It's enough to shock a mere mortal into action."

"I much prefer your quiet counsel to Lucy Hunt's calling me an idiot."

"We each have our own ways, Lucy and I, but it seems we agree that you should see your wife."

"Is she coming back?"

"She'll be at the Huntingtons' ball tomorrow night."

CHAPTER FORTY-FOUR

The Huntingtons' ballroom was ablaze with the light of a thousand candles in chandeliers high above the dance floor. The space was filled with the *ton*'s best, wearing their fine clothing, expensive gowns, and priceless jewels, talking and laughing and having a grand time. Meg was there in a jade-green gown. Sarah had seen to it that her hair had been straightened again, and she wore emeralds, both a necklace and earbobs, borrowed from Sarah this time.

More than once on the way back from Northumbria Sarah had told Meg she must be strong. "Hart detests weakness. You must show him you refuse to cower to him."

"Of course I refuse to cower to him," Meg had replied, indignant that her friend thought she'd be anything other than adamant in her refusal to kowtow to Hart.

"You two are making this far too complicated. All

you have to do is let him know you're willing to talk to him. He'll handle the rest," Christian had added from his seat next to his wife on the way to the ball tonight.

"Ladies adore making things far too complicated, didn't you know that, Christian?" Sarah said with a laugh. "Oh goodness, I'm beginning to sound like Lucy."

"You are a bit," Meg agreed, but she couldn't bring herself to laugh. She was far too nervous about what awaited her in the ballroom. Christian was confident that Hart was in love with her, or at least could be in love with her, but Meg wasn't confident. As the coach rambled closer to their destination, her confidence slipped more and more.

She was bolstered, however, when Lucy rushed over the moment she entered the Huntingtons' ballroom. "I've told him he's an idiot," she announced. "You're quite welcome."

Meg lifted her chin. She'd prepared herself for this moment, too. "Lucy, I appreciate all you've done, but I no longer require your help. I intend to handle my marriage myself from now on."

"Brava!" Sarah clapped her hands.

"I understand." Lucy bowed her head. "I leave you to it. He's here." Lucy lifted her chin. "Over by the refreshment table. I suggest you mingle for a while and allow him to come to *you*."

Hart stood with Harlborough, Norcross, and Wenterley on the sidelines discussing horseflesh and the latest sales at Tatt's when Norcross elbowed him. "Don't look now, Highgate, but if I don't mistake my guess your wife is back."

Hart spun around. By God, it was . . . Meg. She wore

a green gown that hugged her breasts and fell in soft folds from the high waist. Her hair was straightened, as it had been that first night he'd seen her at the Hodges' ball. She still looked like a goddess. Even better than he remembered. He realized . . . he had missed her.

Had Berkeley told her he'd be here? Did she want to talk to him, too? His eyes scanned over her, taking in her glorious golden locks and her trim figure. Their night together flooded back through his mind, making him hard.

"Apparently, becoming a future countess has made her sought after, even with the scandal surrounding your marriage," Norcross said.

Norcross was right. At least a dozen people floated around her, talking and laughing and vying for her attention.

"No one cares about a scandal once a nice tidy marriage takes place," Harlborough said with a laugh. "Besides, a future countess is a future countess, especially when she's as stunning as Lady Highgate."

Hart was barely listening. Instead, he scanned the faces of the men surrounding his wife. "Damn it. That had better not be who I think it is with her," he ground out.

"Who?" Wenterley craned his neck to get a better view.

"Be discreet for heaven's sake, Went." Harlborough took a surreptitious glance himself.

Hart clenched his fist around his brandy glass. "That sop, Sir Winford."

"That's exactly who it is," Wenterley provided helpfully. "I thought I recognized him. I heard he recently got himself engaged."

"I don't care. I'm going to rip that blighter limb from

limb." Hart pressed his still-full glass into Wenterley's hand.

"I thought you didn't get jealous, Highgate?" Harlborough raised a brow.

Hart growled and stalked off through the crowd to claim his wife.

Hart knew the moment she saw him. Meg's bright-green eyes widened almost imperceptibly before she went back to laughing at whatever Winford, that dolt, had said. Engaged or not, how dare the man ogle his wife? How dare any of these men ogle her? She was so perfect and pretty.

Hart wanted to gather her in his arms and take her out of here and make love to her. He felt like he wanted to vomit. He felt like he wanted to crush the skulls of the other men surrounding his wife. By God, he was consumed with jealousy. Bloody hell, Harlborough was right, and it was exactly as Berkeley described it. He was jealous, of all bloody unlikely things. Damn it, he was turning into his father. His father was right, too. It was the worst feeling in the world.

Hart was about to barrel into the center of the group and drag his wife bodily away when Sarah caught his eye. She stood in the crowd surrounding Meg, and motioned for him to follow her to the side of the room. He remained frozen, keeping an eye on his wife. Despite his clawing desire to whisk Meg away from her admirers, his common sense argued he'd better hear from Sarah, first. If what Lucy had told him was true, Sarah would know. Reluctantly, he headed toward his sister.

"When did you get back?" he asked Sarah in a harsh tone as soon as they were far enough from the crowd to not be overheard.

"This morning." Sarah had her arms crossed in front of her and gave him a sour expression.

"You didn't see fit to tell me?" he ground out.

Sarah shrugged. "It was Meg's choice, not mine. Lucy tells me she spoke with you."

Hart pressed a knuckle to his forehead. "I suppose that's one way to put it. She read me the riot act is more like it. She called me an idiot." He couldn't help but glance over his sister's shoulder at Meg, who smiled and laughed with the group surrounding her. A knife twisted in Hart's gut. Would it cause a hideous scandal if he called out Winford? Yes, damn it. Yes it would.

Hart scrubbed a hand across his forehead. "Is it true, Sarah?" He searched his sister's face.

"Is what true?"

"Is it true that the reason Meg went out to Lucy's garden that night was because she had something important to tell me?"

Sarah's gaze swung to the marble floor. "Yes, it's true."

Hart swore under his breath. "What was she going to say?"

"That's not for me to tell, and I don't necessarily agree with Lucy for telling you."

But he already had his answer. Lucy had been telling the truth. Meg had something to say to him. But what? What could possibly have been so important? What could possibly make this entire fiasco all right? He obviously would have to ask Meg.

Hart turned on his heel.

"Wait," Sarah called.

"I'm through waiting," Hart tossed over his shoulder

as he strode back to where his wife was holding court.
He pushed his way through the crowd surrounding her.
Approaching from behind, he bent and whispered in her
ear, "I need to talk to you. Now."

CHAPTER FORTY-FIVE

Meg did her best to keep her breathing steady and her face blank, but her heart was pounding what felt like a thousand beats a minute. Hart's familiar scent filled her nostrils, and he needed to talk to her.

Christian was at least right about Hart being ready to talk, but God only knew what he meant to say. She'd thought after all these weeks she was ready for this, but she wasn't. Not at all. "Perhaps later," she trilled in as nonchalant a voice as she could muster. "I'm enjoying myself at the moment."

"Make your excuses," he growled in her ear. "Because I'm not above dragging you out of here."

Meg swallowed. He was serious. Quite serious. "Excuse us, won't you, everyone," she said to the group. A round of unhappy voices saying good-byes ensued, and she was on her way with Hart's hand on her elbow, walking briskly toward the foyer. When they reached the corridor outside of the ballroom, Sarah hurried up to them, her blue skirts hoisted in her gloved hand.

Sarah let her skirts drop and planted both fists on her hips. "What do you think you're doing? You're acting positively medieval. Let go of Meg."

"Get out of here, Sarah," Hart growled.

"Meg?" Sarah asked, her voice high and worried. "Are you all right?" She searched her friend's face.

"I don't know," Meg replied. "I suppose I should ask my *husband* if he intends to take me home and beat me. Is that your intention, *darling*?" she sneered. "Oh, my apologies, darling is the name your *lover* calls you, isn't it?"

"Beating isn't my style," Hart drawled. He didn't slow his pace, forcing both Meg and Sarah to lift their skirts and half run to keep up with him.

"Promise me you won't say or do anything rash," Sarah cried. "I cannot allow you to leave here with Meg if you won't promise."

"She's my wife," he bit out, still not slowing his pace.

"She's my closest friend."

They entered the foyer and Hart ordered a footman to fetch his coach. The young man scampered off. Hart let go of Meg's arm and paced around the space like a caged animal while Meg watched, wondering what he intended to say to her when he got her alone.

"I'm waiting," Sarah said. "Promise me you will treat Meg properly or I swear I'll make a bigger scene than you ever dreamed of. I'll bring the entire ballroom running with my screams."

"For God's sake, don't be so dramatic." Hart looked out the narrow window flanking the door for the coach.

"I'm not going to hurt her. You should know I don't have that in me."

"You're not going to say anything hurtful to her, either?" Sarah prompted.

Hart turned on his heel and glared at his sibling. He opened his mouth to speak, but Meg stepped between them. She faced Sarah. "It's fine, Sarah, really. I can face going home with my *husband* and having a conversation."

Sarah continued to give Hart a suspicious look. "Are you certain, Meggie?"

"I can handle blustering and fits. I've dealt with it from my mother my entire life."

Damn it. She was comparing him to her *mother*. Perhaps he was being an ass, but jealousy had got the better of him. Hart waved his hand in the air. "You hear that? She's certain."

"Very well." Sarah lifted her chin. "But if I hear tomorrow that you've done anything you shouldn't have . . ." Sarah wagged a finger at her brother menacingly before giving Meg a quick hug.

The coach came around and Hart pushed open the door to allow Meg to precede him outside. He helped her into the coach and climbed in after her, sitting across from her on the burgundy velvet squabs.

He didn't say a word as they rode to their town house. He merely glared at her like an ass while she sat calmly watching him, her hands crossed over her middle.

Finally Meg said, "Are you proud of yourself? Acting like a bully?"

"I wouldn't have acted like a bully if you hadn't been holding court with all those men."

Her mouth fell open. "You dare to question *my* actions? The last time I saw you, you were flirting with your mistress!"

"Ex-mistress," he ground out.

"A minor detail," she retorted.

They sat in charged silence the rest of the way home. Hart stared out one window into the darkness. Meg stared out the other. When the coach pulled to stop in front of their house, Meg allowed the groomsmen to help her down. Without stopping, she lifted her skirts and strode up the front steps into the house and up the inside staircase to her bedchamber. She didn't give a damn if her husband followed her or not. As she climbed the stairs, Hart said, "I'm going to have a drink first, and then I'll be up."

"Of course you are," she tossed over her shoulder, not breaking her stride.

Hart stomped into the study and slammed the door. *Of course you are?* What the bloody hell did she mean by that? Did she think he drank too much? It was none of her bloody business. He strode to the sideboard and grabbed the bottle of brandy. The nearly *empty* bottle of brandy. By God, did he drink too much? He ripped open the credenza and grabbed a snifter from the sideboard. He pulled the stopper off the bottle and splashed what was left into the glass.

He lifted it to his mouth but stopped before tipping it back. Taking that drink would make him feel . . . what? Better? Worse? He didn't know anymore. He'd been drinking to excess for more years that he cared to admit but these last several days while Meg had been gone, he'd felt . . . different. He wanted her back. He wanted to see her, even being angry with her and knowing she was angry with him. It was as if life was incomplete without her. Which was an entirely mad thought because he'd lived years, most of his life, without her. Certainly without thinking about her all the bloody time like he seemed to now. What the hell was wrong with him?

Seeing her tonight in the middle of those men, including Sir Winford, had made Hart's blood boil. She was his. *His.* Those other men had no right to her. God he wanted this drink. When the hell had he become jealous? Was this how his father felt? No, couldn't be. Meg hadn't cheated on him but he was jealous all the same.

Hart set the glass on the desk and glared at it. He'd wanted a drink to clear his head, to gather his thoughts. Now it only made him sick of himself. In that moment, he realized. He'd been just like his bloody father. Drinking and keeping his heart guarded. All these years he'd thought he was being the opposite of the old man. Instead, he'd become just like him. Hart pushed the drink away. He didn't need a bloody drink to talk to his wife. He strode out of the study and up the stairs. He'd talk to her now. Sober.

He shoved open the door to his bedchamber, and it cracked against the wall. He strode straight to the door that separated his bedchamber from Meg's as he ripped off his cravat. He slammed open the door to her room.

"Done drinking so soon?" Meg sat at her dressing table, pulling off the emerald earbobs. She was already wearing her blue dressing gown. Her maid had obviously helped her remove the ball gown and hurried away with it.

"I told you," he barked. "We need to talk." He knew he was being an ass but couldn't seem to help himself.

She looked up at him in the mirror, not at all affected by his raised voice and anger. Was she mentally comparing him to her mother again?

"Talk, then," she said.

He began unbuttoning his shirt. "Why did you leave town?"

Her green eyes sparkled in the looking glass. "Wasn't it obvious?"

He clenched his jaw. She wasn't going to make this conversation easy. "Because you saw me with Maria?"

She swiveled on the tufted stool. "Among other things."

He pulled his shirt out of his breeches, his bare chest visible beneath the flaps. "I didn't touch Maria."

Meg arched a brow at him. "Do you think that makes me feel better? Do you want praise for that?" She swiveled back around.

He slammed the side of his fist against the wall, making a nearby painting bounce. "Damn it, Meg, I haven't touched another woman since . . ."

She turned her head to the side as if she'd been slapped. "Spare me."

"Since before the Hodges' ball. The night I saw you and wanted you so badly."

Her gaze met his in the mirror. "What?"

"You heard me. I wanted you that night. I wanted you before that. I want to make love to you right now. Desperately."

Her gaze held his in the mirror. Tears rushed to her eyes. She swiveled on her seat once more. "Don't lie to me, Hart."

"I would never lie about this. I saw you with those other men tonight and I wanted to kill them. I've never been jealous before. I don't know what to do. I don't know how to do this."

She stood and took two steps toward him. "Do what?"

He pulled her into his arms. "Be a husband." He pushed his fingers through her hair. "What were you going to tell me that night? In the gardens at Lucy's house?" he asked, searching her face, loving every freckle on her slender nose.

Uneasiness flashed through her eyes. "Who told you I was going to tell you something that night?"

"First Lucy did, then Sarah. Tell me, Meg."

"They had no right to say anything to you."

"Perhaps, but I remember, too. You kept trying to tell me something. I wouldn't let you. I kept interrupting."

She shook her head. "It doesn't matter anymore."

"Lucy and Sarah seem to think it matters a great deal."

"It doesn't," she insisted. "Kiss me."

His mouth swooped down to capture hers and he rained kisses down her neck. "It matters to me," he murmured against her throat.

She grabbed his head. "Not tonight, Hart. Tonight let's just do this." She pulled her dressing gown over both shoulders and let it drop. Her naked body gleamed in the candlelight.

Hart's breathing hitched and he scooped her into his arms and carried her to the bed. He laid her down and she pulled him down atop her. He fumbled with his breeches and kicked them off. He pushed open her knees and hovered over her. "Tell me you want me, Meg."

"I want you," she breathed.

"Let me show you something," Hart panted.

Meg was ravenous for him. She pulled his hips toward hers, wanting him inside her. Now. But Hart moved down her body. She nearly sobbed as his hips moved away from hers. "No," she cried, trying to pull him back up to her.

"Wait," he murmured, kissing the tops of her breasts, her belly, the inside of her thigh. When he spread her legs with his hands on her knees, she bit the back of her hand. What was he planning to . . . ?

Oh God.

His tongue dipped into her cleft and Meg's eyes rolled back in her head. Lucy had never told her anything about *this*. His hot tongue stroked her in wave after wave, nudging at the spot that made her thighs tense.

"Tell me you want me," he murmured again into her softness.

"I want you," she echoed, crying out and biting the back of her hand to keep from being too loud so the servants wouldn't hear.

His tongue kept up its gentle assault as wave after wave of lust shot through her. His hands held her knees apart while his mouth worked against her soft flesh. His tongue dipped inside again and again. He moved back up to lick her in that perfect spot over and over and over until she cried out in pure ecstasy. She panted and her breathing hitched when Hart moved back up her body and hovered over her again.

"Tell me you want me," she demanded, grabbing his head by the hair at the nape of his neck.

"I want you," he said, pressing her knees apart this time with his thighs. He nudged at the entrance to her body and then there was the smooth slick slide of him as he entered her. She cried out against his shoulder and moved her head back and forth on the pillow. He slid into her and pulled out. "No," she cried, not wanting him to leave her.

"I want you," he growled against her throat, sliding into her again.

He stroked into her again. "I want you." And again. "I want you." And again. "I want you."

The next morning, Hart was pulling on his breeches when Meg rolled over and stroked his back. He closed his eyes. The touch of her hand was pure torture. He wanted her again. She hadn't told him she loved him last night. He hadn't said it, either. God, did he even know what love was?

She also had refused to tell him whatever it was she'd been planning to in Lucy's gardens that fateful night. Damn it. He clenched his jaw and steeled himself. She made him jealous of other men. She made him crazy with lust. She made him want her again and again. He'd never get enough, but if she couldn't trust him to tell him what she'd been planning to say, what sort of future did they have together? Trust had to be given and received. If he gave her his heart, if she knew she had it, he would be completely vulnerable to her. He made his way toward his bedchamber.

"Where are you going?" Meg's voice was still sleep-muffled. He glanced at her—she was gorgeous, his wife. Their children would be gorgeous, too.

"To the club."

"Again?"

"Yes."

"I thought . . ." She bowed her head and pulled the sheets higher. "Things had changed between us."

"I thought so, too."

CHAPTER FORTY-SIX

That night, Meg picked out a skin-colored gown she'd had made during her time in Northumbria. The garment hugged every curve, was tight in the bodice, and looked as if it were a second skin. It was nearly indecent, unlike anything else she'd ever worn. It was perfect for her purposes.

Sarah had employed a team of dressmakers from the nearby village to come to Berkeley Hall. She'd instructed them on the latest London fashions. The dressmakers had been happy for the work and the information, and Meg had ended up with a lovely new wardrobe purchased on her husband's credit. At least her time in Northumbria had been good for something other than ruminating on her messy marriage.

The gown was a concoction she and Sarah had designed to make Hart salivate. The décolletage was decadent, the embroidery, expensive, and the pearls she wore with it, picked out by Sarah, who insisted Hart owed them to her.

Emily had straightened Meg's hair again. She had just dismissed the maid and was dabbing passion-flower perfume behind both ears when Hart came into her bedchamber wearing casual attire. Clearly, he wasn't planning to go out this evening.

"Where are you going?" His eyes narrowed on the tops of her breasts.

"A ball." She concentrated on keeping her voice even, calm.

He placed his fists on his hips. "You're not going out of this house dressed like that."

She set the vial of perfume back on her dressing table. "You're not about to stop me."

"Yes, I am," he said through clenched teeth. "I am your husband."

She swiveled on her stool and crossed her arms over her chest. "We don't need to be in each other's pockets," she shot back. "Isn't that what you said to me once?"

He clenched his jaw and a muscle ticked there. "What do you want from me, Meg?"

She stood and strode over to the window, crossing her arms over her chest. She couldn't fight him anymore. Tears trickled down her cheeks, but she savagely wiped them away. "I'll tell you what I want from you, Hart. I want love. That's all I ever wanted from you. Do you know what I was going to say to you that night? That night when you didn't give me a chance to say it? I've loved you since I was sixteen! I've wanted you to be my husband since then, but I also want a marriage full of love and children and happiness."

She barely registered the fact that his face had gone pale. He held his breath. "Meg." Hart took two large steps toward her and pulled her into his arms. She was beyond listening to him.

"On our wedding night," she continued. "You reminded me of how I said I wanted a child, a family, but you forgot that I'd also said I wanted love. I've always loved you, Hart. Always. If you haven't realized that by now, you're either blind or stupid or both!"

"Meg." He cradled her face in both hands.

"All Lucy and I were doing was attempting to get you to finally notice me."

"Meg, stop."

She furiously wiped away her tears with the backs of her hands, and her voice held a note of steely resolve. She pushed him away with both hands. "No! I refuse to stop. I'm through holding in what I want to say, what I need to say. I've done that my entire life. I've sat in the corner and been a good girl and done what I was told. I refuse to do it anymore. Here's how it will be. I'm leaving here tonight. I'm going to a ball with Sarah and Lucy. You and I, we're going to love each other and respect each other and be equals. If you want the same thing, you know where I'll be. If you don't want that, *don't* come for me."

CHAPTER FORTY-SEVEN

Meg hurried down the corridor in the Litchfields' town house. She clutched a note in her hand that said, "Meg, meet me in the silver drawing room in five minutes. Come alone."

It had to be Hart. He'd come for her after all. Her heart raced as she neared the door. Just before entering she took a deep breath. This was it. The next few moments might decide their entire future together. She pushed open the door and raced inside.

She stopped and gasped.

Standing in the middle of the room, a glass of brandy in his hand, was Hart's father, the Earl of Highfield.

"Miss Timmons," he said, turning toward her.

"It's Lady Highgate," she intoned. "Or have you forgotten?" She turned to leave. She knew how Hart's father felt about her. She had no intention of listening to his insults.

"Not for long," he sneered.

She swiveled on her heel to face him again. "What is *that* supposed to mean?"

"I have it on good authority from one of the servants that you and Hart haven't consummated your marriage. Hart's spent every night since your marriage in his bed alone. You even left for Northumbria for the better part of a month. Isn't that true?"

Good God, the man had hired all the servants. No wonder there were spies in their midst. "Even if that *were* true, what business is it of yours?" she retorted.

"What business is it? Why, it's all of my business," the older man scoffed. "I intend to see this marriage annulled."

"Have you gone mad?"

"My son was enamored enough of you temporarily to marry you, but now that I know he refuses to touch you, I'm certain I can convince him to seek an annulment."

"Why would you want that? It would only bring more scandal on your family."

"So you admit it?"

"I admit nothing. I'm trying to understand your twisted thinking."

"Do you know what it's like? Seeing my son make the same mistake I made? My wife never wanted me. She wanted my money, just like you. I know how much money Hart has spent on you and your hideous family, and it sickens me."

She narrowed her eyes on the earl. "What money?"

"Don't play dumb, my dear. It doesn't suit you." He took a hefty swallow of brandy.

She crossed her arms over her chest. "I have no idea what you're talking about."

"Hart settled a huge sum on your father. He paid off all his debts."

"What? No." Meg shook her head.

"It's true." The earl downed the rest the brandy and set the empty glass on the sideboard.

Meg's mind raced. Her parents *had* decided to stay in London. She had noticed her mother wearing a new gown. "Even if it is true, I fail to see how it's any of your business."

The earl's face turned purplish red. "It's my business because it's my money."

Meg turned to leave. "If you have a problem, I suggest you take it up with your son."

"I don't think so, Viscountess. I've already hired a solicitor to begin the process of the annulment."

"You're insane. Do you even know what the grounds for annulment are?"

"One of them is a failure to consummate the marriage."

"Because of *impotence*. Do you truly think Hart will admit to that?"

"He'll thank me for this one day."

"You don't know your son at all."

"And you do?"

"Yes. I know he's kind to servants and he adores his sister. I know he has tiny laugh lines around his eyes and when he's tired he rubs them. I know he's been far too accommodating to you and your wife over the years, even after you've frightened him half out of his wits over the prospect of marriage. And I know without a doubt that all four of our parents aren't half the people Hart and Sarah and I have become and we certainly don't have any of you to thank for it."

The earl rolled his eyes. "A pretty little speech, but a useless one. I've whispered news of the annulment into the ears of the *ton*'s biggest gossips at this ball tonight. By the time you return to the ballroom, you'll be scorned by the people who've been pretending to be your friends."

"You've lost your mind."

"I only called you in here to give you a warning. Leave now. Go back to Northumbria or wherever you can go to hide from the gossip. If I were you, I'd talk your parents into going to the Continent after all."

"I'll do no such thing." Meg picked up her skirts and turned toward the door.

"So be it," the earl replied. "Don't say I didn't warn you." His deranged laughter followed her from the room.

CHAPTER FORTY-EIGHT

Hart had watched Meg leave for the ball nearly half an hour earlier. By God, she was magnificent, his wife, and she had been right. He was blind. He was stupid. He was both, and he had been all this time. Berkeley's words from a few nights ago blazed through his mind: "It's a surprising thing when you realize a happy marriage is within your reach. It's enough to shock a mere mortal into action."

By God, Hart was human, too. He *did* have such a chance. A happy marriage was within his reach. By some mad twist of fate, he had managed to marry a woman who loved him, truly loved him, not for his title or future estate, but for himself. He wasn't his father and Meg wasn't his mother. Meg wouldn't cuckold him. Meg was perfect, and he'd done nothing but push her away.

All of the times he'd seen her since she was sixteen paraded through his mind. It was true he hadn't paid much attention, but she'd blushed, she'd laughed, she'd giggled a bit too much. Sarah had often glanced back and forth between them, something he'd noted but had never given much thought to. Now his memory filled with moments when Meg stuttered in his presence or turned silent when he entered the room. She'd known his horse's name. Had been at his bedside when he'd broken his leg last autumn. She'd always been there, on the sidelines, quietly watching him. And waiting, apparently, for him to wise up and notice her. He'd been a blind jackass all these years.

"If you don't want a marriage full of love and laughter and happiness," she had said, "don't come for me." By God, he *was* going after her—right now! He took the stairs two at a time, flying down them to find her lady's maid to ask which ball Meg was attending.

"Send for the carriage," he called to the butler as he ran.

After speaking to her maid, he rushed back upstairs and summoned his valet. He needed to dress, immediately.

One half hour later, Hart strode through the Litchfields' ball, pushing people aside, ignoring both acquaintances and friends, desperately searching for his wife. He'd looked everywhere. She was nowhere to be found. Finally, he spotted Sarah. "Where is she?" he asked in a tone that made Sarah know exactly who he was looking for.

Sarah stepped toward him and lowered her voice. "Hart, Father's in a mood. He discovered you paid off Meg's father's debts and he wants to speak with you. He's been—"

"I don't give a bloody damn about Father right now. Where is she?" he repeated.

"You must listen, Hart. Father's been telling the entire party and anyone who'll listen that you're going to get your marriage annulled. That your marriage hasn't been consummated, that Meg isn't truly your wife, that—"

"What? Where is she?" Hart searched desperately this time. If he found his father first, he'd rip the bastard limb from limb.

Sarah sighed and pointed toward the wall. Hart's gaze followed her finger. There she was. A wallflower again. Just like the night he'd first danced with her. Because of what his father had been telling people? He'd kill the son of a bitch.

Meg's fingers plucked at her reticule strings. She looked toward her feet. She was so beautiful and vulnerable and heartbreakingly perfect that he realized . . . he loved her. He loved her desperately. She was so fragile and lovely, exactly as she had been that night at the Hodges' ball. Only this time she was his wife. His wife whom he couldn't live without, didn't want to at any rate. He strode up to her, his heart in his throat. What if she wouldn't forgive him? What if she could no longer love him back?

She turned as he approached. "Hart!" Her voice was tentative and she looked frightened, like a hare who might bolt at any moment.

Out of the corner of his eye, he saw his father approach. "Hart," his father intoned. "I need a word with you. Now."

"Get out of here, Father," Hart ground out, unwilling to leave Meg's side.

"I must speak with you, *privately*," his father intoned. "There's something you need to know."

"No," Hart replied through clenched teeth. "Why did you allow Meg to sit in the corner? No one allows Meg to sit in the corner."

His father narrowed his eyes on him. "You're being emotional. She's nothing but—"

"My wife!" Hart shouted. He raised his voice so the entire ballroom could hear. "She is my wife, Father, and I love her desperately. Furthermore, I don't care what you or Mother or anyone else thinks. If you cannot accept Meg, get out of my sight."

His father held up both hands conciliatorily. "I can see you're not in any mood to be reasonable tonight."

The people around them were watching with intense interest and a hush had come over the ballroom as more and more of the partygoers turned to stare.

Hart's voice remained raised. "I'll never be in a mood to discuss this with you. Sarah told me you've been telling people our marriage hasn't been consummated. Is that true?"

His father replied with a jerky nod. His face was turning red.

Hart pulled Meg up to stand next to him. He lifted his booted foot and climbed onto the chair she'd been sitting in. "Listen to me!" he shouted. "My father has been making up lies, ugly, dirty lies about me and my wife." He glanced down at Meg and gave her a tender smile. "Meg Highgate is the best wife a man could ever hope to have and I'm lucky to call her mine. Furthermore, I'm happy to announce that we have, in fact, consummated our marriage more than once and hopefully will do so again, tonight, if she forgives me for making this scene."

Meg's face was bright pink. She pulled him by the hand off the chair and he wrapped his arms around her.

Hart's father, spluttering with mortification, his face crimson, pushed his way through the crowd.

Hart picked up Meg and spun her around. The he set her in front of him on the floor.

Meg's voice was slight, quiet. "Does this mean . . . ?"

Hart nodded and swallowed the lump in his throat, searching her face. He fell to one knee. "Meg Highgate, I love you more than anything in this world. I don't deserve you. I've never come close to deserving you, but I want a marriage full of happiness and laughter and fun and love. And children. Lots of children. An indecent amount of children. At least half a score of them. For the rest of my life I will do anything in my power to make you happy."

"Only half a score of children?" The tiny smile at the crook of her mouth might not be noticeable to someone else, but he noticed and he knew. He'd won.

"Do you still love me?" he ventured.

Her eyes were bright with unshed tears. "I told you, I've loved you since I was sixteen."

He wiped her tears from her cheeks with his thumbs. "No. You only thought you loved me back then. I'm much more worthy of your love now. This minute. You've always been what I always wanted. I just never knew it until now."

"I love you no matter what, you dolt." Meg smiled through her tears.

"That's more like it." He lowered his voice. "Will you come with me, now?"

A sly smile appeared on her face. "I don't know. It depends upon where you're headed. I'm having an awfully good time being a wallflower. I'm quite used to it, you know."

He leered at her and leaned down to whisper. "To bed?"

"In that case, can we leave immediately?"

He grinned from ear to ear, scooped her up in his arms and strode away with her, careless of the spectacle he was making. "My darling, I can promise you, you'll *never* be a wallflower again."

CHAPTER FORTY-NINE

Later that night, after having been thoroughly made love to by her gorgeous husband who loved her, Meg rolled over, lifted up on an elbow, and kissed him on his rough cheek.

Hart laughed, rolled atop her, and kissed her on the lips. He lifted her hand to his mouth and soundly kissed the back of it.

"I can't believe you came to the Litchfields' ball and made such a scene," Meg said with a snicker. "Especially in front of your father. We'll never live it down."

"A scene a long time coming. I should have grabbed you and demanded you marry me last summer after I kissed you in the gardens by your father's house."

Meg slapped at his shoulder playfully. "You thought I was your mistress."

Hart rolled to his side to face her, his elbow braced on the mattress, his head resting on his palm. "Yes, but I soon realized my mistake, and imagine my surprise when I realized my sister's closest friend could kiss like *that*."

Meg slapped at his shoulder again. "You wouldn't even look at me in the coach the next day after Sarah ran out of the church."

"I didn't know where to look. If I had, I'd have been staring at your delectable mouth."

Meg wrapped her arms around his shoulders. He'd come for her. He'd really come for her. And he'd told her he loved her. She might think it had been a dream if the man wasn't lying next to her, his glorious chest bared, and a wide grin on his handsome lips.

"Hart, tell me something."

"Anything, my love." He leaned down and kissed her bare shoulder.

"You know why our parents fought, don't you?"

The smile faded from his face. "Yes."

Meg leaned up on her elbow, the sheets covering her chest. She clutched them to her. "Why? Tell me."

Hart took a deep breath. "It's an ugly story, love."

"I must know."

Hart scrubbed a hand through his hair. "Very well. Before my parents were married, my mother was madly in love with your father. They almost married. Then my mother met my father. A wealthy earl trumps a baron, I'm afraid."

Meg nodded. "I suspected it was something like that, but that was years ago. I specifically remember them having a falling-out when I was a teen."

"Yes," Hart replied. "Apparently, they'd all been out drinking together and my father and your mother stumbled upon my mother and your father kissing each other in a drawing room."

"No!" Meg gasped. She covered her hand with her mouth.

"I'm afraid it's true."

"When did it . . . I never knew."

"I only found out because my father liked to drink and tell me about Mother's indiscretions. Not details, thank God. Just the fact that she hadn't been faithful to him since soon after Sarah was born. Said she produced an heir and a spare and was through with him."

"Oh, that's . . . that's awful."

"Father has been telling me these stories since I was a teen. It haunted me."

Meg shook her head. "No wonder you were afraid of marriage."

"Petrified."

"Oh, please let's never be like them. I couldn't stand it if we were as nasty to each other as our parents are."

"I agree. I don't want a life where I am constantly worried about who my wife is with."

"I can promise you, you'll never have to worry about that with me."

"I know. I love you, Meg."

"I love you, too," she replied, tracing a finger along his cheekbone. "May I ask you one more thing?"

He nuzzled his face in the crook of her neck and kissed it. "Anything, my love."

"Did you pay off my father's debts?"

Hart's eyes widened. "How did you—?"

"Your father told me, tonight. He threatened me. I had my suspicions, of course, especially after my father said they wouldn't be leaving the country after all. I noticed repairs going on at the house, and Mother had a new gown."

"I've taken over all your father's books, and he and I will meet monthly to ensure he's not racking up more debt. He's promised he won't."

"Your father was furious," Meg said. "He said it was his money."

"I don't give a damn if he approves and it's not his money, it's mine. I have a large sum settled on me from my grandmother."

"Your father told me he'd see our marriage annulled if it was the last thing he did."

"If he tries, it *will* be the last thing he does. But he doesn't scare me. His bark has always been worse than his bite. He'll want this scandal to die down as quickly as possible. It wouldn't surprise me if the next time he sees you, he acts like he's adored you all along."

Meg was quiet for a moment. "You saved my father." Tears filled her eyes. "You saved him even when you hated me."

Hart gathered her into his arms. "I never hated you, love. I was merely a blind, stupid ass. My pride wouldn't let me realize what was obvious."

"Which was?"

"I was falling in love with you." He rubbed his fingertip along the freckles on the bridge of her nose.

Meg stroked her palm against his rough cheek. "Thank you. Thank you for saving my father. I'm certain he's quite appreciative of your help, too."

"Your mother didn't seem thankful."

"I don't know if she's capable of that emotion. I haven't known her to be happy a day in her life."

"A pity."

"But we will be happy. Every day. To think, none of this would have happened if it weren't for Lucy Hunt."

"Yes," Hart replied. "She's still not my favorite person. It may take a bit for me to forgive her for calling me an idiot, but she is an expert matchmaker. I'll give her that."

"She says we're like Romeo and Juliet. Without the poison of course."

Hart's bark of laughter followed. "Speaking of Lucy, that reminds me. Her disciple, Delilah Montebank, asked me to give you a message."

"Really? What's that?"

"She said she's awfully sorry she ruined your life and hopes you'll forgive her one day."

Meg laughed. "Already forgiven. The truth is that she saved my life. Though I must say if I'd known what you were like in bed, I would have demanded you marry me after you kissed me at the Hodges' ball."

"When I cured your hiccups?"

"Precisely."

Hart's laughter cracked across the room. "You must have thought me a rogue."

She grinned at him. "I already knew you were a rogue, my darling, but I also knew you were the *right* kind of rogue."

Thank you for reading *The Right Kind of Rogue*.
Ever since they stepped onto the page in *The Legendary Lord*, Meg and Hart have been one of my most beloved couples. I hope you enjoyed their story.

I'd love to keep in touch.

- Visit my website for information about upcoming books, excerpts, and to sign up for my email newsletter: www.ValerieBowmanBooks.com or at www.ValerieBowmanBooks.com/subscribe.
- Join me on Facebook: http://Facebook.com/ValerieBowmanAuthor.
- Follow me on Twitter at @ValerieGBowman, https://twitter.com/ValerieGBowman.
- Reviews help other readers find books. I appreciate all reviews, whether positive or negative. Thank you so much for considering it!

Look for the next Playful Brides novel from

VALERIE BOWMAN

A Duke Like No Other

Coming soon from
St. Martin's Paperbacks

Stay updated at
www.valeriebowmanbooks.com